SCIENCE FICTION

THE MYSTERY

BY

STEWART EDWARD WHITE

AND

SAMUEL HOPKINS ADAMS

ARNO PRESS

A New York Times Company

New York — 1975

Reprint Edition 1974 by Arno Press Inc.

Copyright © 1907 by McClure, Phillips & Co.

Reprinted by permission of Doubleday & Company, Inc.

Reprinted from a copy in The Library
of the University of California, Riverside

SCIENCE FICTION
ISBN for complete set: 0-405-06270-2
See last pages of this volume for titles.

Manufactured in the United States of America

———◆———

Library of Congress Cataloging in Publication Data

White, Stewart Edward, 1873-1946.
    The mystery.

    (Science fiction)
    Reprint of the ed. published by Grosset & Dunlap,
New York.
    I. Adams, Samuel Hopkins, 1871-1958, joint author.
II. Title.   III. Series.
PZ3.W585My8 [PS3545.H6]   813'.5'2   74-16525
ISBN 0-405-06317-2

THE MYSTERY

"And you know a heap too much"

[Page 201]

THE MYSTERY

BY

STEWART EDWARD WHITE

AND

SAMUEL HOPKINS ADAMS

Illustrations by Will Crawford

NEW YORK
GROSSET & DUNLAP
PUBLISHERS

CONTENTS

PART ONE

THE SEA RIDDLE

PART TWO

THE BRASS BOUND CHEST

Being the story told by Ralph Slade, Free Lance, to the officers of the United States Cruiser " Wolverine."

CONTENTS

PART THREE

THE MAROON

ILLUSTRATIONS

THE MYSTERY

PART ONE

THE SEA RIDDLE

I

DESERT SEAS

THE late afternoon sky flaunted its splendour of blue and gold like a banner over the Pacific, across whose depths the trade wind droned in measured cadence. On the ocean's wide expanse a hulk wallowed sluggishly, the forgotten relict of a once brave and sightly ship, possibly the Sphinx of some untold ocean tragedy, she lay black and forbidding in the ordered procession of waves. Half a mile to the east of the derelict hovered a ship's cutter, the turn of her crew's heads speaking expectancy. As far again beyond, the United States cruiser *Wolverine* outlined her severe and trim silhouette against the horizon. In all the spread of wave and sky no other thing was visible. For this was one of the desert parts of the Pacific, three hundred miles north of the steamship route from Yokohama to Honolulu, five hundred miles from the nearest land, Gardner Island, and more than seven hundred northwest of the Hawaiian group.

On the cruiser's quarter-deck the officers lined the starboard rail. Their interest was focussed on the derelict.

"Looks like a heavy job," said Ives, one of the junior lieutenants. "These floaters that lie with deck almost awash will stand more hammering than a mud fort."

" Wish they'd let us put some six-inch shells into her," said Billy Edwards, the ensign, a wistful expression on his big round cheerful face. " I'd like to see what they would do."

" Nothing but waste a few hundred dollars of your Uncle Sam's money," observed Carter, the officer of the deck. " It takes placed charges inside and out for that kind of work."

" Barnett's the man for her then," said Ives. " He's no economist when it comes to getting results. There she goes! "

Without any particular haste, as it seemed to the watchers, the hulk was shouldered out of the water, as by some hidden leviathan. Its outlines melted into a black, outshowering mist, and from that mist leaped a giant. Up, up, he towered, tossed whirling arms a hundred feet abranch, shivered, and dissolved into a widespread cataract. The water below was lashed into fury, in the midst of which a mighty death agony beat back the troubled waves of the trade wind. Only then did the muffled double boom of the explosion reach the ears of the spectators, presently to be followed by a whispering, swift-skimming wavelet that swept irresistibly across the bigger surges and lapped the ship's side, as for a message that the work was done.

Here and there in the sea a glint of silver, a patch of purple, or dull red, or a glistening apparition of black showed where the unintended victims of the explosion, the gay-hued open-sea fish of the warm waters, had succumbed to the force of the shock. Of the intended victim there was no sign, save a few fragments of wood bobbing in a swirl of water.

When Barnett, the ordnance officer in charge of the destruction, returned to the ship, Carter complimented him.

"Good clean job, Barnett. She was a tough customer, too."

"What was she?" asked Ives.

"The *Caroline Lemp,* three-masted schooner. Anyone know about her?"

Ives turned to the ship's surgeon, Trendon, a grizzled and brief-spoken veteran, who had at his finger's tips all the lore of all the waters under the reign of the moon.

"What does the information bureau of the Seven Seas know about it?"

"Lost three years ago—spring of 1901—got into ice field off the tip of the Aleutians. Some of the crew froze. Others got ashore. Part of survivors accounted for. Others not. Say they've turned native. Don't know myself."

"The Aleutians!" exclaimed Billy Edwards. "Great Cats! What a drift! How many thousand miles would that be?"

"Not as far as many another derelict has wandered in her time, son," said Barnett.

The talk washed back and forth across the hulks of classic sea mysteries, new and old; of the *City of Boston,* which went down with all hands, leaving for record only a melancholy scrawl on a bit of board to meet the wondering eyes of a fisherman on the far Cornish coast; of the *Great Queensland,* which set out with five hundred and sixty-nine souls aboard, bound by a route unknown to a tragic end; of the *Naronic,*

with her silent and empty lifeboats alone left, drifting
about the open sea, to hint at the story of her fate;
of the *Huronian,* which, ten years later, on the same
day and date, and hailing from the same port as the
Naronic, went out into the void, leaving no trace; of
Newfoundland captains who sailed, roaring with
drink, under the arches of cathedral bergs, only to
be prisoned, buried, and embalmed in the one icy em-
brace; of craft assailed by the terrible one-stroke
lightning clouds of the Indian Ocean found days
after, stone blind, with their crews madly hauling at
useless sheets, while the officers clawed the compass
and shrieked; of burnings and piracies; of pest ships
and slave ships, and ships mad for want of water; of
whelming earthquake waves, and mysterious suctions,
drawing irresistibly against wind and steam power
upon unknown currents; of stout hulks deserted in
panic although sound and seaworthy; and of others
so swiftly dragged down that there was no time for
any to save himself; and of a hundred other strange,
stirring and pitiful ventures such as make up the inevitable peril and incorrigible romance of the ocean.
In a pause Billy Edwards said musingly:

"Well, there was the *Laughing Lass.*"

"How did you happen to hit on her?" asked Barnett quickly.

"Why not, sir? It naturally came into my head.
She was last seen somewhere about this part of the
world, wasn't she?" After a moment's hesitation he
added: "From something I heard ashore I judge
we've a commission to keep a watch out for her as well
as to destroy derelicts."

"What about the *Laughing Lass?*" asked Mc-Guire, the paymaster, a New Englander, who had been in the service but a short time.

"Good Lord! don't you remember the *Laughing Lass* mystery and the disappearance of Doctor Schermerhorn?"

"Karl Augustus Schermerhorn, the man whose experiments to identify telepathy with the Marconi wireless waves made such a furore in the papers?"

"Oh, that was only a by-product of his mind. He was an original investigator in every line of physics and chemistry, besides most of the natural sciences," said Barnett. "The government is particularly interested in him because of his contributions to aërial photography."

"And he was lost with the *Laughing Lass?*"

"Nobody knows," said Edwards. "He left San Francisco two years ago on a hundred-foot schooner, with an assistant, a big brass-bound chest, and a ragamuffin crew. A newspaper man named Slade, who dropped out of the world about the same time, is supposed to have gone along, too. Their schooner was last sighted about 450 miles northeast of Oahu, in good shape, and bound westward. That's all the record of her that there is."

"Was that Ralph Slade?" asked Barnett.

"Yes. He was a free-lance writer and artist."

"I knew him well," said Barnett. "He was in our mess in the Philippine campaign, on the *North Dakota*. War correspondent then. It's strange that I never identified him before with the Slade of the *Laughing Lass*."

" What was the object of the voyage? " asked Ives.

" They were supposed to be after buried treasure," said Barnett.

" I've always thought it more likely that Doctor Schermerhorn was on a scientific expedition," said Edwards. " I knew the old boy, and he wasn't the sort to care a hoot in Sheol for treasure, buried or un-buried."

" Every time a ship sets out from San Francisco without publishing to all the world just what her business is, all the world thinks it's one of those wild-goose hunts," observed Ives.

" Yes," agreed Barnett. " Flora and fauna of some unknown island would be much more in the Schermerhorn line of traffic. Not unlikely that some of the festive natives collected the unfortunate professor."

Various theories were advanced, withdrawn, refuted, defended, and the discussion carried them through the swift twilight into the darkness which had been hastened by a high-spreading canopy of storm-clouds. Abruptly from the crow's-nest came startling news for those desolate seas: " Light—ho! Two points on the port bow."

The lookout had given extra voice to it. It was plainly heard throughout the ship.

The group of officers stared in the direction indicated, but could see nothing. Presently Ives and Edwards, who were the keenest-sighted, made out a faint, suffused radiance. At the same time came a second hail from the crow's-nest.

" On deck, sir."

"Hello," responded Carter, the officer of the deck.

"There's a light here I can't make anything out of, sir."

"What's it like?"

"Sort of a queer general glow."

"General glow, indeed!" muttered Forsythe, among the group aft. "That fellow's got an imagination."

"Can't you describe it better than that?" called Carter.

"Don't make it out at all, sir. 'Tain't any regular and proper light. Looks like a lamp in a fog."

Among themselves the officers discussed it interestedly, as it grew plainer.

"Not unlike the electric glow above a city, seen from a distance," said Barnett, as it grew plainer.

"Yes: but the nearest electric-lighted city is some eight hundred miles away," objected Ives.

"Mirage, maybe," suggested Edwards.

"Pretty hard-working mirage, to cover that distance" said Ives. "Though I've seen 'em——"

"Great heavens! Look at that!" shouted Edwards.

A great shaft of pale brilliance shot up toward the zenith. Under it whirled a maelstrom of varied radiance, pale with distance, but marvellously beautiful. Forsythe passed them with a troubled face, on his way below to report, as his relief went up.

"The quartermaster reports the compass behaving queerly," he said.

Three minutes later the captain was on the bridge. The great ship had swung, and they were speeding direct for the phenomenon. But within a few minutes the light had died out.

"Another sea mystery to add to our list," said Billy Edwards. "Did anyone ever see a show like that before? What do you think, Doc?"

"Humph!" grunted the veteran. "New to me. Volcanic, maybe."

II

THE *LAUGHING LASS*

THE falling of dusk on June the 3d found tired eyes aboard the *Wolverine*. Every officer in her complement had kept a private and personal lookout all day for some explanation of the previous night's phenomenon. All that rewarded them were a sky filmed with lofty clouds, and the holiday parade of the epauletted waves.

Nor did evening bring a repetition of that strange glow. Midnight found the late stayers still deep in the discussion.

" One thing is certain," said Ives. " It wasn't volcanic."

" Why so? " asked the paymaster.

" Because volcanoes are mostly stationary, and we headed due for that light."

" Yes; but did we keep headed? " said Barnett, who was navigating officer as well as ordnance officer, in a queer voice.

" What do you mean, sir? " asked Edwards eagerly.

" After the light disappeared the compass kept on varying. The stars were hidden. There is no telling just where we were headed for some time."

" Then we might be fifty miles from the spot we aimed at."

"Hardly that," said the navigator. "We could guide her to some extent by the direction of wind and waves. If it was volcanic we ought certainly to have sighted it by now."

"Always some electricity in volcanic eruptions," said Trendon. "Makes compass cut didoes. Seen it before."

"Where?" queried Carter.

"Off Martinique. Pelée eruption. Needle chased its tail like a kitten."

"Are there many volcanoes hereabouts?" somebody asked.

"We're in 162 west, 31 north, about," said Barnett. "No telling whether there are or not. There weren't at last accounts, but that's no evidence that there aren't some since. They come up in the night, these volcanic islands."

"Just cast an eye on the charts," said Billy Edwards. "Full of E. D.'s and P. D.'s all over the shop. Every one of 'em volcanic."

"E. D.'s and P. D.'s?" queried the paymaster.

"Existence doubtful, and position doubtful," explained the ensign. "Every time the skipper of one of these wandering trade ships gets a speck in his eye, he reports an island. If he really does bump into a rock he cuts in an arithmetic book for his latitude and longitude and lets it go at that. That's how the chart makers make a living, getting out new editions every few months."

"But it's a fact that these seas are constantly changing," said Barnett. "They're so little travelled that no one happens to be around to see an island born.

I don't suppose there's a part on the earth's surface more liable to seismic disturbances than this
region."

"Seismic!" cried Billy Edwards, "I should say
it was seismic! Why, when a native of one of these
island groups sets his heart on a particular loaf of
bread up his bread-fruit tree, he doesn't bother to
climb after it. Just waits for some earthquake to happen along and shake it down to him."

"Good boy, Billy," said Dr. Trendon, approvingly.
"Do another."

"It's a fact," said the ensign, heatedly. "Why, a
couple of years back there was a trader here stocked
up with a lot of belly-mixture in bottles. Thought he
was going to make his pile because there'd been a colic
epidemic in the islands the season before. Bottles were
labelled 'Do not shake.' That settled his business.
Might as well have marked 'em 'Keep frozen' in this
part of the world. Fellow went broke."

"In any case," said Barnett, "such a glow as that
we sighted last night I've never seen from any
volcano."

"Nor I," said Trendon. "Don't prove it mightn't
have been."

"I'll just bet the best dinner in San Francisco that
it isn't," said Edwards.

"You're on," said Carter.

"Let me in," suggested Ives.

"And I'll take one of it," said McGuire.

"Come one, come all," said Edwards cheerily.
"I'll live high on the collective bad judgment of this
outfit."

"To-night isn't likely to settle it, anyhow," said Ives. "I move we turn in."

Expectant minds do not lend themselves to sound slumber. All night the officers of the *Wolverine* slept on the verge of waking, but it was not until dawn that the cry of "Sail-ho!" sent them all hurrying to their clothes. Ordinarily officers of the U. S. Navy do not scuttle on deck like a crowd of curious schoolgirls, but all hands had been keyed to a high pitch over the elusive light, and the bet with Edwards now served as an excuse for the betrayal of unusual eagerness. Hence the quarter-deck was soon alive with men who were wont to be deep in dreams at that hour.

They found Carter, whose watch on deck it was, reprimanding the lookout.

"No, sir," the man was insisting, "she didn't show no light, sir. I'd 'a' sighted her an hour ago, sir, if she had."

"We shall see," said Carter grimly. "Who's your relief?"

"Sennett."

"Let him take your place. Go aloft, Sennett."

As the lookout, crestfallen and surly, went below, Barnett said in subdued tones:

"Upon my word, I shouldn't be surprised if the man were right. Certainly there's something queer about that hooker. Look how she handles herself."

The vessel was some three miles to windward. She was a schooner of the common two-masted Pacific type, but she was comporting herself in a manner uncommon on the Pacific, or any other ocean. Even as Barnett spoke, she heeled well over, and came rush-

A schooner comporting herself in a manner uncommon
on the Pacific

ing up into the wind, where she stood with all sails
shaking. Slowly she paid off again, bearing away
from them. Now she gathered full headway, yet edged
little by little to windward again.

"Mighty queer tactics," muttered Edwards. "I
think she's steering herself."

"Good thing she carries a weather helm," commented Ives, who was an expert on sailing rigs.
"Most of that type do. Otherwise she'd have jibed
her masts out, running loose that way."

Captain Parkinson appeared on deck and turned his
glasses for a full minute on the strange schooner.

"Aloft there," he hailed the crow's-nest. "Do you
make out anyone aboard?"

"No, sir," came the answer.

"Mr. Carter, have the chief quartermaster report
on deck with the signal flags."

"Yes, sir."

"Aren't we going to run up to her?" asked Mc-
Guire, turning in surprise to Edwards.

"And take the risk of getting a hole punched in our
pretty paint, with her running amuck that way? Not
much!"

Up came the signal quartermaster to get his orders,
and there ensued a one-sided conversation in the preg-
nant language of the sea.

"What ship is that?"

No answer.

"Are you in trouble?" asked the cruiser, and
waited. The schooner showed a bare and silent main-
peak.

"Heave to." Now Uncle Sam was giving orders.

But the other paid no heed.

"We'll make that a little more emphatic," said Captain Parkinson. A moment later there was the sharp crash of a gun and a shot went across the bows of the sailing vessel. Hastened by a flaw of wind that veered from the normal direction of the breeze the stranger made sharply to windward, as if to obey.

"Ah, there she comes," ran the comment along the cruiser's quarter-deck.

But the schooner, after standing for a moment, all flapping, answered another flaw, and went wide about on the opposite tack.

"Derelict," remarked Captain Parkinson. "She seems to be in good shape, too, Dr. Trendon!"

"Yes, sir." The surgeon went to the captain, and the others could hear his deep, abrupt utterance in reply to some question too low for their ears.

"Might be, sir. Beri-beri, maybe. More likely smallpox if anything of that kind. But *some* of 'em would be on deck."

"Whew! A plague ship!" said Billy Edwards. "Just my luck to be ordered to board her." He shivered slightly.

"Scared, Billy?" said Ives. Edwards had a record for daring which made this joke obvious enough to be safe.

"I wouldn't want to have my peculiar style of beauty spoiled by smallpox marks," said the ensign, with a smile on his homely, winning face. "And I've a hunch that that ship is not a lucky find for this ship."

"Then I've a hunch that your hunch is a wrong

one," said Ives. "How long would you guess that craft to be?"

They were now within a mile of the schooner. Edwards scrutinised her calculatingly.

"Eighty to ninety feet."

"Say 150 tons. And she's a two-masted schooner, isn't she?" continued Ives, insinuatingly.

"She certainly is."

"Well, I've a hunch that that ship is a lucky find for any ship, but particularly for this ship."

"Great Cæsar!" cried the ensign excitedly. "Do you think it's *her?*"

A buzz of electric interest went around the group. Every glass was raised; every eye strained toward her stern to read the name as she veered into the wind again. About she came. A sharp sigh of excited disappointment exhaled from the spectators. The name had been painted out.

"No go," breathed Edwards. "But I'll bet another dinner——"

"Mr. Edwards," called the captain. "You will take the second cutter, board that schooner, and make a full investigation."

"Yes, sir."

"Take your time. Don't come alongside until she is in the wind. Leave enough men aboard to handle her."

"Yes, sir."

The cruiser steamed to within half a mile of the aimless traveller, and the small boat put out. Not one of his fellows but envied the young ensign as he left the ship, steered by Timmins, a veteran bo's'n's mate, wise in all the ins and outs of sea ways. They saw him board, neatly running the small boat under the schooner's counter; they saw the· foresheet eased off and the ship run up into the wind; then the foresail dropped and the wheel lashed so that she would stand so. They awaited the reappearance of Edwards and the bo's'n's mate when they had vanished below decks, and with an intensity of eagerness they followed the return of the small boat.

Billy Edwards's face as he came on deck was a study. It was alight with excitement; yet between the eyes two deep wrinkles of puzzlement quivered. Such a face the mathematician bends above his paper when some obstructive factor arises between him and his solution.

"Well, sir?" There was a hint of effort at restraint in the captain's voice.

"She's the *Laughing Lass,* sir. Everything shipshape, but not a soul aboard."

"Come below, Mr. Edwards," said the captain. And they went, leaving behind them a boiling cauldron of theory and conjecture.

III

THE DEATH SHIP

BILLY EDWARDS came on deck with a line of irritation right-angling the furrows between his eyes.

"Go ahead," the quarter-deck bade him, seeing him aflush with information.

"The captain won't believe me," blurted out Edwards.

"Is it as bad as that?" asked Barnett, smiling.

"It certainly is," replied the younger man seriously. "I don't know that I blame him. I'd hardly believe it myself if I hadn't——"

"Oh, go on. Out with it. Give us the facts. Never mind your credibility."

"The facts are that there lies the *Laughing Lass,* a little weather-worn, but sound as a dollar, and not a living being aboard of her. Her boats are all there. Everything's in good condition, though none too orderly. Pitcher half full of fresh water in the rack. Sails all O. K. Ashes of the galley fire still warm. I tell you, gentlemen, that ship hasn't been deserted more than a couple of days at the outside."

"Are you sure all the boats are there?" asked Ives.

"Dory, dingy, and two surf boats. Isn't that enough?"

"Plenty."

" Been over her, inside and out. No sign of collision. No leak. No anything, except that the starboard side is blistered a bit. No evidence of fire anywhere else. I tell you," said Billy Edwards pathetically, " it's given me a headache."

" Perhaps it's one of those cases of panic that Forsythe spoke of the other night," said Ives. " The crew got frightened at something and ran away, with the devil after them."

" But crews don't just step out and run around the corner and hide, when they're scared," objected Barnett.

" That's true, too," assented Ives. " Well, perhaps that volcanic eruption jarred them so that they jumped for it."

" Pretty wild theory, that," said Edwards.

" No wilder than the facts, as you give them," was the retort.

" That's so," admitted the ensign gloomily.

" But how about pestilence? " suggested Barnett.

" Maybe they died fast and the last survivor, after the bodies of the rest were overboard, got delirious and jumped after them."

" Not if the galley fire was hot," said Dr. Trendon, briefly. " No; pestilence doesn't work that way."

" Did you look at the wheel, Billy? " asked Ives.

" Did I! There's another thing. Wheel's all right, but compass is no good at all. It's regularly bewitched."

" What about the log, then? "

" Couldn't find it anywhere. Hunted high, low, jack, and the game; everywhere except in the big, brass-bound chest I found in the captain's cabin. Couldn't break into that."

"Dr. Schermerhorn's chest!" exclaimed Barnett. "Then he was aboard."

"Well, he isn't aboard now," said the ensign grimly. "Not in the flesh. And that's all," he added suddenly.

"No; it isn't all," said Barnett gently. "There's something else. Captain's orders?"

"Oh, no. Captain Parkinson doesn't take enough stock in my report to tell me to withhold anything," said Edwards, with a trace of bitterness in his voice. "It's nothing that I believe myself, anyhow."

"Give *us* a chance to believe it," said Ives.

"Well," said the ensign hesitantly, "there's a sort of atmosphere about that schooner that's almost uncanny."

"Oh, you had the shudders before you were ordered to board," bantered Ives.

"I know it. I'd have thought it was one of those fool presentiments if I were the only one to feel it. But the men were affected, too. They kept together like frightened sheep. And I heard one say to another: 'Hey, Boney, d'you feel like someone was a-buzzin' your nerves like a fiddle-string?' Now," demanded Edwards plaintively, "what right has a jackie to have nerves?"

"That's strange enough about the compass," said Barnett slowly. "Ours is all right again. The schooner must have been so near the electric disturbance that her instruments were permanently deranged."

"That would lend weight to the volcanic theory," said Carter.

"So the captain didn't take kindly to your go-look-see?" questioned Ives of Edwards.

"As good as told me I'd missed the point of the thing," said the ensign, flushing. "Perhaps he can make more of it himself. At any rate, he's going to try. Here he is now."

"Dr. Trendon," said the captain, appearing. "You will please to go with me to the schooner."

"Yes, sir," said the surgeon, rising from his chair with such alacrity as to draw from Ives the sardonic comment:

"Why, I actually believe old Trendon is excited."

For two hours after the departure of the captain and Trendon there were dull times on the quarter-deck of the *Wolverine*. Then the surgeon came back to them.

"Billy was right," he said.

"But he didn't tell us anything," cried Ives. "He didn't clear up the mystery."

"That's what," said Trendon. "One thing Billy said," he added, waxing unusually prolix for him, "was truer than maybe he knew."

"Thanks," murmured the ensign. "What was that?"

"You said 'Not a living being aboard.' Exact words, hey?"

"Well, what of it?" exclaimed the ensign excitedly. "You don't mean you found dead——?"

"Keep your temperature down, my boy. No. You were exactly right. Not a living being aboard."

"Thanks for nothing," retorted the ensign.

"Neither human nor other," pursued Trendon.

"What!"

"Food scattered around the galley. Crumbs on the mess table. Ever see a wooden ship without cockroaches?"

"Never particularly investigated the matter."

"Don't believe such a thing exists," said Ives.

"Not a cockroach on the *Laughing Lass*. Ever know of an old hooker that wasn't overrun with rats?"

"No; nor anyone else. Not above water."

"Found a dozen dead rats. No sound or sign of a live one on the *Laughing Lass*. No rats, no mice. No bugs. Gentlemen, the *Laughing Lass* is a charnel ship."

"No wonder Billy's tender nerves went wrong," said Ives, with irrepressible flippancy. "She's probably haunted by cockroach wraiths."

"He'll have a chance to see," said Trendon. "Captain's going to put him in charge."

"By way of apology, then," said Barnett. "That's pretty square."

"Captain Parkinson wishes to see you in his cabin, Mr. Edwards," said an orderly, coming in.

"A pleasant voyage, Captain Billy," said Ives. "Sing out if the goblins git yer."

Fifteen minutes later Ensign Edwards, with a quartermaster, Timmins, the bo's'n's mate, and a crew, was heading a straight course toward his first command, with instructions to "keep company and watch for signals"; and intention to break into the brass-bound chest and ferret out what clue lay there, if it took dynamite. As he boarded, Barnett and Trendon, with both of whom the lad was a favourite, came to a sinister conclusion.

"It's poison, I suppose," said the first officer.

"And a mighty subtle sort," agreed Trendon. "Don't like the looks of it." He shook a solemn head. "Don't like it for a damn."

IV

THE SECOND PRIZE CREW

In semi-tropic Pacific weather the unexpected so seldom happens as to be a negligible quantity. The *Wolverine* met with it on June 5th. From some unaccountable source in that realm of the heaven-scouring trades came a heavy mist. Possibly volcanic action, deranging by its electric and gaseous outpourings the normal course of the winds, had given birth to it. Be that as it may, it swept down upon the cruiser, thickening as it approached, until presently it had spread a curtain between the warship and its charge. The wind died. Until after fall of night the *Wolverine* moved slowly, bellowing for the schooner, but got no reply. Once they thought they heard a distant shout of response, but there was no repetition.

" Probably doesn't carry any fog horn," said Carter bitterly, voicing a general uneasiness.

" No log; compass crazy; without fog signal; I don't like that craft. Barnett ought to have been ordered to blow the damned thing up, as a peril to the high seas."

" We'll pick her up in the morning, surely," said Forsythe. " This can't last for ever."

Nor did it last long An hour before midnight a pounding shower fell, lashing the sea into phosphorescent whiteness. It ceased, and with the growl of a

leaping animal a squall furiously beset the ship. Soon
the great steel body was plunging and heaving in the
billows. It was a gloomy company about the wardroom table. Upon each and all hung an oppression of
spirit. Captain Parkinson came from his cabin and
went on deck. Constitutionally he was a nervous and
pessimistic man with a fixed belief in the conspiracy
of events, banded for the undoing of him and his.
Blind or dubious conditions racked his soul, but real
danger found him not only prepared, but even eager.
Now his face was a picture of foreboding.

"Parky looks as if Davy Jones was pulling on his
string," observed the flippant Ives to his neighbour.

"Worrying about the schooner. Hope Billy Edwards saw or heard or felt that squall coming," replied Forsythe, giving expression to the anxiety that
all felt.

"He's a good sailor man," said Ives, "and that's a
staunch little schooner, by the way she handled
herself."

"Oh, it will be all right," said Carter confidently.
"The wind's moderating now."

"But there's no telling how far out of the course
this may have blown him."

Barnett came down, dripping.

"Anything new?" asked Dr. Trendon.

The navigating officer shook his head.

"Nothing. But the captain's in a state of mind," he
said.

"What's wrong with him?"

"The schooner. Seems possessed with the notion
that there's something wrong with her."

" Aren't you feeling a little that way yourself? "
said Forsythe. " I am. I'll take a look around before
I turn in."

He left behind him a silent crowd. His return was
prompt and swift.

" Come on deck," he said.

Every man leaped as to an order. There was that
in Forsythe's voice which stung. The weather had
cleared somewhat, though scudding wrack still blew
across them to the westward. The ship rolled heavily.
Of the sea naught was visible except the arching waves,
but in the sky they beheld again, with a sickening sense
of disaster, that pale and lovely glow which had so
bewildered them two nights before.

" The aurora! " cried McGuire, the paymaster.

" Oh, certainly," replied Ives, with sarcasm. " Dead
in the west. Common spot for the aurora. Particularly on the edge of the South Seas, where they are
thick! "

" Then what is it? "

Nobody had an answer. Carter hastened forward
and returned to report.

" It's electrical anyway," said Carter. " The compass is queer again."

" Edwards ought to be close to the solution of it,"
ventured Ives. " This gale should have blown him just
about to the centre of interest."

" If only he isn't involved in it," said Carter anxiously.

" What could there be to involve him? " asked Mc-
Guire.

" I don't know," said Carter slowly. " Somehow

I feel as if the desertion of the schooner was in some formidable manner connected with that light."

For perhaps fifteen minutes the glow continued. It seemed to be nearer at hand than on the former sighting; but it took no comprehensible form. Then it died away and all was blackness again. But the officers of the *Wolverine* had long been in troubled slumber before the sensitive compass regained its exact balance, and with the shifting wind to mislead her, the cruiser had wandered, by morning, no man might know how far from her course.

All day long of June 6th the *Wolverine,* baffled by patches of mist and moving rain-squalls, patrolled the empty seas without sighting the lost schooner. The evening brought an envelope of fog again, and presently a light breeze came up from the north. An hour of it had failed to disperse the mist, when there was borne down to the warship a flapping sound as of great wings. The flapping grew louder—waned— ceased—and from the lookout came a hail.

" Ship's lights three points on the starboard quarter."

" What do you make it out to be? " came the query from below.

" Green light's all I can see, sir." There was a pause.

" There's her port light, now. Looks to be turning and bearing down on us, sir. Coming dead for us "— the man's voice rose—" close aboard; less'n two ship's lengths away! "

As for a prearranged scene, the fog-curtain parted. There loomed silently and swiftly the *Laughing Lass.*

Down she bore upon the greater vessel until it seemed as if she must ram; but all the time she was veering to windward, and now she ran into the wind with a castanet rattle of sails. So close aboard was she that the eager eyes of Uncle Sam's men peered down upon her empty decks—for she was void of life.

Behind the cruiser's blanketing she paid off very slowly, but presently caught the breeze full and again whitened the water at her prow. Forgetting regulations, Ives hailed loudly:

"Ahoy, *Laughing Lass!* Ahoy, Billy Edwards!"

No sound, no animate motion came from aboard that apparition, as she fell astern. A shudder of horror ran across the *Wolverine's* quarter-deck. A wraith ship, peopled with skeletons, would have been less dreadful to their sight than the brisk and active desolation of the heeling schooner.

"Been deserted since early last night," said Trendon hoarsely.

"How can you tell that?" asked Barnett.

"Both sails reefed down. Ready for that squall. Been no weather since to call for reefs. Must have quit her during the squall."

"Then they jumped," cried Carter, "for I saw her boats. It isn't believable."

"Neither was the other," said Trendon grimly.

A hurried succession of orders stopped further discussion for the time. Ives was sent aboard the schooner to lower sail and report. He came back with a staggering dearth of information. The boats were all there; the ship was intact—as intact as when Billy Edwards had taken charge—but the cheery, lovable ensign and his men had vanished without trace or clue. As to the how or the wherefore they might rack their brains without guessing. There was the beginning of a log in the ensign's handwriting, which Ives had found with high excitement and read with bitter disappointment.

"*Had squall from northeast,*" it ran. "*Double reefed her and she took it nicely. Seems a seaworthy, quick ship. Further search for log. No result. Have ordered one of crew who is a bit of a mechanic to work at the brass-bound chest till he gets it open. He reports marks on the lock as if somebody had been trying to pick it before him.*"

There was no further entry.

"Dr. Trendon is right," said Barnett. "Whatever happened—and God only knows what it could have been—it happened just after the squall."

"Just about the time of the strange glow," cried Ives.

It was decided that two men and a petty officer should be sent aboard the *Laughing Lass* to make her fast with a cable, and remain on board over night. But when the order was given the men hung back. One of them protested brokenly that he was sick. Trendon, after examination, reported to the captain.

"Case of blue funk, sir. Might as well be sick. Good for nothing. Others aren't much better."

"Who was to be in charge?"

"Congdon," replied the doctor, naming one of the petty officers.

"He's my coxswain," said Captain Parkinson. "A

A man who was a bit of a mechanic was set to work
to open the chest

first-class man. I can hardly believe that he is afraid.
We'll see."

Congdon was sent for.

" You're ordered aboard the schooner for the night,
Congdon," said the captain.

" Yes, sir."

" Is there any reason why you do not wish to go?"

The man hesitated, looking miserable. Finally he
blurted out, not without a certain dignity:

" I obey orders, sir."

" Speak out, my man," urged the captain kindly.

" Well, sir: it's Mr. Edwards, then. You couldn't
scare him off a ship, sir, unless it was something—
something——"

He stopped, failing of the word.

" You know what Mr. Edwards was, sir, for
pluck," he concluded.

" *Was!*" cried the captain sharply. " What do you
mean?

" The schooner got him, sir. You don't make no
doubt of that, do you, sir?" The man spoke in a
hushed voice, with a shrinking glance back of him.

" Will you go aboard under Mr. Ives?"

" Anywhere my officer goes I'll go, and gladly,
sir."

Ives was sent aboard in charge. For that night, in
a light breeze, the two ships lay close together, the
schooner riding jauntily astern. But not until morning illumined the world of waters did the *Wolverine's*
people feel confident that the *Laughing Lass* would not
vanish away from their ken like a shape of the mist.

V

THE DISAPPEARANCE

WHEN Barnett come on deck very early in the morning of June 7th, he found Dr. Trendon already up and staring moodily out at the *Laughing Lass*. As the night was calm the tow had made fair time toward their port in the Hawaiian group. The surgeon was muttering something which seemed to Barnett to be in a foreign tongue.

" Thought out any clue, doctor? " asked the first officer.

" *Petit Chel*—Pshaw! *Jolie Celimene!* No," muttered Trendon. " *Marie—Marie*—I've got it! The *Marie Celeste*."

" Got what? What about her? "

" Parallel case." said Trendon. " Sailed from New York back in the seventies. Seven weeks out was found derelict. Everything in perfect order. Captain's wife's hem on the machine. Boats all accounted for. No sign of struggle. Log written to within forty-eight hours."

" What became of the crew? "

" Wish I could tell you. Might help to unravel our tangle." He shook his head in sudden, unwonted passion.

" Evidently there's something criminal in her record," said Barnett, frowning at the fusty schooner astern. " Otherwise the name wouldn't be painted out."

" Painted out long ago. See how rusty it is. Scher-merhorn's work maybe," replied Trendon. " Secret ex-pedition, remember."

" In the name of wonders, why should he do it? "

" Secret expedition, wasn't it? "

" Um-ah; that's true," said the other thoughtfully. " It's quite possible."

" Captain wishes to see both of you gentlemen in the ward room, if you please," came a message.

Below they found all the officers gathered. Captain Parkinson was pacing up and down in ill-controlled agitation.

" Gentlemen," he said, " we are facing a problem which, so far as I know, is without parallel. It is my intention to bring the schooner which we have in tow to port at Honolulu. In the present unsettled weather we cannot continue to tow her. I wish two officers to take charge. Under the circumstances I shall issue no orders. The duty must be voluntary."

Instantly every man, from the veteran Trendon to the youthful paymaster, volunteered.

" That is what I expected," said Captain Parkinson quietly. " But I have still a word to say. I make no doubt in my own mind that the schooner has twice been beset by the gravest of perils. Nothing less would have driven Mr. Edwards from his post. All of us who know him will appreciate that. Nor can I free myself from the darkest forebodings as to his fate and that of his companions. But as to the nature of the peril I am unable to make any conjecture worthy of consideration. Has anyone a theory to offer? "

There was a dead silence.

"Mr. Barnett? Dr. Trendon? Mr. Ives?"

"Is there not possibly some connection between the unexplained light which we have twice seen, and the double desertion of the ship?" suggested the first officer, after a pause.

"I have asked myself that over and over. Whatever the source of the light and however near to it the schooner may have been, she is evidently unharmed."

"Yes, sir," said Barnett. "That seems to vitiate that explanation."

"I thank you, gentlemen, for the promptitude of your offers," continued the captain. "In this respect you make my duty the more difficult. I shall accept Mr. Ives because of his familiarity with sailing craft and with these seas." His eyes ranged the group.

"I beg your pardon, Captain Parkinson," eagerly put in the paymaster, "but I've handled a schooner yacht for several years and I'd appreciate the chance of——"

"Very well, Mr. McGuire, you shall be the second in command."

"Thank you, sir."

"You gentlemen will pick a volunteer crew and go aboard at once. Spare no effort to find records of the schooner's cruise. Keep in company and watch for signals. Report at once any discovery or unusual incident, however slight."

Not so easily was a crew obtained. Having in mind the excusable superstition of the men, Captain Parkinson was unwilling to compel any of them to the duty.

Awed by the mystery of their mates' disappearance, the sailors hung back. Finally by temptation of extra prize money, a complement was made up.

At ten o'clock of a puffy, mist-laden morning a new and strong crew of nine men boarded the *Laughing Lass*. There were no farewells among the officers. Forebodings weighed too heavy for such open expression.

All the fates of weather seemed to combine to part the schooner from her convoy. As before, the fog fell, only to be succeeded by squally rain-showers that cut out the vista into a checkerboard pattern of visible sea and impenetrable greyness. Before evening the *Laughing Lass,* making slow way through the mists, had become separated by a league of waves from the cruiser. One glimpse of her between mist areas the *Wolverine* caught at sunset. Then wind and rain descended in furious volume from the southeast. The cruiser immediately headed about, following the probable course of her charge, which would be beaten far down to leeward. It was a gloomy mess on the warship. In his cabin, Captain Parkinson was frankly sea-sick: a condition which nothing but the extreme of nervous depression ever induced in him.

For several hours the rain fell and the gale howled. Then the sky swiftly cleared, and with the clearing there rose a great cry of amaze from stem to stern of the *Wolverine.* For far toward the western horizon appeared such a prodigy as the eye of no man aboard that ship had ever beheld. From a belt of marvellous, glowing gold, rich and splendid streamers of light spiralled up into the blackness of the heavens.

In all the colours of the spectrum they rose and fell; blazing orange, silken, wonderful, translucent blues, and shimmering reds. Below, a broad band of paler hue, like sheet lightning fixed to rigidity, wavered and rippled. All the auroras of the northland blended in one could but have paled away before the splendour of that terrific celestial apparition.

On board the cruiser all hands stood petrified, bound in a stricture of speechless wonder. After the first cry, silence lay leaden over the ship. It was broken by a scream of terror from forward. The quartermaster who had been at the wheel came clambering down the ladder and ran along the deck, his fingers splayed and stiffened before him in the intensity of his panic.

"The needle! The compass!" he shrieked.

Barnett ran to the wheel house with Trendon at his heels. The others followed. The needle was sway-ing like a cobra's head. And as a cobra's head spits venom, it spat forth a thin, steel-blue stream of lucent fire. Then so swiftly it whirled that the sparks scat-tered from it in a tiny shower. It stopped, quivered, and curved itself upward until it rattled like a fairy drum upon the glass shield. Barnett looked at Trendon.

"Volcanic?" he said.

"'Mine eyes have seen the coming of the glory of the Lord,'" muttered the surgeon in his deep bass, as he looked forth upon the streaming, radiant heavens. "It's like nothing else."

In the west the splendour and the terror shot to the zenith. Barnett whirled the wheel. The ship re-sponded perfectly.

" I though she might be bewitched, too," he murmured.

" You may head her for the light, Mr. Barnett," said Captain Parkinson calmly. He had come from his cabin, all his nervous depression gone in the face of an imminent and visible danger.

Slowly the great mass of steel swung to the unknown. For an hour the unknown guided her. Then fell blackness, sudden, complete. After that radiance the dazzled eye could make out no stars, but the look-out's keen vision discerned something else.

" Ship afire," he shouted hoarsely.

" Where away? "

" Two points to leeward, near where the light was, sir."

They turned their eyes to the direction indicated, and beheld a majestic rolling volume of purple light. Suddenly a fiercer red shot it through.

" That's no ship afire," said Trendon. " Volcano in eruption."

" And the other? " asked the captain.

" No volcano, sir."

" Poor Billy Edwards wins his bet," said Forsythe, in a low voice.

" God grant he's on earth to collect it," replied Barnett solemnly.

No one turned in that night. When the sun of June 8th rose, it showed an ocean bare of prospect except that on the far horizon where the chart showed no land there rose a smudge of dirty rolling smoke. Of the schooner there was neither sign nor trace.

VI

THE CASTAWAYS

"THIS ship," growled Carter, the second officer, to Dr. Trendon, as they stood watching the growing smoke-column, "is a worse hot-bed of rumours than a down-east village. That's the third sea-gull we've had officially reported since breakfast."

As he said, three distinct times the *Wolverine* had thrilled to an imminent discovery, which, upon nearer investigation, had dwindled to nothing more than a floating fowl. Upon the heels of Carter's complaint came another hail.

"Boat ahoy. Three points on the starboard bow."

"If that's another gull," muttered Carter, "I'll have something to say to you, my festive lookout."

The news ran electrically through the cruiser, and all eyes were strained for a glimpse of the boat. The ship swung away to starboard.

"Let me know as soon as you can make her out," ordered Carter.

"Aye, aye, sir."

"There's certainly something there," said Forsythe, presently. "I can make out a speck rising on the waves."

"Bit o' wreckage from Barnett's derelict," muttered Trendon, scowling through his glasses.

"Rides too high for a spar or anything of that sort," said the junior lieutenant.

"She's a small boat," came in the clear tones of the lookout, "driftin' down."

"Anyone in her?" asked Carter.

"Can't make out yet, sir. No one's in charge though, sir."

Captain Parkinson appeared and Carter pointed out the speck to him.

"Yes. Give her full speed," said the captain, replying to a question from the officer of the deck.

Forward leapt the swift cruiser, all too slow for the anxious hearts of those aboard. For there was not one of the *Wolverines* who did not expect from this aimless traveller of desert seas at the least a leading clue to the riddle that oppressed them.

"Aloft there!"

"Aye, aye, sir."

"Can you make out her build?"

"Rides high, like a dory, sir."

"Wasn't there a dory on the *Laughing Lass?*" cried Forsythe.

"On her stern davits," answered Trendon.

"It is hardly probable that unattached small boats should be drifting about these seas," said Captain Parkinson, thoughtfully. "If she's a dory, she's the *Laughing Lass's* boat."

"That's what she is," said Barnett. "You can see her build plain enough now."

"Mr. Barnett, will you go aloft and keep me posted?" said the captain.

The executive officer climbed to join the lookout.

As he ascended, those below saw the little craft rise high and slow on a broad swell.

"Same dory," said Trendon. "I'd swear to her in Constantinople."

"What else could she be?" muttered Forsythe.

"Somethin' that looks like a man in the bottom of her," sang out the crow's-nest. "Two of 'em, I think."

For five minutes there was stillness aboard, broken only by an occasional low-voiced conjecture. Then from aloft:

"Two men rolling in the bottom."

"Are they alive?"

"No, sir; not that I can see."

The wind, which had been extremely variable since dawn, now whipped around a couple of points, swinging the boat's stern to them. Barnet, putting aside his glass for a moment, called down:

"That's the one, sir. I can make out the name."

"Good," said the captain quietly. "We should have news, at least."

"Ives or McGuire," suggested Forsythe, in low tones.

"Or Billy Edwards," amended Carter.

"Not Edwards," said Trendon.

"How do you know?" demanded Forsythe.

"Dory was aboard when we found her the second time, after Edwards had left."

"Can you make out which of the men are in her?" hailed the captain.

"Don't think it's any of our people," came the astonishing reply from Barnett.

"Are you sure?"

"I can see only one man's face, sir. It isn't Ives or McGuire. He's a stranger to me."

"It must be one of the crew, then."

"No, sir, beg your parding," called the lookout. "Nothin' like that in our crew, sir."

The boat came down upon them swiftly. Soon the quarter-deck was looking into her. She was of a type common enough on the high seas, except that a step for a mast showed that she had presumably been used for skimming about open shores. Of her passengers, one lay forward, prone and quiet. A length of sail cloth spread over him made it impossible to see his garb. At his breast an ugly protuberance, outlined vaguely, hinted a deformity.

The other sprawled aft, and at a nearer sight of him some of the men broke out into nervous titters. There was some excuse, for surely such a scarecrow had never before been the sport of wind and wave. A thing of shreds he was, elaborately ragged, a face overrun with a scrub of beard, and preternaturally drawn, surmounted by a stiff-dried, dirty, cloth semi-turban, with a wide, forbidding stain along the side, worked out the likeness to a make-up.

"My God!" cackled Forsythe with an hysterical explosion; and again, "My God!"

A long-drawn, irrepressible aspiration of expectancy rose from the warship's decks as the stranger raised his haggard face, turned eyes unseeingly upon them, and fell back. The forward occupant stirred not, save as the boat rolled.

From between decks someone called out, sharply, an order. In the grim silence it seemed strangely incongruous that the measured business of a ship's life should be going forward as usual. Something within the newcomer's consciousness stirred to that voice of authority. Mechanically, like some huge, hideous toy, he raised first one arm, then the other, and hitched himself halfway up on the stern seat. His mouth opened. His face wrinkled. He seemed groping for the meaning of a joke at which he knew he ought to laugh. Suddenly from his lips in surprising volume, raucous, rasping, yet with a certain rollicking deviltry fit to set the head a-tilt, burst a chanty:

" Oh, their coffin was their ship, and their grave it was
        the sea:
        Blow high, blow low, what care we!
And the quarter that we gave them was to sink them in
        the sea:
        Down on the coast of the high Barbaree-ee."

Long-drawn, like the mockery of a wail, the minor cadence wavered through the stillness, and died away.

" The High Barbaree! " cried Trendon.

" You know it? " asked the captain, expectant of a clue.

" One of those cursed tunes you can't forget," said the surgeon. " Heard a scoundrel of a beach-comber sing it years ago. Down in New Zealand, that was. When the fever rose on him he'd pipe up. Used to beat time with a steel hook he wore in place of a hand. The thing haunted me till I was sorry I hadn't let the rascal die. This creature might have learned it from him. Howls it out exactly like."

"I don't see that that helps us any," said Forsythe, looking down on the preparations that were making to receive the unexpected guests.

With a deftness which had made the *Wolverine* famous in the navy for the niceties of seamanship, the great cruiser let down her tackle as she drew skilfully alongside, and made fast, preparatory to lifting the dory gently to her broad deck. But before the order came to hoist away, one of the jackies who had gone down drew the covering back from the still figure forward, and turned it over. With a half-stifled cry he shrank back. And at that the tension of soul and mind on the *Wolverine* snapped, breaking into outcries and sudden, sharp imprecations. The face revealed was that of Timmins, the bo's'n's mate, who had sailed with the first vanished crew. A life preserver was fastened under his arms. He was dead.

"I'm out," said the surgeon briefly, and stood with mouth agape. Never had the disciplined *Wolverines* performed a sea duty with so ragged a routine as the getting in of the boat containing the live man and the dead body. The dead seaman was reverently disposed and covered. As to the survivor there was some hesitancy on the part of the captain, who was inclined to send him forward until Dr. Trendon, after a swift scrutiny, suggested that for the present, at least, he be berthed aft. They took the stranger to Edwards's vacant room, where Trendon was closeted with him for half an hour. When he emerged he was beset with questions.

"Can't give any account of himself yet," said the surgeon. "Weak and not rightly conscious."

" What ails him? "

" Enough. Gash in his scalp. Fever. Thirst and exhaustion. Nervous shock, too, I think."

" How came he aboard the *Laughing Lass?* " " Does he know anything of Billy? " " Was he a stow-away? " " Did you ask him about Ives and Mc-Guire? " " How came he in the small boat? " " Where are the rest? "

" Now, now," said the veteran chidingly. " How can I tell? Would you have me kill the man with questions? "

He left them to look at the body of the bo's'n's mate. Not a word had he to say when he returned. Only the captain got anything out of him but growling and unintelligible expressions, which seemed to be objurgatory and to express bewildered cogitation.

" How long had poor Timmins been drowned? " the captain had asked him, and Trendon replied:

" Captain Parkinson, the man wasn't drowned. No water in his lungs."

" Not drowned! Then how came he by his death? "

" If I were to diagnose it under any other conditions I should say that he had inhaled flames."

Then the two men stared at each other in blank impotency. Meantime the scarecrow was showing signs of returning consciousness and a message was dispatched for the physician. On his way he met Barnett, who asked and received permission to accompany him. The stranger was tossing restlessly in his bunk, opening and shutting his parched mouth in silent, piteous appeal for the water that must still be doled to him parsimoniously.

"I think I'll try him with a little brandy," said Trendon, and sent for the liquor.

Barnett raised the patient while the surgeon held the glass to his lips. The man's hand rose, wavered, and clasped the glass.

"All right, my friend. Take it yourself, if you like," said Trendon.

The fingers closed. Tremulously held, the little glass tilted and rattled against the teeth. There was one deep, eager spasm of swallowing. Then the fevered eyes opened upon the face of the *Wolverine's* first officer.

"Prosit, Barnett," said the man, in a voice like the rasp of rusty metal.

The navy man straightened up as from a blow under the jaw.

"Be careful what you are about," warned Trendon, addressing his superior officer sharply, for Barnett had all but let his charge drop. His face was a puckered mask of amaze and incredulity.

"Did you hear him speak my name—or am I dreaming?" he half whispered.

"Heard him plain enough. Who is he?"

The man's eyes closed, but he smiled a little—a singular, wry-mouthed, winning smile. With that there sprung from behind the brush of beard, filling out the deep lines of emaciation, a memory to the recognition of Barnett; a keen and gay countenance that whisked him back across seven years time to the days of Dewey and the Philippines.

"Ralph Slade, by the Lord!" he exclaimed.

"Of the *Laughing Lass?*" cried Trendon.

" Of the *Laughing Lass.*"

Such a fury of eagerness burned in the face of Barnett that Trendon cautioned him. " See here, Mr. Barnett, you're not going to fire a broadside of disturbing questions at my patient yet a while. He's in no condition."

But it was from the other that the questions came. Opening his eyes he whispered, " The sailor? Where?"

" Dead," said Trendon bluntly. Then, breaking his own rule of repression, he asked:

" Did he come off the schooner with you?"

" Picked him up," was the straining answer. " Drifting."

The survivor looked around him, then into Barnett's face, and his mind too, traversed the years.

"*North Dakota?*" he queried.

" No; I've changed my ship," said Barnett. " This is the *Wolverine.*"

" Where's the *Laughing Lass?*"

Barnett shook his head.

" Tell me," begged Slade.

" Wait till you're stronger," admonished Trendon.

" Can't wait," said the weak voice. The eyes grew wild.

" Mr. Barnett, tell him the bare outline and make it short," said the surgeon.

" We sighted the *Laughing Lass* two days ago. She was in good shape, but deserted. That is, we thought she was deserted."

The man nodded eagerly.

" I suppose you were aboard," said Barnett, and

Trendon made a quick gesture of impatience and re-
buke.

"No," said Slade. "Left three—four—don't know
how many nights ago."

The officers looked at each other. "Go on," said
Trendon to his companion.

"We put a crew aboard in command of an ensign,"
continued Barnett, "and picked up the schooner the
next night, deserted. You must know about it. Where
is Billy Edwards?"

"Never heard of him," whispered the other.

"Ives and McGuire, then. They were there
after—— Great God, man!" he cried, his agitation
breaking out, "Pull yourself together! Give us
something to go on."

"Mr. Barnett!" said the surgeon peremptorily.

But the suggestion was working in the sick man's
brain. He turned to the officers a face of horror.

"Your man, Edwards—the crew—they left her? In
the night?"

"What does he mean?" cried Barnett.

"The light! You saw it?"

"Yes; we saw a strange light," answered Trendon
soothingly. Slade half rose. "Lost; all lost!" he
cried, and fell back unconscious. Trendon exploded
into curses. "See what you've done to my patient,"
he fumed. Barnett looked at him with contrite eyes.

"Better get out before he comes to," growled the
surgeon. "Nice way to treat a man half dead of exhaustion."

It was nearly an hour before Slade came back to
the world again. The doctor forbade him to attempt

speech. But of one thing he would not be denied. There was a struggle for utterance, then:

"The volcano?" he rasped out.

"Dead ahead," was the reply.

"Stand by!" grasped Slade. He strove to rise, to say something further, but endurance had reached its limit. The man was utterly done.

Dr. Trendon went on deck, his head sunk between his shoulders. For a minute he was in earnest talk with the captain. Presently the *Wolverine's* engines slowed down, and she lay head to the waves, with just enough turn of the screw to hold her against the sea-way.

VII

THE FREE LANCE

By the following afternoon Dr. Trendon reported his patient as quite recovered.

"Starved for water," proffered the surgeon. "Tissues fairly dried out. Soaked him up. Fed him broth. Put him to sleep. He's all right. Just wakes up to eat; then off again like a two-year old. Wonderful constitution."

"The gentleman wants to know if he can come on deck, sir," saluted an orderly.

"Waked up, eh. Come on, Barnett. Help me boost him on deck."

The two officers disappeared to return in a moment arm-in-arm with Ralph Slade.

Nearly twenty-four hours' rest and skilful treatment had done wonders. He was still a trifle weak and uncertain, was still a little glad to lean on the arms of his companions, but his eye was bright and alert, and his hollow cheeks mounted a slight colour. This, with the clothes lent him by Barnett, transformed his appearance, and led Captain Parkinson to congratulate himself that he had not obeyed his first impulse to send the castaway forward with the men.

The officers pressed forward.

"Mighty glad to see you out." "Hope you've got

your pins under you again." "Old man, I'm mighty glad we came along."

The chorus of greeting was hearty enough, but the journalist barely paid the courtesy of acknowledgment. His eye swept the horizon eagerly until it rested on the cloud of volcanic smoke billowing up across the setting sun. A sigh of relief escaped him.

"Where are we?" he asked Barnett. "I mean since you picked me up. How long ago was that, anyway?"

"Yesterday," replied the navigating officer. "We've stood off and on, looking for some of our men."

"Then that's the same volcano——"

Barnett laughed softly. "Well, they aren't quite holding a caucus of volcanoes down in this country. One like that is enough."

But Slade brushed the remark aside.

"Head for it!" he cried excitedly. "We may be in time! There's a man on that island."

"A man!" "Another!" "Not Billy Edwards?" "Not some of our boys?"

Slade stared at them bewildered.

"Hold on," interposed Dr. Trendon authoritatively. "What's his name?" he inquired of the journalist.

"Darrow," replied the latter. "Percy Darrow. Do you know him?"

"Who in Kamschatka is Percy Darrow?" demanded Forsythe.

"Why, he's the assistant. "It's a long story——"

"Of course, it's a long story. There's a lot we want to know," interrupted Captain Parkinson. "Quartermaster, head for the volcano yonder. Mr. Slade, we want to know where you came from; and why you left the schooner, and who Percy Darrow is. And there's dinner, so we'll just adjourn to the messroom and hear what you can tell us. But there's one thing we're all anxious to know; how came you in the dory which we found and left on the *Laughing Lass* no later than two days ago?"

"I haven't set eyes on the *Laughing Lass* for— well, I don't know how long, but it's five days anyway, perhaps more," replied Slade.

They stared at him incredulously.

"Oh, I see!" he burst out suddenly; "there were twin dories on the schooner. The other one's still there, I suppose. Did you find her on the stern davits?"

"Yes."

"That's it, then. You see when I left——"

Captain Parkinson's raised hand checked him. "If you will be so good, Mr. Slade, let us have it all at once, after mess."

At table the young officers, at a sharp hint from Dr. Trendon, conversed on indifferent subjects until the journalist had partaken heartily of what the physician allowed him. Slade ate with keen appreciation.

"I tell you, that's good," he sighed, when he had finished. "Real, live, after-dinner coffee, too. Why, gentlemen, I haven't eaten a civilised meal, with all the trimmings, for over two years. Doctor, do you think a little of the real stuff would hurt me? It's a pretty dry yarning."

"One glass," growled the surgeon, "no more."

" Scotch high-ball, then," voted Slade, " the higher the better."

The steward brought a tall glass with ice, in which the newcomer mixed his drink. Then for quite a minute he sat silent, staring at the table, his fingers aimlessly rubbing into spots of wetness the water beads as they gathered on the outside of his glass. Suddenly he looked up.

" I don't know how to begin," he confessed. " It's too confounded improbable. I hardly believe it myself, now that I'm sitting here in human clothes, surrounded by human beings. Old Scrubs, and the Nigger, and Handy Solomon, and the Professor, and the chest, and the—well, they were real enough when I was caught in the mess. But I warn you, you are not going to believe me, and hanged if I blame you a bit."

" We've seen marvels ourselves in the last few days," encouraged Captain Parkinson.

" Fire ahead, man," advised Barnett impatiently. " Just begin at the beginning and let it go at that."

Slade sipped at his glass reflectively.

" Well," said he at length, " the best way to begin is to show you how I happened to be mixed up in it at all."

The officers unconsciously relaxed into attitudes of greater ease. Overhead the lamps swayed gently to the swell. The dull throb of the screw pulsated. Stewards clad in white moved noiselessly, filling the glasses, deferentially striking lights for the smokers, clearing away the last dishes of the repast.

" I'm a reporter by choice, and a detective by instinct," began Slade, with startling abruptness. "Furthermore, I'm pretty well off. I'm what they call a free lance, for I have no regular desk on any of the journals. I generally turn my stuff in to the *Star* because they treat me well. In return it is pretty well understood between us that I'm to use my judgment in regard to 'stories' and that they'll stand back of me for expenses. You see, I've been with them quite a while."

He looked around the circle as though in appeal to the comprehension of his audience. Some of the men nodded. Others sipped from their glasses or drew at their cigars.

"I loaf around here and there in the world, having a good time travelling, visiting, fooling around. Every once in a while something interests me. The thing is a sort of instinct. I run it down. If it's a good story, I send it in. That's all there is to it." He laughed slightly. "You see, I'm a sort of magazine writer in method, but my stuff is newspaper stuff. Also the game suits me. That's why I play it. That's why I'm here. I have to tell you about myself this way so you will understand how I came to be mixed up in this *Laughing Lass* matter."

"I remember," commented Barnett, "that when you came aboard the *South Dakota,* you had a little trouble making Captain Arnold see it." He turned to the others with a laugh. "He had all kinds of papers of ancient date, but nothing modern—letter from the *Star* dated five years back, recommendations to everybody on earth, except Captain Arnold, certificate of bravery in Apache campaign, bank identifications, and all the rest. 'Maybe you're the *Star's* correspondent, and maybe you're not,' said the Captain, 'I don't see anything here to prove it.' Slade argued an hour; no go. Remember how you caught him?" he inquired of Slade.

The reporter grinned assent.

" After the old man had turned him down for good, Slade fished down in his warbag and hauled out an old tattered document from an oilskin case. 'Hold on a minute,' said he, 'you old shellback. I've proved to you that I can write; and I've proved to you that I have fought, and now here I'll prove to you that I can sail. If writing, fighting, and sailing don't fit me adequately to report any little disturbances your antiquated washboiler may blunder into, I'll go to raising cabbages.' With that he presented a master's certificate! Where did you get it, anyway? I never found out."

" Passed as ' fresh-water ' on the Great Lakes," replied Slade briefly.

" Well, the spunk and the certificate finished the captain. He was an old square rigger himself in the Civil War."

" So much for myself," Slade continued. " As for the *Laughing Lass*——"

PART TWO

THE BRASS BOUND CHEST

Being the story told by Ralph Slade, Free Lance, to the officers of the United States cruiser Wolverine.

I

THE BARBARY COAST

A COINCIDENCE got me aboard her. I'll tell you how
it was. One evening late I was just coming out of
a dark alley on the Barbary Coast, San Francisco.
You know—the water front, where you can hear more
tongues than at Port Said, see stranger sights, and
meet adventure with the joyous certainty of mediæval
times. I'd been down there hunting up a man reported,
by a wharf-rat of my acquaintance, to have just returned from a two years' whaling voyage. He'd been
" shanghaied " aboard, and as a matter of fact, was
worth nearly a million dollars. Landed in the city
without a cent, could get nobody to believe him, nor
trust him to the extent of a telegram East. Wharf-
rat laughed at his yarn; but I believe it was true. Good
copy anyway——

Just at the turn of the alley I nearly bumped into
two men. On the Barbary Coast you don't pass men
in narrow places until you have reconnoitered a little.
I pulled up, thanking fortune that they had not seen
me. The first words were uttered in a voice I knew
well.

You've all heard of Dr. Karl Augustus Schermerhorn. He did some big things, and had in mind
still bigger. I'd met him some time before in connection with his telepathy and wireless waves theory.

57

It was picturesque stuff for my purpose, but wasn't in it with what the old fellow had really done. He showed me—well, that doesn't matter. The point is, that good, staid, self-centred, or rather science-centred, Dr. Schermerhorn was standing at midnight in a dark alley on the Barbary Coast in San Francisco talking to an individual whose facial outline at least was not ornamental.

My curiosity, or professional instinct, whichever you please, was all aroused. I flattened myself against the wall.

The first remark I lost. The reply came to me in a shrill falsetto. So grotesque was the effect of this treble from a bulk so squat and broad and hairy as the silhouette before me that I almost laughed aloud.

" I guess you've made no mistake on that. I'm her master, and her owner too."

" Well, I haf been told you might rent her," said the Doctor.

" Rent her! " mimicked the falsetto. " Well, that —hell, yes, I'll *rent* her! " he laughed again.

" Doch recht." The Doctor was plainly at the end of his practical resources.

After waiting a moment for something more definite, the falsetto inquired rather drily:

" How long? What to? What for? Who are you, anyway? "

" I am Dr. Schermerhorn," the latter answered.

" Seen pieces about you in the papers."

" How many men haf you in the crew? "

" Me and the mate and the cook and four hands."

" And you could go—soon? "

"Soon as you want—*if* I go."

"I wish to leaf to-morrow."

"If I can get the crew together, I might make it. But say, let's not hang out here in this run of darkness. Come over to the grog shop yonder where we can sit down."

To my relief, for my curiosity was fully aroused— Dr. Schermerhorn's movements are usually productive —this proposal was vetoed.

"No, no!" cried the Doctor, with some haste, "this iss well! Somebody might oferhear."

The huge figure stirred into an attitude of close attention. After a pause the falsetto asked deliberately:

"Where we goin'?"

"I brefer not to say."

"H'm! How long a cruise?"

"I want to rent your schooner and your crew as-long-as I-please-to remain."

"H'm! How long's that likely to be?"

"Maybe a few months; maybe seferal years."

"H'm! Unknown port; unknown cruise. See here, anything crooked in this?"

"No, no! Not at all! It iss simply business of my own."

"Not that I care," commented the other easily, "only risks is worth paying for."

"There shall not be risk."

"Pearls likely?" hazarded the other, without much heed to the assurance. "Them Jap gunboats is getting pretty hard to dodge of late years. However, I've dodged 'em before."

" Now as to pay—how mooch iss your boat worth? "

I could almost follow the man's thoughts as he pondered how much he dared ask.

" Well, you see, for a proposition like that—don't know where we're going, when we're going to get back,—and them gunboats—how would a hundred and twenty-five a month strike you? "

" Double it up. I want you to do ass I say, and I will also give your crew double wages. Bud I want goot men, who will stay, and who will keep the mouth shut."

" Gosh all fish-hooks! They'd go to hell with you for that! "

" Now you can get all you want of Adams & Marsh. Tell them it iss for me. Brovisions for three years, anyhow. Be ready to sail to-morrow."

" Tide turns at eight in the evening."

" I will send some effects in the morning."

The master hesitated.

" That's all right, Doctor, but how do I know it's all right? Maybe by morning you'll change your mind."

" That cannot be. My plans are all——"

" It's the usual thing to pay something——"

" Ach, but yes. I haf forgot. Darrow told me. I will make you a check. Let us go to the table of which you spoke."

They moved away, still talking. I did not dare follow them into the light, for I feared that the Doctor would recognise me. I'd have given my eye teeth, though, to have gathered the name of the schooner, or that of her master. As it was, I hung around until the two had emerged from the corner saloon. They paused outside, still talking earnestly. I ventured a hasty interview with the bar-keeper.

" Did you notice the two men who were sitting at the middle table?" I asked him.

" Sure!" said he, shoving me my glass of beer.

" Know them?" I inquired.

" Never laid eyes on 'em before. Old chap looked like a sort of corn doctor or corner spell-binder. Other was probably one of these longshore abalone men."

"Thanks," I muttered, and dodged out again, leaving the beer untouched.

I cursed myself for a blunderer. When I got to the street the two men had disappeared. I should have shadowed the captain to his vessel.

The affair interested me greatly. Apparently Dr. Schermerhorn was about to go on a long voyage. I prided myself on being fairly up to date in regard to the plans of those who interested the public; and the public at that time was vastly interested in Dr. Schemerhorn. I, in common with the rest of the world, had imagined him anchored safely in Philadelphia, immersed in chemical research. Here he bobbed up at the other end of the continent, making shady bargains with obscure shipping captains, and paying a big premium for absolute secrecy. It looked good.

Accordingly I was out early the next morning. I had not much to go by; schooners are as plenty as tadpoles in San Francisco harbour. However, I was sure I could easily recognise that falsetto voice; and

I knew where the supplies were to be purchased.
Adams & Marsh are a large firm, and cautious. I
knew better than to make direct inquiries, or to appear in the salesroom. But by hanging around the
door of the shipping room I soon had track of the
large orders to be sent that day. In this manner I
had no great difficulty in following a truck to Pier 10,
nor to identify a consignment to Captain Ezra Selover
as probably that of which I was in search.

The mate was in charge of the stowage, so I could
not be quite sure. Here, however, was a schooner—of
about a hundred and fifty tons burden. I looked her
over.

You're all acquainted with the *Laughing Lass* and
the perfection of her lines. You have not known her
under Captain Ezra Selover. She was the cleanest
ship I ever saw. Don't know how he accomplished it,
with a crew of four and the cook; but he did. The deck
looked as though it had been holystoned every morning by a crew of jackies; the stays were whipped and
tarred, the mast new-slushed, and every foot of running gear coiled down shipshape and Bristol fashion.
There was a good deal of brass about her; it shone
like gold, and I don't believe she owned an inch of
paint that wasn't either fresh or new-scrubbed.

I gazed for some time at this marvel. It's unusual
enough anywhere, but aboard a California hooker it
is little short of miraculous. The crew had all turned
up, apparently, and a swarm of stevedores were hus-
tling every sort of provisions, supplies, stock, spars,
lines and canvas down into the hold. It was a rush
job, and that mate was having his hands full. I didn't

wonder at his language nor at his looks, both of which were somewhat mussed up. Then almost at my elbow I heard that shrill falsetto squeal, and turned just in time to see the captain ascend the after gangplank.

He was probably the most dishevelled and untidy man I ever laid my eyes on. His hair and beard were not only long, but tangled and unkempt, and grew so far toward each other as barely to expose a strip of dirty brown skin. His shoulders were bowed and enormous. His arms hung like a gorilla's, palms turned slightly outwards. On his head was jammed a linen boating hat that had once been white; gaping away from his hairy chest was a faded dingy checked cotton shirt that had once been brown and white; his blue trousers were spotted and splashed with dusty stains; he was chewing tobacco. A figure more in contrast to the exquisitely neat vessel it would be hard to imagine.

The captain mounted the gangplank with a steadiness that disproved my first suspicion of his having been on a drunk. He glanced aloft, cast a speculative eye on the stevedores trooping across the waist of the ship, and ascended to the quarter-deck where the mate stood leaning over the rail and uttering directed curses from between sweat-beaded lips. There the big man roamed aimlessly on what seemed to be a tour of casual inspection. Once he stopped to breathe on the brass binnacle and to rub it bright with the dirtiest red bandana handkerchief I ever want to see.

His actions amused me. The discrepancy between his personal habits and his particularity in the matter of his surroundings was exceedingly interesting. I have often noticed that such discrepancies seem to indicate exceptional characters. As I watched him, his whole frame stiffened. The long gorilla arms contracted, the hairy head sunk forward in the tenseness of a serpent ready to strike. He uttered a shrill falsetto shriek that brought to a standstill every stevedore on the job, and sprang forward to seize his mate by the shoulder.

Evidently the grasp hurt. I can believe it might, from those huge hands. The man wrenched himself about with an oath of inquiry and pain. I could hear one side of what followed. The captain's high-pitched tones carried clearly; but the grumble and growl of the mate were indistinguishable at that distance.

" How far is it to the side of the ship, you hound of hell? " shrieked the captain.

Mumble—surprised—for an answer.

" Well, I'll tell you, you *swab!* It's just two fathom from where you stand. Just two fathom! How long would it take you to walk there? How long? Just about six seconds! There and back! You——" I won't bother with all the epithets, although by now I know Captain Selover's vocabulary fairly well. " And you couldn't take six seconds off to spit over the side! Couldn't walk two fathom! Had to spit on my quarter-deck, did you! "

Rumble from the mate.

" No, by God, you won't call up any of the crew. You'll get a swab and do it yourself. You'll get a *hand* swab and get down on your knees, damn you! I'll teach you to be lazy! "

The mate said something again.

" It don't matter if we ain't under way. That has nothing to do with it. The quarter-deck is clean, if the waist ain't, and nobody but a damn misbegotten son-of-a-sea-lawyer would spit on deck anyhow! " From this Captain Selover went on into a good old-fashioned deep-sea " cussing out," to the great joy of the stevedores.

The mate stood it pretty well, but there comes a time when further talk is useless even in regard to a most heinous offense. And, of course, as you know, the mate could hardly consider himself very seriously at fault. Why, the ship was not yet at sea, and in all the clutter of charging. He began to answer back. In a moment it was a quarrel. Abruptly it was a fight. The mate marked Selover beneath the left eye. The captain with beautiful simplicity crushed his antagonist in his gorilla-like squeeze, carried him to the side of the vessel, and dropped him limp and beaten to the pier. And the mate was a good stout specimen of a sea-farer, too.

Then the captain rushed below, emerging after an instant with a chest which he flung after his subordinate. It was followed a moment later by a stream of small stuff,—mingled with language—projected through an open port-hole. This in turn ceased. The captain reappeared with a pail and brush, scrubbed feverishly at the offending spot, mopped it dry with that same old red bandana handkerchief, glared about him,—and abruptly became as serene and placid as a noon calm. He took up the direction of the stevedores. It was all most astounding.

Nobody paid any attention to the mate. He looked toward the ship once or twice, thought better of it, and began to pick up his effects, muttering savagely. In a moment or so he threw his chest aboard an outgoing truck and departed.

It was now nearly noon and I was just in the way of going for something to eat, when I caught sight of another dray laden with boxes and crated affairs which I recognised as scientific apparatus. It was followed in quick succession by three others. Ignorant as I was of the requirements of a scientist, my common sense told me this could be no exploring outfit. I revised my first intention of going to the club, and bought a sandwich or two at the corner coffee house. I don't know why, but even then the affair seemed big with mystery, with the portent of tragedy. Perhaps the smell of tar was in my nostrils and the sea called. It has always possessed for me an extraordinary allurement——

A little after two o'clock a cab drove to the after gangplank and stopped. From it alighted a young man of whom I shall later have occasion to tell you more, followed by Dr. Schermerhorn. The young man carried only a light leather " serviette," such as students use abroad; while the doctor fairly staggered under the weight of a square, brass-bound chest without handles. The singularity of this unequal division of labour struck me at once.

It struck also one of the dock men, who ran forward, eager for a tip.

" Kin I carry th' box for you, boss? " he asked, at the same time reaching for it.

The doctor's thin figure seemed fairly to shrink at the idea.

"No, no!" he cried. "It iss not for you to carry!"

He hastened up the gangplank, clutching the chest close. At the top Captain Selover met him.

"Hello, doctor," he squeaked. "Here in good time. We're busy, you see. Let me carry your chest for you."

"No, no!" Dr. Schermerhorn fairly glared.

"It's almighty heavy," insisted the captain. "Let me give you a hand."

"You must not *touch!*" emphatically ordered the scientist. "Where iss the cabin?"

He disappeared down the companionway clasping his precious load. The young man remained on deck to superintend the stowing of the scientific goods and the personal baggage.

All this time I had been thinking busily. I remembered distinctly one other instance when Dr. Schermerhorn had disappeared. He came back inscrutably, but within a week his results on aërial photography were public property. I told myself that in the present instance his lavish use of money, the elaborate nature of his preparations, the evident secrecy of the expedition as evidenced by the fact that he had negotiated for the vessel only the day before setting sail, the importance of personal supervision as proved by the fact that he—notoriously impractical in practical matters, and notoriously disliking anything to do with business—had conducted the affair himself instead of delegating it,—why, gentlemen, don't you see that all this was more than enough to wake me up, body and soul? Suddenly I came to a definite resolution. Captain Selover had descended to the pier. I approached him.

"You need a mate," said I.

He looked me over.

"Perhaps," he admitted. "Where's your man?"

"Right here," said I.

His eyes widened a little. Otherwise he showed no sign of surprise. I cursed my clothes.

Fortunately I had my master's certificate with me— I'd passed fresh-water on the Great Lakes—I always carry that sort of document on the chance that it may come handy. It chanced to have a couple of naval endorsements, results of the late war.

"Look here," I said before I gave it to him. "You don't believe in me. My clothes are too good. That's all right. They're all I have that are good. I'm broke. I came down here wondering whether I'd better throw myself in the drink."

"You look like a dude," he squeaked. "Where did you ever ship?"

I handed him my certificate. The endorsements from Admiral Keays and Captain Arnold impressed him. He stared at me again, and a gleam of cunning crept into his eyes.

"Nothing crooked about this?" he breathed softly.

I had the key to this side of his character. You remember I had overheard the night before his statement of his moral scruples. I said nothing, but looked knowing.

"What was it?" he murmured. "Plain desertion, or something worse?"

I remained inscrutable.

"Well," he conceded, "I do need a mate; and a naval man—even if he is wantin' to get out of sight——"

"He won't spit on your decks, anyway," I broke in boldly.

Captain Selover's hairy face bristled about the mouth. This I subsequently discovered was symptom of a grin.

"You saw that, eh?" he trebled.

"Aren't you afraid he'll bring down the police and delay your sailing?" I asked.

He grinned again, with a cunning twinkle in his eye.

"You needn't worry. There ain't goin' to be any police. He had his advance money, and he won't risk it by tryin' to come back."

We came to an agreement. I professed surprise at the wages. The captain guardedly explained that the expedition was secret.

"What's our port?" I asked, to test him.

"Our papers are made out for Honolulu," he replied.

We adjourned to sign articles.

"By the way," said I, "I wish you wouldn't make them out in my own name. 'Eagen' will do."

"All right," he laughed, "I *sabe*. Eagen it is."

"I'll be aboard at six," said I. "I've got to make some arrangements."

"Wish you could help with the lading," said he. "Still, I can get along. Want any advance money?"

"No," I replied; then I remembered that I was supposed to be broke. "Yes," I amended.

He gave me ten dollars.

"I guess you'll show up," he said. "Wouldn't do this to everybody. But a naval man—even if he is dodgin' Uncle Sam——"

"I'll be here," I assured him.

At that time I wore a pointed beard. This I shaved. Also I was accustomed to use eye-glasses. The trouble was merely a slight astigmatism which bothered me only in reading or close inspection. I could get along perfectly well without the glasses, so I discarded them. I had my hair cut rather close. When I had put on sea boots, blue trousers and shirt, a pea jacket and a cap I felt quite safe from the recognition of a man like Dr. Schermerhorn. In fact, as you shall see, I hardly spoke to him during all the voyage out.

Promptly at six, then, I returned with a sea chest, bound I knew not whither, to be gone I knew not for how long, and pledged to act as second officer on a little hundred-and-fifty-ton schooner.

II

THE GRAVEN IMAGE

I HAD every reason to be satisfied with my disguise,—
if such it could be called. Captain Selover at first failed
to recognise me. Then he burst into his shrill cackle.

"Didn't know you," he trebled. "But you look
shipshape. Come, I'll show you your quarters."

Immediately I discovered what I had suspected before; that on so small a schooner the mate took rank
with the men rather than the afterguard. Cabin accommodations were of course very limited. My own
lurked in the waist of the ship—a tiny little airless
hole.

"Here's where Johnson stayed," proffered Selover.
"You can bunk here, or you can go in the foc'sle
with the men. They's more room there. We'll get under way with the turn of the tide."

He left me. I examined the cabin. It was just a
trifle larger than its single berth, and the berth was just
a trifle larger than myself. My chest would have to be
left outside. I strongly suspected that my lungs would
have to be left outside also; for the life of me I could
not see where the air was to come from. With a mental reservation in favour of investigating the forecastle,
I went on deck.

The *Laughing Lass* was one of the prettiest little
schooners I ever saw. Were it not for the lines of her

bilges and the internal arrangement of her hold, it might be imagined she had been built originally as a pleasure yacht. Even the rake of her masts, a little forward of the plumb, bore out this impression, which a comparatively new suit of canvas, well stopped down, brass stanchions forward, and two little guns under tarpaulins, almost confirmed. One thing struck me as peculiar. Her complement of boats was ample enough. She had two surf boats, a dingy, and a dory slung to the davits. In addition another dory,—the one you picked me up in—was lashed to the top of the deck house.

"They'd mighty near have a boat apiece," I thought, and went forward.

Just outside the forecastle hatch I paused. Some-one below was singing in a voice singularly rich in quality. The words and the quaintness of the minor air struck me immensely and have clung to my memory like a burr ever since.

" ' Are you a man-o'-war or a privateer,' said he.
   Blow high, blow low, what care we!
' Oh, I am a jolly pirate, and I'm sailing for my fee.'
   Down on the coast of the high Barbare-e-e."

I stepped to the companion. The voice at once ceased. I descended.

A glimmer of late afternoon struggled through the deadlights. I found myself in a really commodious space,—extending far back of where the forward bulk-heads are usually placed,—accommodating rows and row of bunks—eighteen of them, in fact. The un-

lighted lamp cast its shadow on wood stained black
by much use, but polished like ebony from the continued friction of men's garments. I wish I could con-
vey to you the uncanny effect, this—of dropping from
the decks of a miniature craft to the internal arrangements of a square-rigged ship. It was as though,
entering a cottage door, you were to discover yourself on the floor of Madison Square Garden. A fresh
sweet breeze of evening sucked down the hatch. I immediately decided on the forecastle. Already it was
being borne in on me that I was little more than a
glorified bo's'n's mate. The situation suited me, however. It enabled me to watch the course of events more
safely, less exposed to the danger of recognition.

I stood for a moment at the foot of the companion
accustoming my eyes to the gloom. After a moment,
with a shock of surprise, I made out a shining pair of
bead-points gazing at me unblinkingly from the
shadow under the bitts. Slowly the man defined himself, as a shape takes form in a fog. He was leaning
forward in an attitude of attention, his elbows resting on his knees, his forearms depending between
them, his head thrust out. I could detect no faintest
movement of eyelash, no faintest sound of breathing.
The stillness was portentous. The creature was exactly like a wax figure, one of the sort you meet in
corridors of cheap museums and for a moment mistake for living beings. Almost I thought to make out
the customary grey dust lying on the wax of his
features.

I am going to tell you more of this man, because, as
you shall see, he was destined to have much to do with

my life, the fate of Dr. Karl Augustus Schermerhorn, and the doom of the *Laughing Lass*.

He wore on his head a red bandana handkerchief. I never saw him with other covering. From beneath it straggled oily and tangled locks of glossy black. His face was long, narrow, hook-nosed and sinister; his eyes, as I have described them, a steady and beady black. I could at first glance ascribe great activity, but only moderate strength to his slender, wiry figure. In this I was mistaken. His sheer physical power was second only to that of Captain Selover. One of his forearms ended in a steel hook. At the moment I could not understand this; could not see how a man so maimed could be useful aboard a ship. Later I wished we had more as handy. He knew a jam hitch which he caught over and under his hook quicker than most men can grasp a line with the naked hand. It would render one way, but held fast the other. He told me it was a cinch-hook hitch employed by mule packers in the mountains, and that he had used it on swamp-hooks in the lumber woods of Michigan. I shouldn't wonder. He was a Wandering Jew.—His name was Anderson, but I never heard him called that. It was always " Handy Solomon " with men and masters.

We stared at each other, I fascinated by something, some spell of the ship, which I have never been able to explain to myself—nor even describe. It was a mystery, a portent, a premonition such as overtakes a man sometimes in the dark passageways of life. I cannot tell you of it, nor make you believe—let it pass——

Then by a slow process of successive perceptions I

Slowly the man defined himself as a shape takes form in a fog

became aware that I was watched by other eyes, other wax figures, other human beings with unwavering gaze. They seemed to the sense of mystic apprehension that for the moment held possession of me, to be everywhere—in the bunks, on the floor, back in the shadows, watching, watching, watching from the advantage of another world.

I don't know why I tell you this; why I lay so much stress on the first weird impression I got of the forecastle. It means something to me now—in view of all that happened subsequently. Almost can I look back and see, in that moment of occultism, a warning, an enlightenment—— But the point is, it meant something to me then. I stood there fascinated, unable to move, unable to speak.

Then the grotesque figure in the corner stirred.

"Well, mates," said the man, "believe or not believe, it's in the book, and it stands to reason, too. We have gold mines here in Californy and Nevada and all them States; and we hear of gold mines in Mexico and Australia, too, but did you ever hear tell of gold mines in Europe? Tell me that! And where did the gold come from then, before they discovered America? Tell me that! Why they *made* it, just as the man that wrote this-here says, and you can kiss the Book on that."

"How about that place, Ophir, I read about?" asked a voice from the bunks.

The man shot a keen glance thither from beneath his brows.

"Know last year's output from the mines of Ophir, Thrackles?" he inquired in silky tones.

"Why, no," stammered the man addressed as Thrackles.

"Well I do," pursued the man with the steel hook, "and it's just the whole of nothing, and you can kiss the Book on that too! There ain't any gold output, because there ain't any mines, and there never have been. They *made* their gold."

He tossed aside a book he had been holding in his left hand. I recognised the fat little paper duodecimo with amusement, and some wonder. The only other copy I had ever laid my eyes on is in the Astor Library. It is somewhat of a rarity, called *The Secret of Alchemy, or the Grand Doctrine of Transmutation Fully Explained,* and was written by a Dr. Edward Duvall,—a most extraordinary volume to have fallen into the hands of seamen.

I stepped forward, greeting and being greeted. Besides the man I have mentioned they were four. The cook was a bullet-headed squat negro with a broken nose. I believe he had a name,—Robinson, or something of that sort. He was to all of us, simply the Nigger. Unlike most of his race, he was gloomy and taciturn.

Of the other two, a little white-faced, thin-chested youth named Pulz, and a villainous-looking Mexican called Perdosa, I shall have more to say later.

My arrival broke the talk on alchemy. It resumed its course in the direction of our voyage. Each discovered that the others knew nothing; and each blundered against the astounding fact of double wages.

"All I know is the pay's good; and that's enough," concluded Thrackles, from a bunk.

"The pay's too good," growled Handy Solomon. "This ain't no job to go look at the 'clipse of the moon, or the devil's a preacher!"

"W'at you maik heem, den?" queried Perdosa.

"It's treasure, of course," said Handy Solomon shortly.

"He, he, he!" laughed the negro, without mirth.

"What's the matter with you, Doctor?" demanded Thrackles.

"Treasure!" repeated the Nigger. "You see dat box he done carry so cairful? You see dat?"

A pause ensued. Somebody scratched a match and lit a pipe.

"No, I don't see that!" broke out Thrackles finally, with some impatience. "I *sabe* how a man goes *after* treasure with a box; but why should he take treasure away *in* a box? What do you think, Bucko?" he suddenly appealed to me.

I looked up from my investigation of the empty berths.

"I don't think much about it," I replied, "except that by the look of the stores we're due for more than Honolulu; and from the look of the light we'd better turn to on deck."

An embarrassed pause fell.

"Who are you, anyway?" bluntly demanded the man with the steel hook.

"My name is Eagen," I replied; "I've the berth of mate. Which of these bunks are empty?"

They indicated what I desired with just a trace of sullenness. I understood well enough their resentment at having a ship's officer quartered on them,—the forec'stle they considered as their only liberty when at sea, and my presence as a curtailment to the freedom of speech. I subsequently did my best to overcome this feeling, but never quite succeeded.

At my command the Nigger went to his galley. I ascended to the deck. Dusk was falling, in the swift Californian fashion. Already the outlines of the wharf houses were growing indistinct, and the lights of the city were beginning to twinkle. Captain Selover came to my side and leaned over the rail, peering critically at the black water against the piles.

" She's at the flood," he squeaked. " And here comes the *Lucy Belle*."

The tug took us in charge and puffed with us down the harbour and through the Golden Gate. We had sweated the canvas on her, even to the flying jib and a huge club topsail she sometimes carried at the main, for the afternoon trades had lost their strength. About midnight we drew up on the Farallones.

The schooner handled well. Our crew was divided into three watches—an unusual arrangement, but comfortable. Two men could sail her handily in most sorts of weather. Handy Solomon had the wheel. Otherwise the deck was empty. The man's fantastic headgear, the fringe of his curling oily locks, the hawk outline of his face momentarily silhouetted against the phosphorescence astern as he glanced to windward, all lent him an appearance of another day. I could almost imagine I caught the gleam of silver-butted horse pistols and cutlasses at his waist.

I brooded in wonder at what I had seen and how little I had explained. The number of boats, sufficient for a craft of three times the tonnage; the capacity of the forec'stle with its eighteen bunks, enough for a passenger ship,—what did it mean? And this wild, unkempt, villainous crew with its master and his almost ridiculous contrast of neatness and filth;—did Dr. Schermerhorn realise to what he had trusted himself and his precious expedition, whatever it might be?

The lights of shore had sunk; the *Laughing Lass* staggered and leaped joyously with the glory of the open sea. She seemed alone on the bosom of the ocean; and for the life of me I could not but feel that I was embarked on some desperate adventure. The notion was utterly illogical; that I knew well. In sober thought, I, a reporter, was shadowing a respectable and venerable scientist, who in turn was probably about to investigate at length some little-known deep-sea conditions or phenomena of an unexplored island. But that did not suffice to my imagination. The ship, its surroundings, its equipment, its crew—all read fantastic. So much the better story, I thought, shrugging my shoulders at last.

III

THE TWELVE REPEATING RIFLES

AFTER my watch below the next morning I met Percy Darrow. In many ways he is, or was, the most extraordinary of my many acquaintances. During that first half hour's chat with him I changed my mind at least a dozen times. One moment I thought him clever, the next an utter ass; now I found him frank, open, a good companion, eager to please,—and then a droop of his blond eyelashes, a lazy, impertinent drawl of his voice, a hint of half-bored condescension in his manner, convinced me that he was shy and affected. In a breath I appraised him as intellectual, a fool, a shallow mind, a deep schemer, an idler, and an enthusiast. One result of his spasmodic confidences was to throw a doubt upon their accuracy. This might be what he desired; or with equal probability it might be the chance reflection of a childish and aimless amiability.

He was tall and slender and pale, languid of movement, languid of eye, languid of speech. His eyes drooped, half-closed beneath blond brows; a long wiry hand lazily twisted a rather affected blond moustache, his voice drawled his speech in a manner either insufferably condescending and impertinent, or ineffably tired,—who could tell which?

I found him leaning against the taffrail, his languid graceful figure supported by his elbows, his chin

propped against his hand. As I approached the binnacle, he raised his eyes and motioned me to him. The
insolence of it was so superb that for a moment I was
angry enough to ignore him. Then I reflected that I
was here, not to stand on my personal dignity, but to
get information. I joined him.

" You are the mate? " he drawled.

" Since I am on the quarter-deck," I snapped back
at him.

He eyed me thoughtfully, while he rolled with one
hand a corn-husk Mexican cigarette.

" Do you know where you are going? " he inquired at length.

" Depends on the moral character of my future
actions," I rejoined tartly.

He allowed a smile to break and fade, then lighted
his cigarette.

" The first mate seems to have a remarkable command of language," said he.

I did not reply.

" Well, to tell you the truth *I* don't know where we
are going," he continued. " Thought you might be
able to inform me. Where did this ship and its precious gang of cutthroats come from, anyway? "

" Meaning me? "

" Oh, meaning you too, for all I know," he
shrugged wearily. Suddenly he turned to me and laid
his hand on my shoulder with one of those sudden
bursts of confidence I came later to recognise and look
for, but in which I could never quite believe—nor
disbelieve.

" I am eaten with curiosity," he stated in the least

curious voice in the world. " I suppose you know who his Nibs is?"

" Dr. Schermerhorn, do you mean?"

" Yes. Well, I've been with him ten years. I am his right-hand man. All his business I transact down to the last penny. I even order his meals. His discoveries have taken shape in my hands. Suddenly he gets a freak. He will go on a voyage. Where? I shall know in good time. For how long? I shall know in good time. For what purpose? Same answer. What accommodations shall I engage? I experience the worst shock of my life;—he will engage them himself. What scientific apparatus? Shock number two;—he will attend to that. Is there anything I can do? What do you suppose he says?"

" How should I know?" I asked.

" You should know in the course of intelligent conversation with me," he drawled. " Well, he, good old staid Schermie with the vertebrated thoughts gets kittenish. He says to me, ' Joost imachin, Percy, you are all-alone-on-a-desert-island placed; and that you will sit on those sands and wish within yourself all you would buy to be comfortable. Go out and buy me those things—in abundance.' Those were my directions."

He puffed.

" What does he pay you?" he asked.

" Enough," I replied.

" More than enough, by a good deal, I'll bet," he rejoined. " The old fool! He ought to have left it to me. What is this craft? Have you ever sailed on her before?"

" No."

" Have any of the crew? "

I replied that I believed all of them were Selover's men. He threw the cigarette butt into the sea and turned back.

" Well, I wish you joy of your double wages," he mocked.

So he knew that, after all! How much more of his ignorance was pretended I had no means of guessing. His eye gleamed sarcastically as he sauntered toward the companion-way. Handy Solomon was at the wheel, steering easily with one foot and an elbow. His steel hook lay fully exposed, glittering in the sunlight. Darrow glanced at it curiously, and at the man's headgear.

" Well, my genial pirate," he drawled, " if you had a line to fit that hook, you'd be equipped for fishing." The man's teeth bared like an animal's, but Darrow went on easily as though unconscious of giving offence. " If I were you, I'd have it arranged so the hook would turn backward as well as forward. It would be handier for some things,—fighting, for instance."

He passed on down the companion. Handy Solomon glared after him, then down at his hook. He bent his arm this way and that, drawing the hook toward him softly, as a cat does her claws. His eyes cleared and a look of admiration crept into them.

" By God, he's right! " he muttered, and after a moment; " I've wore that ten year and never thought of it. The little son of a gun! "

He remained staring for a moment at the hook.

Then he looked up and caught my eye. His own turned quizzical. He shifted his quid and began to hum:

> " The bos'n laid aloft, aloft laid he,
>> *Blow high, blow low! What care we?*
> ' There's a ship upon the wind'ard, a wreck upon the lee,'
>> *Down on the coast of the high Barbare-e-e.*"

We had entered the trades and were making good time. I was content to stay on deck, even in my watch below. The wind was strong, the waves dashing, the sky very blue. From under our forefoot the flying fish sped, the monsters pursued them. A tingle of spray was in the air. It was all very pleasant. The red handkerchief around Solomon's head made a pretty spot of colour against the blue of the sky and the darker blue of the sea. Silhouetted over the flawless white of the deck house was the sullen, polished profile of the Nigger. Beneath me the ship swerved and leaped, yielded and recovered. I breathed deep, and saw cutlasses in harmless shadows. It was two years ago. I was young—then——

At the mess hour I stood in doubt. However, I was informed by the captain's falsetto that I was to eat in the cabin. As the only other officer, I ate alone, after the others had finished, helping myself from the dishes left on the table. It was a handsome cabin, well kept, with white woodwork spotlessly clean, leather cushions—much better than one would expect. I afterwards found that the neatness of this cabin and of the three staterooms was maintained by the Nigger—at peril of his neck. A rack held a dozen rifles, five revolvers, and,—at last—my cutlasses. I examined the lot with interest. They were modern weapons,—the new high power 30-40 box-magazine rifle, shooting government ammunition,—and had been used. The revolvers were of course the old 45 Colt's. This was an extraordinary armament for a peaceable schooner of one hundred and fifty tons burden.

The rest of the cabin's fittings were not remarkable. By the configuration of the ship I guessed that two of the staterooms must be rather large. I could make out voices within.

On deck I talked with Captain Selover.

" She's a snug craft," I approached him.

He nodded.

" You have armed her well."

He muttered something of pirates and the China seas.

I laughed.

" You have arms enough to give your crew about two magazine rifles apiece—unless you filled all your berths forward! "

Captain Selover looked me direct in the eye.

" Talk straight, Mr. Eagen," said he.

" What is this ship, and where is she bound? " I asked, with equal simplicity.

He considered.

" As for the ship," he replied at length, " I don't mind saying. You're my first officer, and on you I depend if it comes to—well, the small arms below. If the ship's a little under the shade, why, so are you.

She's by way of being called a manner of hard names by some people. I do not see it myself. It is a matter of conscience. If you would ask some interested, they would call her a smuggler, a thief, a wrecker, and all the other evil titles in the catalogue. She has taken in Chinks by way of Santa Cruz Island—if that is smuggling. The country is free, and a Chink is a man. Besides, it paid ten dollars a head for the landing. She has carried in a cargo or so of junk; it was lying on the beach where a fool master had piled it, and I took what I found. I couldn't keep track of the underwriters' intentions."

" But the room forward——?" I broke in.

" Well, you see, last season we were pearl fishing."

" But you needed only your diver and your crew," I objected.

" There was the matter of a Japanese gunboat or so," he explained.

" Poaching!" I cried.

" So some call it. The shells are there. The islands are not inhabited. I do not see how men claim property beyond the tide water. I have heard it argued——"

" Hold on!" I cried. " There was a trouble last year in the Ishigaki Jima Islands where a poacher beat off the *Oyama*. It was a desperate fight."

Captain Selover's eye lit up.

" I've commanded a black brigantine, name of *The Petrel*," he admitted simply. " She was a brigantine aloft, but *alow* she had much the same lines as the *Laughing Lass*." He whirled on his heel to roll to one of the covered yacht's cannon. " Looks like a

harmless little toy to burn black powder, don't she?"
he remarked. He stripped off the tarpaulin and the
false brass muzzle to display as pretty a little Maxim
as you would care to see. "Now you know all about
it," he said.

"Look here, Captain Selover," I demanded, "don't
you know that I could blow your whole shooting-
match higher than Gilderoy's kite. How do you know
I won't do it when I get back? How do you know I
won't inform the doctor at once what kind of an outfit he has tied to?"

He planted far apart his thick legs in their soiled
blue trousers, pushed back his greasy linen boating hat
and stared at me with some amusement.

"How do you know I won't blow on Lieutenant
or Ensign Ralph Slade, U. S. N., when *I* get back?"
he demanded. I blessed that illusion, anyway. "Besides, I know my man. You won't do anything of
the sort." He walked to the rail and spat carefully
over the side.

"As for the doctor," he went on, "*he* knows all
about it. He told me all about myself, and everything
I had ever done from the time I'd licked Buck Jones
until last season's little diversion. Then he told me
that was why he wanted me to ship for this cruise."
The captain eyed me quizzically.

I threw out my hands in a comic gesture of sur-
render.

"Well, where are we bound, anyway?"

The dirty, unkempt, dishevelled figure stiffened.

"Mr. Eagen," its falsetto shrilled, "you are mate
of this vessel. Your duty is to see that my orders as

to sailing are carried out. Beyond that you do not
go. As to navigation, and latitude and longitude and
where the hell we are, that is outside your line of duty.
As to where we are bound, you are getting double
wages not to get too damn curious. Remember to
earn your wages, Mr. Eagen!"

He turned away to the binnacle. In spite of his
personal filth, in spite of the lawless, almost piratical,
character of the man, in that moment I could not but
admire him. If Percy Darrow was ignorant of the
purposes of this expedition, how much more so Captain
Selover. Yet he accepted his trust blindly, and as far
as I could then see, intended to fulfil it faithfully. I
liked him none the worse for snubbing me. It indicated a streak in his moral nature akin to and quite as
curious as his excessive neatness regarding his immediate surroundings.

IV

THE STEEL CLAW

DURING the next few days the crew discussed our destination. Discipline, while maintained strictly, was not conventional. During the dog watches, often, every man aboard would be below, for at that period Captain Selover loved to take the wheel in person, a thick cigar between his lips, the dingy checked shirt wide open to expose his hairy chest to the breeze. In the twilight of the forecastle we had some great sea-lawyer's talks—I say " We," though I took little part in them. Generally I lay across my bunk smoking my pipe while Handy Solomon held forth, his speech punctuated by surly speculations from the Nigger, with hesitating deep-sea wisdom from the hairy Thrackles, or with voluminous bursts of fractured English from Perdosa. Pulz had nothing to offer, but watched from his pale green eyes. The light shifted and wavered from one to the other as the ship swayed: garments swung; the empty berths yawned cavernous. I could imagine the forecastle filled with the desperate men who had beaten off the *Oyama*. The story is told that they had swept the gunboat's decks with her own rapid-fires, turned in.

No one knew where we were going, nor why. The doctor puzzled them, and the quantity of his belongings.

"It ain't pearls," said Handy Solomon. "You can kiss the Book on that, for we ain't a diver among us. It ain't Chinks, for we are cruising sou'-sou'-west. Likely it's trade,—trade down in the Islands."

We were all below. The captain himself had the wheel. Discipline, while strict, was not conventional.

"Contrabandista," muttered the Mexican, "for dat he geev us double pay."

"We don't get her for nothing," agreed Thrackles. "Double pay and duff on Wednesday generally means get your head broke."

"No trade," said the Nigger gloomily.

They turned to him with one accord.

"Why not?" demanded Pulz, breaking his silence.

"No trade," repeated the Nigger.

"Ain't you got a reason, Doctor?" asked Handy Solomon.

"No trade," insisted the Nigger.

An uneasy silence fell. I could not but observe that the others held the Nigger's statements in a respect not due them as mere opinions. Subsequently I understood a little more of the reputation he possessed. He was believed to see things hidden, as their phrase went.

Nobody said anything for some time; nobody stirred, except that Handy Solomon, his steel claw removed from its socket, whittled and tested, screwed and turned, trying to fix the hook so that, in accordance with the advice of Percy Darrow, it would turn either way.

"What is it, then, Doctor?" he asked softly at last.

"Gold," said the Nigger shortly. "Gold—treasure."

"That's what I said at first!" cried Handy Solomon triumphantly. It was extraordinary, the unquestioning and entire faith with which they accepted as gospel fact the negro's dictum.

There followed much talk of the nature of this treasure, whether it was to be sought or conveyed, bought, stolen, or ravished in fair fight. No further soothsaying could they elicit from the Nigger. They followed their own ideas, which led them nowhere. Someone lit the forecastle lamp. They settled themselves. Pulz read aloud.

This was the programme every day during the dog watch. Sometimes the watch on deck was absent, leaving only Handy Solomon, the Nigger and Pulz, but the order of the day was not on that account varied. They talked, they lit the lamp, they read. Always the talk was of the treasure.

As to the reading, it was of the sort usual to seamen, cowboys, lumbermen, and miners. Thrackles had a number of volumes of very cheap love stories. Pulz had brought some extraordinary garish detective stories. The others contributed sensational literature with paper covers adorned lithographically. By the usual incongruity a fragment of *The Marble Faun* was included in the collection. The Nigger has his copy of *Duvall on Alchemy*. I haven't the slightest idea where he could have got it.

While Pulz read, Handy Solomon worked on the alteration of his claw. He could never get it to hold, and I remember as an undertone to Pulz's reading, the rumble of strange, exasperated oaths. Whatever the evening's lecture, it always ended with the book on alchemy. These men had no perspective by which to judge such things. They accepted its speculations and theories at their face value. Extremely laughable were the discussions that followed. I often wished the shade of old Duvall could be permitted to see these, his last disciples, spelling out dimly his teachings, mispronouncing his grave utterances, but believing utterly.

Dr. Schermerhorn appeared on deck seldom. When he did, often his fingers held a pen which he had forgotten to lay aside. I imagined him preoccupied by some calculation of his own, but the forecastle, more picturesquely, saw him as guarding constantly the heavy casket he had himself carried aboard. He breathed the air, walked briskly, turned with the German military precision at the end of his score of strides, and re-entered his cabin at the lapse of the half hour. After he had gone, remained Percy Darrow leaning indolently against the taffrail, his graceful figure swaying with the ship's motion, smoking always the corn-husk Mexican cigarettes which he rolled with one hand. He seemed from that farthest point aft to hold in review the appliances, the fabric, the actions, yes, even the very thoughts, of the entire ship. From them he selected that on which he should comment or with which he should play, always with a sardonic, half-serious, quite wearied and indifferent manner. His inner knowledge, viewed by the light of this manner or mannerism, was sometimes uncanny, though perhaps the sources of his information were commonplace enough, after all. Certainly he always viewed with amusement his victim's wonder.

Thus one evening at the close of our day-watch on deck, he approached Handy Solomon. It was at the end of ten days, on no one of which had the seaman failed to tinker away at his steel claw. Darrow balanced in front of him with a thin smile.

"Too bad it doesn't work, my amiable pirate," said he. "It would be so handy for fighting—— See here," he suddenly continued, pulling some object from his pocket, "here's a pipe; present to me; I don't smoke 'em. Twist her halfway, like that, she comes out. Twist her halfway, like this, she goes in. That's your principle. Give her back to me when you get through."

He thrust the briar pipe into the man's hand, and turned away without waiting for a reply. The seaman looked after him in open amazement. That evening he worked on the socket of the steel hook, and in two days he had the job finished. Then he returned the pipe to Darrow with some growling of thanks.

"That's all right," said the young man, smiling full at him. "Now what are you going to fight?"

V

THE PHILOSOPHER'S STONE

Captain Selover received as his due the most absolute and implicit obedience imaginable. When he condescended to give an order in his own person, the men fairly jumped to execute it. The matter had evidently been threshed out long ago. They did not love him, not they; but they feared him with a mighty fear, and did not hesitate to say so, vividly, and often, when in the privacy of the forecastle. The prevailing spirit was that of the wild beast, cowed but snarling still. Pulz and Thrackles in especial had a great deal to say of what they were or were not going to do, but I noticed that their resolution always began to run out of them when first foot was set to the companion ladder.

One day we were loafing along, everything drawing well, and everybody but the doctor on deck to enjoy the sun. I was in the crow's-nest for my pleasure. Below me on the deck Captain Selover roamed here and there, as was his custom, his eye cocked out like a housewife's for disorder. He found it, again in the evidence of expectoration, and as Perdosa happened to be handiest, fell on the unfortunate Mexican.

Perdosa protested that he had had nothing to do with it, but Captain Selover, enraged as always when his precious deck was soiled, would not listen. Finally the Mexican grew sulky and turned away as though refusing to hear more. The captain thereupon felled him to the deck, and began brutally to kick him in the face and head.

Perdosa writhed and begged, but without avail. The other members of the crew gathered near. After a moment, they began to murmur. Finally Thrackles ventured, most respectfully, to intervene.

"You'll kill him, sir," he interposed. "He's had enough."

"Had enough, has he?" screeched the captain. "Well, you take what's left."

He marked Thrackles heavily over the eye. There was a breathless pause; and then Thrackles, Pulz, the Nigger, and Perdosa attacked at once.

They caught the master unawares, and bore him to the deck. I dropped at once to the ratlines, and commenced my descent. Before I had reached the deck, however, Selover was afoot again, the four hanging to him like dogs. In a moment more he had shaken them off; and before I could intervene, he had seized a belaying pin in either hand, and was hazing them up and down the deck.

"Mutiny, would you?" he shrilled. "You poor swabs! Forgot who was your captain, did ye? Well, it's Captain Ezra Selover, and you can lay to that! It would need about eight fathom of *stuff* like you to tie me down."

He chased them forward, and he chased them aft, and every time the pins fell, blood followed. Finally they dived like rabbits into the forecastle hatch. Captain Selover leaned down after them.

"Now tie yourselves up," he advised, "and then

come on deck and clean up after yourselves!" He turned to me. "Mr. Eagen, turn out the crew to clean decks."

I descended to the forecastle, followed immediately by Handy Solomon. The latter had taken no part in the affair. We found the men in horrible shape, what with the bruises and cuts, and bleeding freely.

"Now you're a nice-looking Sunday school!" observed Handy Soloman, eyeing them sardonically. "Tackel Old Scrubs, will ye? Well, some needs a bale of cotton to fall on 'em afore they learns anything. Enjoyed your little diversions, mates? And w'at do you expect to gain? I asks you that, now. You poor little infants! Ain't you never tackled him afore? Don't remember a little brigatine, name of the *Petrel!* My eye, but you *are* a pack of damn fools!"

To this he received no reply. The men sullenly assisted each other. Then they went immediately on deck and to work.

After this taste of his quality, Captain Selover enjoyed a quiet ship. We made good time, but for a long while nothing happened. Finally the monotony was broken by an incident.

One evening before the night winds I sat in the shadow of the extra dory on top of the deck house. The moon was but just beyond the full, so I suppose I must have been practically invisible. Certainly the Nigger did not know of my presence, for he came and stood within three feet of me without giving any sign. The companion was open. In a moment some door below was opened also, and a scrap of conversation came up to us very clearly.

"You haf dem finished?" the doctor's voice inquired. "So, that iss well,"—papers rustled for a few moments. "And the r-result—ah—exactly—it iss that exactly. Percy, mein son, that maigs the experiment exact. We haf the process——"

"I don't see, sir, quite," replied the voice of Percy Darrow, with a tinge of excitement. "I can follow the logic of the experiment, of course—so can I follow the logic of a trip to the moon. But when you come to apply it—how do you get your re-agent? There's no known method——"

Dr. Schermerhorn broke in: "Ach, it iss that I haf perfected. Pardon me, my boy, it iss the first I haf worked from you apart. It iss for a surprise. I haf made in small quantities the missing ingredient. It will form a perfect interruption to the current. Now we go——"

"Do you mean to say," almost shouted Darrow, "that you have succeeded in freeing it in the metal?"

"Yes," replied the doctor simply.

I could hear a chair overturned.

"Why, with that you can——"

"I can do efferything," broke in the doctor. "The possibilities are enormous."

"And you can really produce it in quantity?"

"I think so; it iss for us to discover."

A pause ensued.

"Why!" came the voice of Percy Darrow, awe-stricken. "With fifty centigrammes only you could— you could transmute any substance—why, you could make anything you pleased almost! You could make

enough diamonds to fill that chest! It is the philosopher's stone!"

"Diamonds—yes—it is possible," interrupted the
doctor impatiently, "if it was worth while. But
you should see the real importance——"

The ship careened to a chance swell; a door
slammed; the voices were cut off. I looked up. The
Nigger's head was thrust forward fairly into the glow
from the companionway. The mask of his sullenness
had fallen. His eyes fairly rolled in excitement, his
thick lips were drawn back to expose his teeth, his
powerful figure was gathered with the tensity of a
bow. When the door slammed, he turned silently to
glide away. At that instant the watch was changed,
and in a moment I found myself in my bunk.

Ten seconds later the Nigger, detained by Captain
Selover for some trifling duty, burst into the forecastle. He was possessed by the wildest excitement.
This in itself was enough to gain the attention of the
men, but his first words were startling.

"I found de treasure!" he almost shouted. "I
know where he kept!"

They leaped at him—Handy Solomon and Pulz—
and fairly shook out of him what he thought he knew.
He babbled in the forgotten terms of alchemy, dress-
ing modern facts in the garments of mediæval thought
until they were scarcely to be recognised.

"And so he say dat he fine him, de Philosopher
Stone, and he keep him in dat heavy box we see him
carry aboard, and he don' have to make gol' with it—
he can make diamon's—*diamon's*—he say it too easy
to fill dat box plum full of diamon's."

They gesticulated and exclaimed and breathed hard, full of the marvel of such a thought. Then abruptly the clamour died to nothing. I felt six eyes bent on me, six unwinking eyes moving restless in motionless figures, suspicious, deadly as cobras——

Up to now my standing with the men had been well enough. Now they drew frankly apart. One of the most significant indications of this was the increased respect they paid my office. It was as though by prompt obedience, instant deference, and the emphasising of ship's etiquette they intended to draw sharply the line between themselves and me. There was much whispering apart, many private talks and consultations in which I had no part. Ordinarily they talked freely enough before me. Even the reading during the dog watch was intermitted—at least it was on such days as I happened to be in the watch below. But twice I caught the Nigger and Handy Solomon consulting together over the volume on alchemy.

I was in two minds whether to report the whole matter to Captain Selover. The only thing that restrained me was the vagueness of the intention, and the fact that the afterguard was armed, and was four to the crew's five. An incident, however, decided me. One evening I was awakened by a sound of violent voices. Captain Selover occasionally juggled the watches for variety's sake, and I now had Handy Solomon and Perdosa. The Nigger, being cook, stood no watch.

"You drunken Greaser swab!" snarled Handy Solomon. "You misbegotten son of a Yaqui! I'll learn you to step on a seaman's foot, and you can kiss the Book on that! I'll cut your heart out and feed it to the sharks!"

"Potha!" sneered Perdosa. "You cut heem you finger wid your knife."

They wrangled. At first I thought the quarrel genuine, but after a moment or so I could not avoid a sort of reminiscent impression of the cheap melodrama. It seemed incredible, but soon I could not dodge the conclusion that it was a made-up quarrel designed to impress me.

Why should they desire to do so? I had to give it up, but the fact itself was obvious enough. I laughed to see them. The affair did not come to blows, but it did come to black looks on meeting, muttered oaths, growls of emnity every time they happened to pass each other on the deck. Perdosa was not so bad; his Mexican blood inclined him to the histrionic, and his Mexican cast lent itself well to evil looks. But Handy Solomon, for the first time in, my acquaintance with him, was ridiculous.

About this time we crossed into frequent thunders. One evening just at dark we made out a heavy black squall. Not knowing exactly what weight lay behind it, I called up all hands. We ducked the staysail and foresail, lowered the peak of the mainsail, and waited to feel of it—a rough and ready seamanship often used in these little California wind-jammers. I was pretty busy, but I heard distinctly Handy Solomon's voice behind me.

" I'll kill you sure, you Greaser, as soon as my hands are free!"

And some muttered reply from the Mexican.

The wind hit us hard, held on a few moments, and moderated to a stiff puff. There followed the rain, so of course I knew it would amount to nothing. I was just stooping to throw the stops off the staysail when I felt myself seized from behind, and forced rapidly toward the side of the ship.

Of course I struggled. The Japanese have a little trick to fool a man who catches you around the waist from behind. It is part of the jiu-jitsu taught the Samurai—quite a different proposition from the ordinary "policeman jiu-jitsu." I picked it up from a friend in the nobility. It came in very handy now, and by good luck a roll of the ship helped me. In a moment I stood free, and Perdosa was picking himself out of the scuppers.

The expression of astonishment was fairly well done—I will say that for him—but I was prepared for histrionics.

"Señor!" he gasped. "Eet is you! *Sacrosanta Maria!* I thought you was dat Solomon! Pardon me, señor! Pardon! Have I hurt you?"

He approached me almost wheedling. I could have laughed at the villain. It was all so transparent. He no more mistook me for Handy Solomon than he felt any real enmity for that person. But being angry, and perhaps a little scared, I beat him to his quarters with a belaying pin.

On thinking the matter over, however, I failed to see all the ins and outs of it. I could understand a desire to get rid of me; there would be one less of the afterguard, and then, too, I knew too much of the men's sentiments, if not of their plans. But why all this elaborate farce of the mock quarrel and the alleged mistake? Could it be to guard against possible failure? I could hardly think it worth while. My only theory was that they had wished to test my strength and determination. The whole affair, even on that supposition, was childish enough, but I referred the exaggerated cunning to Handy Solomon, and considered it quite adequately explained. It is a minor point, but subsequently I learned that this surmise was correct. I was to be saved because none of the conspirators understood navigation.

The next morning I approached Captain Selover.

"Captain," said I, "I think it my duty to report that there is trouble brewing among the crew."

"There always is," he replied, unmoved.

"But this is serious. Dr. Schermerhorn came aboard with a chest which the men think holds treasure. The other evening Robinson overheard him tell his assistant that he could easily fill the box with diamonds. Of course, he was merely illustrating the value of some scientific experiment, but Robinson thinks, and has made the others think, that the chest contains something to make diamonds with. I am sure they intend to get hold of it. The affair is coming to a head."

Captain Selover listened almost indifferently.

"I came back from the islands last year," he piped, "with three hundred thousand dollars' worth of pearls. There was sixteen in the crew, and every man of them was blood hungry for them pearls. They had three or four shindies and killed one man over the proper way to divide the loot after they had got it. They didn't get it. Why?" He drew his powerful figure to its height and spread his thick arms out in the luxury of stretching. "Why?" he repeated, exhaling abruptly. "Because their captain was Ezra Selover! Well, Mr. Eagen," he went on crisply, "Captain Ezra Selover is their captain, *and they know it!* They'll talk and palaver and git into dark corners, and sharpen their knives, and perhaps fight it out as to which one's going to work the monkey-doodle business in the doctor's chest, and which one's going to tie up the sacks of them diamonds, but they won't git any farther as long as Captain Ezra is on deck."

"Yes," I objected, "but they mean business. Last night in the squall one of them tried to throw me overboard."

Captain Selover grinned.

"What did you do?" he asked.

"Hazed him to his quarters with a belaying pin."

"Well, that's all settled then, isn't it? What more do you want?"

stood undecided.

"I can take care of myself," he went on. "You ought to take care of yourself. Then there's nothing more to do."

He mused a moment.

"You have a gun, of course?" he inquired. "I forgot to ask."

"No," said I.

He whistled.

"Well, no wonder you feel sort of lost and hopeless! Here, take this, it'll make a man of you."

He gave me a Colt's 45, the barrel of which had

been filed down to about two inches of length. It was a most extraordinary weapon, but effective at short range.

"Here's a few loose cartridges," said he. "Now go easy. This is no warship, and we ain't got men to experiment on. Lick 'em with your fists or a pin, if you can; and if you do shoot, for God's sake just wing 'em a little. They're awful good lads, but a little restless."

I took the gun and felt better. With it I could easily handle the members of my own watch, and I did not doubt that with the assistance of Percy Darrow even a surprise would hardly overwhelm us. I did not count on Dr. Schermerhorn. He was quite capable of losing himself in a problem of trajectory after the first shot.

VI

THE ISLAND

I CAME on deck one morning at about four bells to find the entire ship's company afoot. Even the doctor was there. Everybody was gazing eagerly at a narrow, mountainous island lying slate-coloured across the early morning.

We were as yet some twenty miles distant from it, and could make out nothing but its general outline. The latter was sharply defined, rising and falling to a highest point one side of the middle. Over the island, and raggedly clasping its sides, hung a cloud, the only one visible in the sky.

I joined the afterguard.

" You see? " the doctor was exclaiming. " It iss as I haf said. The island iss there. Everything iss as it should be! " He was quite excited.

Percy Darrow, too, was shaken out of his ordinary calm.

" The volcano is active," was his only comment, but it explained the ragged cloud.

" You say there's a harbour? " inquired Captain Selover.

" It should be on the west end," said Dr. Schermerhorn.

Captain Selover drew me one side. He, too was a little aroused.

"Now wouldn't that get you?" he squeaked. "Doctor runs up against a Norwegian bum who tells him about a volcanic island, and gives its bearings. The island ain't on the map at all. Doctor believes it, and makes me lay my course for those bearings. *And here's the island!* So the bum's story was true! I'd like to know what the rest of it was!" His eyes were shining.

"Do we anchor or stand off and on?" I asked.

Captain Selover turned to grip me by the shoulder.

"I have orders from Darrow to get to a good berth, to land, to build shore quarters, and to snug down for a stay of a year at least!"

We stared at each other.

"Joyous prospect," I muttered. "Hope there's something to do there."

The morning wore, and we rapidly approached the island. It proved to be utterly precipitous. The high rounded hills sloped easily to within a hundred feet or so of the water and then fell away abruptly. Where the earth ended was a fantastic filigree border, like the fancy paper with which our mothers used to line the pantry shelves. Below, the white surges flung themselves against the cliffs with a wild abandon. Thousands of sea birds wheeled in the eddies of the wind, thousands of ravens perched on the slopes. With our glasses we could make out the heads of seals fishing outside the surf, and a ragged belt of kelp.

When within a mile we put the helm up, and ran for the west end. A bold point we avoided far out, lest there should be outlying ledges. Then we came in sight of a broad beach and pounding surf.

I was ordered to take a surf boat and investigate for a landing and an anchorage. The swell was running high. We rowed back and forth, puzzled as to how to get ashore with all the freight it would be necessary to land. The ship would lie well enough, for the only open exposure was broken by a long reef over which we could make out the seas tumbling. But inshore the great waves rolled smoothly, swiftly—then suddenly fell forward as over a ledge, and spread with a roar across the yellow sands. The fresh winds blew the spume back to us. We conversed in shouts.

"We can surf the boat," yelled Thrackles, "but we can't land a load."

That was my opinion. We rowed slowly along, parallel to the shore, and just outside the line of breakers.

I don't know exactly how to tell you the manner in which we became aware of the cove. It was as nearly the instantaneous as can be imagined. One minute I looked ahead on a cliff as unbroken as the side of a cabin; the very next I peered down the length of a cove fifty fathoms long by about ten wide, at the end of which was a gravel beach. I cried out sharply to the men. They were quite as much astonished as I. We backed water, watching closely. At a given point the cove and all trace of its entrance disappeared. We could only just make out the line where the headlands dissolved into the background of the cliffs, and that merely because we knew of its existence. The blending was perfect.

We rowed in. The water was still. A faint ebb and flow whispered against the tiny gravel beach at the

end. I noted a practicable way from it to the top of
the cliff, and from the cliff down again to the sand
beach. Everything was perfect. The water was a
beautiful light green, like semi-opaque glass, and from
the indistinctness of its depths waved and beckoned,
rose and disappeared with indescribable grace and deliberation long feathery sea growths. In a moment
the bottom abruptly shallowed. The motion of the
boat toward the beach permitted us to catch a hasty
glimpse of little fish darting, of big fish turning, of
yellow sand and some vivid colour. Then came the
grate of gravel and the scraping of the boat's bottom
on the beach.

We jumped ashore eagerly. I left the men, very re-
luctant, and ascended a natural trail to a high sloping
down over which blew the great Trades. Grass sprung
knee-high. A low hill rose at the back. From below
the fall of the cliff came the pounding of surf.

I walked to the edge. Various ledges, sloping
toward me, ran down to the sea. Against one of them
was a wreck, not so very old, head on, her afterworks
gone. I recognised the name *Golden Horn,* and was
vastly astonished to find her here against this unknown
island. Far up the coast I could see—with the surges
dashing up like the explosion of shells, and the cliffs,
and the rampart of hills grown with grass and cactus.
A bold promontory terminated the coast view to the
north, and behind it I could glimpse a more fertile and
wooded country. The sky was partly overcast by the
volcanic murk. It fled before the Trades, and the red
sun alternately blazed and clouded through it.

As there was nothing more to be seen here, I turned

above the hollow of our cove, skirted the base of the hill, and so down to the beach.

It occupied a wide semicircle where the hills drew back. The flat was dry and grown with thick, coarse grass. A stream emerged from a sort of cañon on its landward side. I tasted it, found it sulphurous, and a trifle worse than lukewarm. A little nearer the cliff, however, was a clear, cold spring from the rock, and of this I had a satisfying drink. When I arose from my knees, I made out an animal on the hill crest looking at me, but before I could distinguish its characteristics it had disappeared.

I returned along the tide sands. The surf dashed and roared, lifting seaweeds of a blood red, so that in places the water looked pink. Seals innumerable watched me from just outside the breakers. As the waves lifted to a semi-transparence, I could make out others playing, darting back and forth, up and down like disturbed tadpoles, clinging to the wave until the very instant of its fall, then disappearing as though blotted out. The salt smell of seaweed was in my nostrils: I found the place pleasant——

With these few and scattered impressions we returned to the ship. It had been warped to a secure anchorage, and snugged down. Dr. Schermerhorn and Darrow were on deck waiting to go ashore.

I made my report. The two passengers disappeared. They carried lunch and would not be back until nightfall. We had orders to pitch a large tent at a suitable spot and to lighten ship of the doctor's personal and scientific effects. By the time this was accomplished, the two had returned.

"It's all right," Darrow volunteered to Captain Selover, as he came over the side. "We've found what we want."

Their clothes were picked by brush and their boots muddy. Next morning Captain Selover detailed me to especial work.

"You'll take two of the men and go ashore under Darrow's orders," said he.

Darrow told us to take clothes for a week, an axe apiece, and a block and tackle. We made up our ditty bags, stepped into one of the surf boats, and were rowed ashore. There Darrow at once took the lead.

Our way proceeded across the grass flat, through the opening of the narrow cañon, and so on back into the interior by way of the bed through which flowed the sulphur stream. The country was badly eroded. Most of the time we marched between perpendicular clay banks about forty feet high. These were occasionally broken by smaller tributary arroyos of the same sort. It would have been impossible to reach the level of the upper country. The bed of the main arroyo was flat, and grown with grasses and herbage of an extraordinary vividness, due, I supposed, to the sulphur water. The stream itself meandered aimlessly through the broader bed. It steadily grew warmer and the sulphur smell more noticeable. Above us we could see the sky and the sharp clay edge of the arroyo. I noticed the tracks of Darrow and Dr. Schermerhorn made the day before.

After a mile of this, the bottom ran up nearly to the level of the sides, and we stepped out on the floor of a little valley almost surrounded by more hills.

It was an extraordinary place, and since much happened there, I must give you an idea of it.

It was round and nearly encircled by naked painted hills. From its floor came steam and a roaring sound. The steam blew here and there among the pines on the floor; rose to eddy about the naked painted hills. At one end we saw intermittently a broad ascending cañon—deep red and blue-black—ending in the cone of a smoking volcano. The other seemed quite closed by the sheer hills; in fact the only exit was the route by which we had come.

For the hills were utterly precipitous. I suppose a man might have made his way up the various knobs, ledges, and inequalities, but it would have required long study and a careful head. I, myself, later worked my way a short distance, merely to examine the texture of their marvellous colour.

This was at once varied and of great body—not at all like the smooth, glossed colour of most rock, but soft and rich. You've seen painters' palettes—it was just like that, pasty and *fat*. There were reds of all shades, from a veritable scarlet to a red umber; greens, from sea-green to emerald; several kinds of blue, and an indeterminate purple-muave. The whole effect was splendid and barbaric.

We stopped and gasped as it hit our eyes. Darrow alone was unmoved. He led the way forward and in an instant had disappeared behind the veil of steam. Thrackles and Perdosa hung back murmuring, but at a sharp word from me gathered their courage in their two hands and proceeded.

We found that the first veil of steam, and a fearful

stench of gases, proceeded from a miniature crater whose edge was heavily encrusted with a white salt. Beyond, close under the rise of the hill, was another. Between the two Percy Darrow had stopped and was waiting.

He eyed us with his lazy, half-quizzical glance as we approached.

"Think the place is going to blow up?" he inquired, with a tinge of irony. "Well, it isn't." He turned to me. "Here's where we shall stay for a while. You and the men are to cut a number of these pine trees for a house. Better pick out the little ones, about three or four inches through: they're easier handled. I'll be back by noon."

We set to work then in the roaring, steaming valley with the vapour swirling about us, sometimes concealing us, sometimes half revealing us gigantic, again in the utterness of exposure showing us dwindled pigmies against the magnitudes about us. The labour was not difficult. By the time Darrow returned we had a pile of the saplings ready for his next direction.

He was accompanied by the Nigger, very much terrified, very much burdened with food and cooking utensils. The assistant was lazily relating tales of voodoos, a glimmer of mischief in his eyes.

VII

CAPTAIN SELOVER LOSES HIS NERVE

I LIVED in the place for three weeks. We were afoot shortly after daybreak, under way by sun-up, and at work before the heats began. Three of us worked on the buildings, and the rest formed a pack train carrying all sorts of things from the shore to the valley. The men grumbled fiercely at this, but Captain Selover drove them with slight regard for their opinions or feelings.

"You're getting double pay," was his only word, "earn it!"

They certainly earned it during those three weeks. The things they brought up were astounding. Besides a lot of scientific apparatus and chests of chemical supplies, everything that could possibly be required, had been provided by that omniscient young man. After we had built a long, low structure, windows were forthcoming, shelves, tables, sinks, faucets, forges, burners, all cut out, fitted and ready to put together, each with its proper screws, nails, clamps, or pipes ready to our hands. When we had finished, we had constructed as complete a laboratory on a small scale as you could find on a college campus, even to the stone pillar down to bed-rock for delicate microscopic experiments, and hot and cold water led from the springs. And we were utterly unskilled. It was all Percy Darrow.

113

I was toward the last engaged in screwing on a fixture for the generation of acetelyne gas.

"Darrow," said I, "there's one thing you've over-looked; you forgot to bring a cupola and a gilt weather-cock for this concern."

After the laboratory was completed, we put up sleeping quarters for the two men, with wide porches well screened, and a square, heavy storeroom. By the end of the third week we had quite finished.

Dr. Schermerhorn had turned with enthusiasm to the unpacking of his chemical apparatus. Almost immediately at the close of the freight-carrying, he had appeared, lugging his precious chest, this time suffering the assistance of Darrow, and had camped on the spot. We could not induce him to leave, so we put up a tent for him. Darrow remained with him by way of safety against the men, whose measure, I believe, he had taken. Now that all the work was finished, the doctor put in a sudden appearance.

"Percy," said he, "now we will have the defence built."

He dragged us with him to the narrow part of the arroyo, just before it rose to the level of the valley.

"Here we will build the stockade-defence," he announced.

Darrow and I stared at each other blankly.

"What for, sir?" inquired the assistant.

"I haf come to be undisturbed," announced the doctor, with owl-like, Teutonic gravity, "and I will not be disturbed."

Darrow nodded to me and drew his principal aside.

They conversed earnestly for several minutes. Then the assistant returned to me.

"No use," he shrugged in complete return to his indifferent manner. "Stockade it is. Better make it of fourteen foot logs, slanted out. Dig a trench across, plant your logs three or four feet, bind them at the top. That's his specification for it. Go at it."

"But," I expostulated, "what's the *use* of it? Even if the men were dangerous, that would just make them think you *did* have something to guard."

"I know that. Orders," replied Percy Darrow.

We built the stockade in a day. When it was finished we marched to the beach, and never, save in the three instances of which I shall later tell you, did I see the valley again. The next day we washed our clothes, and moved ashore with all our belongings.

"I'm not going to have this crew aboard," stated Captain Selover positively, "I'm going to clean her." He himself stayed, however.

We rowed in, constructed a hasty fireplace of stones, spread our blankets, and built an unnecessary fire near the beach.

"Clean her!" grumbled Thrackles, "my eye!"

"I'd rather round the Cape," growled Pulz hopelessly.

"Come, now, it can't be as bad as all that," I tried to cheer them. "It can't be more than a week or ten days' job, even if we careen her."

"You don't know what you're talking about," said Thrackles. "It's worse than the yellow jack. It's six weeks at least. Mind when we last 'cleaned her'?" he inquired of Handy Solomon.

"You can kiss the Book on it," replied he. "Down by the line in that little swab of a sand island. My eye, but *don't* I remember! I sweated my liver white."

They smoked in silence.

"That's a main queer contrivance of the Perfessor's —that stockade-like," ventured Solomon, after a little.

"He doesn't want any intrusion," I said. "These scientific experiments are very delicate."

"Quite like," he commented non-committally.

We slept on the ground that night, and next morning, under Captain Selover's directions, we commenced the task of lightening the ship. He detailed the Nigger and Perdosa for special duty.

"I'll just see to your shore quarters," he squeaked. "You empty her."

All day long we rowed back and forth from the ship to the cove, landing the contents of the hold. These, by good fortune, we did not have to carry over the neck of land, for just above the gravel beach was a wide ledge on which we could pile the stores. We ate aboard, and so had no opportunity of seeing what Captain Selover and his men were about, until evening. Then we discovered that they had collected and lowered to the beach a quantity of stateroom doors from the wreck, and had trundled the galley stove to the edge where it awaited our assistance. We hitched a cable to it, and let it down gently. The Nigger was immensely pleased. After some experiment he got it to draw, and so cooked us our supper on it. After supper, Captain Selover rowed himself back to the ship.

"Eagen," he had said, drawing me aside, "I'm going to leave you with them. It's better that one of us—I think as owner I ought to be aboard——"

"Of course, sir," said I, "it's the only proper place for you."

"I'm glad you think so," he rejoined, apparently relieved. "And anyway," he cried, with a burst of feeling, "I hate the gritty feeling of it under my feet! Solid oak's the only walking for a man."

He left me hastily, as though a trifle ashamed. I thought he seemed depressed, even a little furtive, and yet on analysis I could discover nothing definite on which to base such a conclusion.

It was rather a feeling of difference from the man I had known. In my fatigue it seemed hardly worth thinking about.

The men had rolled themselves in their blankets, tired with the long day.

Next morning Captain Selover was ashore early. He had quite recovered his spirits, and offered me a dram of French brandy, which I refused. We worked hard again; again the master returned at night to his vessel, this time without a word to any of us; again the men, drugged by toil, turned in early and slept like the dead.

We became entangled in a mesh of days like these, during which things were accomplished, but in which was no space for anything but the tasks imposed upon us. The men for the most part had little to say.

"Por Dios, eet is too mooch work!" sighed Perdosa once.

"Why don't you kick to the Old Man, then?" sneered Thrackles.

The silence that followed, and the sullenness with which Perdosa readdressed himself to his work, was significant enough of Captain Selover's past relations with the men.

And how we did clean her! We stripped her of every stitch and sliver until she floated high, an empty hull, even her spars and running rigging ashore. I understood now the crew's grumbling. We literally went at her with a nail brush.

Captain Selover took charge of us when we had reached this period. He and the Nigger and Perdosa had long since finished the installation of the permanent camp. They had built us huts from the wreck, collecting stateroom doors for the sides, and hatches for the roofs, huge and solid, with iron rings in them. The bronze and iron ventilation gratings to the doors gave us glimpses of the coast through fretwork; the rich inlaying of woods surrounded us. We set up on a solid rock the galley stove—with its rails to hold the cooking pots from upsetting, in a sea way. In it we burned the débris of the wreck, all sorts of wood, some sweet and aromatic and spicy as an incensed cathedral. I have seen the Nigger boiling beans over a blaze of sandal wood fragrant as an Eastern shop.

First we scrubbed the *Laughing Lass*, then we painted her, and resized and tarred her standing rigging, resized and rove her running gear, slushed her masts, finally careened her and scraped and painted her below.

When we had quite finished, we had the anchor chain dealt out to us in fathoms, and scraped, pounded and polished that. These were indeed days full of labour.

Being busy from morning until night we knew but little of what was about us. We saw the open sea and the waves tumbling over the reef outside. We saw the headlands, and the bow of the bay and the surf with its watching seals and the curve of yellow sands. We saw the sweep of coast and the downs and the strange huts we had built out of departed magnificence, And that was all; that constituted our world.

In the evening sometimes we lit a big bonfire, sailor fashion, just at the edge of the beach. There we sat at ease and smoked our pipes in silence, too tired to talk. Even Handy Solomon's song was still. Outside the circle of light were mysterious things—strange wavings of white hands, bendings of figures, callings of voices, rustling of feet. We knew them for the surf and the wind in the grasses: but they were not the less mysterious for that.

Logically Captain Selover and I should have passed most of our evenings together. As a matter of fact we so spent very few. Early in the dusk the captain invariably rowed himself out to his beloved schooner. What he did there I do not know. We could see his light now in one part of her, now in the other. The men claimed he was scrubbing her teeth. " Old Scrubs " they called him to his back: never Captain Selover.

" He has to clean up after his own feet, he's so dirty," sagely proffered Handy Solomon. And this was true.

The seaman's prophecy held good. Seven weeks

held us at that infernal job—seven weeks of solid, grinding work. The worst of it was, that we were kept at it so breathlessly, as though our very existence were to depend on the headlong rush of our labour. And then we had fully half the stores to put away again, and the other half to transport painfully over the neck of land from the cove to the beach.

So accustomed had I become to the routine in which we were involved, so habituated to anticipating the coming day as exactly like the day that had gone, that the completion of our job caught me quite by surprise. I had thrown myself down by the fire prepared for the some old half hour of drowsy nicotine, to be followed by the accustomed heavy sleep, and the usual early rising to toil. The evening was warm; I half closed my eyes.

Handy Solomon was coming in last. Instead of dropping to his place, he straddled the fire, stretching his arms over his head. He let them fall with a sharp exhalation.

" ' Lay aloft, lay aloft,' the jolly bos'n cried.
    Blow high, blow low, what care we!
  ' Look ahead, look astern, look a-windward, look a-lee.'
    Down on the coast of the high Barbare-e-e."

The effect was electrical. We all sprang to our feet and fell to talking at once.

" By God, we're *through!*" cried Pulz. " I'd clean forgot it!"

The Nigger piled on more wood. We drew closer about the fire. All the interests in life, so long held in the background, leaped forward, eager for recognition. We spoke of trivialities almost for the first time since our landing, fused into a temporary but complete good fellowship by the relief.

"Wonder how the old doctor is getting on?" ventured Thrackles, after a while.

"The devil's a preacher! I wonder?" cried Handy Solomon.

"Let's make 'em a call," suggested Pulz.

"Don't believe they'd appreciate the compliment," I laughed. "Better let them make first call: they're the longer established." This was lost on them, of course. But we all felt kindly to one another that evening.

I carried the glow of it with me over until next morning, and was therefore somewhat dashed to meet Captain Selover, with clouded brows and an uncertain manner. He quite ignored my greeting.

"By God, Eagen," he squeaked, "can you think of anything more to be done?"

I straightened my back and laughed.

"Haven't you worked us hard enough?" I inquired. "Unless you gild the cabins, I don't see what else there can be to do."

Captain Selover stared me over.

"And you a naval man!" he marvelled. "Don't you see that the only thing that keeps this crew from gettin' restless is keeping them busy? I've sweat a damn sight more with my brain than you have with your back thinking up things to do. I can't see anything ahead, and then we'll have hell to pay. Oh, they're a sweet lot!"

I whistled and my crest fell. Here was a new point of view; and also a new Captain Ezra. Where was the confidence in the might of his two hands?

He seemed to read my thoughts, and went on.

"I don't feel *sure* here on this cussed land. It ain't like a deck where a man has some show. They can scatter. They can hide. It ain't right to put a man ashore alone with such a crew. I'm doing my best, but it ain't goin' to be good enough. I wisht we were safe in 'Frisco harbour——"

He would have maundered on, but I seized his arm and led him out of possible hearing of the men.

"Here, buck up!" I said to him sternly. "There's nothing to be scared of. If it comes to a row, there's three of us and we've got guns. We could even sail the schooner at a pinch, and leave them here. You've stood them off before."

"Not ashore," protested Captain Selover weakly.

"Well, they don't know that. For God's sake don't let them see you've lost your nerve this way." He did not even wince at the accusation. "Put up a front."

He shook his head. The sand had completely run out of him. Yet I am convinced that if he could have felt the heave and roll of the deck beneath him, he would have faced three times the difficulties he now feared. However, I could see readily enough the wisdom of keeping the men at work.

"You can wreck the *Golden Horn*," I suggested. "I don't know whether there's anything left worth salvage; but it'll be something to do."

He clapped me on the shoulder.

"Good!" he cried, "I never thought of it."

"Another thing," said I, "you better give them a day off a week. That can't hurt them and it'll waste just that much more time."

"All right," agreed Captain Selover.

"Another thing yet. You know I'm not lazy, so it ain't that I'm trying to dodge work. But you'd better lay me off. It'll be so much more for the others."

"That's true," said he.

I could not recognise the man for what I knew him to be. He groped, as one in the dark, or as a sea animal taken out of its element and placed on the sands. Courage had given place to fear; decision to wavering; and singleness of purpose to a divided counsel. He who had so thoroughly dominated the entire ship, eagerly accepted advice of me—a man without experience.

That evening I sat apart considerably disturbed. I felt that the ground had dropped away beneath my feet. To be sure, everything was tranquil at present; but now I understood the source of that tranquillity and how soon it must fail. With opportunity would come more scheming, more speculation, more cupidity. How was I to meet it, with none to back me but a scared man, an absorbed man, and an indifferent man?

VIII

WRECKING OF THE *GOLDEN HORN*

PERCY DARROW, unexpected, made his first visit to us the very next evening. He sauntered in with a Mexican corn-husk cigarette between his lips, carrying a lantern; blew the light out, and sat down with a careless greeting, as though he had seen us only the day before.

"Hullo, boys," said he, "been busy?"

"How are ye, sir?" replied Handy Solomon. "Good Lord, mates, look at that!"

Our eyes followed the direction of his forefinger. Against the dark blue of the evening sky to northward glowed a faint phosphorescence, arch-shaped, from which shot, with pulsating regularity, long shafts of light. They beat almost to the zenith, and back again, a half dozen times, then the whole illumination disappeared with the suddenness of gas turned out.

"Now I wonder what that might be!" marvelled Thrackles.

"Northern lights," hazarded Pulz. "I've seen them almost like that in the Behring Seas."

"Northern lights your eye!" sneered Handy Solomon. "You may have seen them in the Behring Seas, but never this far south, and in August, and you can kiss the Book on that."

"What do you think, sir?" Thrackles inquired of the assistant.

"Devil's fire," replied Percy Darrow briefly. "The island's a little queer. I've noticed it before."

"Debbil fire," repeated the Nigger.

Darrow turned directly to him.

"Yes, devil's fire; and devils, too, for all I know; and certainly vampires. Did you ever hear of vampires, Doctor?"

"No," growled the Nigger.

"Well, they are women, wonderful, beautiful women. A man on a long voyage would just smack his lips to see them. They have shiny grey eyes, and lips red as raspberries. When you meet them they will talk with you and go home with you. And then when you're asleep they tear a little hole in your neck with their sharp claws, and they suck the blood with their red lips. When they aren't women, they take the shape of big bats like birds." He turned to me with so beautifully casual an air that I wanted to clap him on the back with the joy of it.

"By the way, Eagen, have you noticed those big bats the last few evenings, over by the cliff? *I* can't make out in the dusk whether they are vampires or just plain bats." He directed his remarks again to the Nigger. "Next time you see any of those big bats, Doctor, just you notice close. If they have just plain, black eyes, they're all right; but if they have grey eyes, with red rims around 'em, they're vampires. I wish you'd let me know, if you do find out. It's interesting."

"Don' get me near no bats," growled the Nigger.

"Where's Selover?" inquired Darrow.

"He stays aboard," I hastened to say. "Wants to keep an eye on the ship."

"That's laudable. What have you been doing?"

"We've been cleaning ship. Just finished yesterday evening."

"What next?"

"We were thinking of wrecking the *Golden Horn*."

"Quite right. Well, if you want any help with your engines or anything of the sort, call on me."

He arose and began to light his lantern.

"I hope as how you're getting on well there above, sir?" ventured Handy Solomon insinuatingly.

"Very well, I thank you, my man," replied Percy Darrow drily. "Remember those vampires, Doctor."

He swung the lantern and departed without further speech. We followed the spark of it until it disappeared in the arroyo.

Behind us bellowed the sea; over against us in the sky was the dull threatening glow of the volcano; about us were mysterious noises of crying birds, barking seals, rustling or rushing winds. I felt the thronging ghosts of all the old world's superstition swirling madly behind us in the eddies that twisted the smoke of our fire.

We wrecked the *Golden Horn*. Forward was a rusted-out donkey engine, which we took to pieces and put together again. It was no mean job, for all the running parts had to be cleaned smooth, and with the exception of a rudimentary knowledge on the part of Pulz and Perdosa, we were ignorant. In fact we should not have succeeded at all had it not been for Percy Darrow and his lantern. The first evening we took him over to the cliff's edge he laughed aloud.

" Jove, boys, how could you guess it *all* wrong," he wondered.

With a few brief words he set us right, Pulz, Perdosa, and I listening intently; the others indifferent in the hopelessness of being able to comprehend. Of course, we went wrong again in our next day's experiments; but Darrow was down two or three times a week, and gradually we edged toward a practical result.

His explanations consumed but a few moments. After they were finished, we adjourned to the fire.

Thus we came gradually to a better acquaintance with the doctor's assistant. In many respects he remained always a puzzle to me. Certainly the men never knew how to take him. He was evidently not only unafraid of them, but genuinely indifferent to them.

Yet he displayed a certain interest in their needs and affairs. His practical knowledge was enormous. I think I have told you of the completeness of his arrangements—everything had been foreseen from grindstones to gas nippers. The same quality of concrete speculation showed him what we lacked in our own lives.

There was, as you remember, the matter of Handy Solomon's steel claw. He showed Thrackles a kind of lanyard knot that deep-sea person had never used. He taught Captain Selover how to make soft soap out of one species of seaweed. Me, he ini-

tiated in the art of fishing with a white bone lure.
Our camp itself he reconstructed on scientific lines so
that we enjoyed less aromatic smoke and more pala-
table dinner. And all of it he did amusedly, as though
his ideas were almost too obvious to need communication.

We became in a manner intimate with him. He
guyed the men in his indolent fashion, playing on their
credulity, their good nature, even their forbearance.
They alternately grinned and scowled. He left always
a confused impression, so that no one really knew
whether he cherished rancour against Percy Darrow
or kindly feeling.

The Nigger was Darrow's especial prey. The assistant had early discovered that the cook was given
to signs, omens, and superstitions.

From a curious scholar s lore he drew fantastics
with which to torment his victim. We heard of all
the witches, warlocks, incubi, succibi, harpies, devils,
imps, and haunters of Avitchi, from all the teachings
of history, sacred and profane, Hindu, Egyptian, Greek,
mediæval, Swedenborg, Rosicrucian, theosophy, the-
ology, with every last ounce of horror, mystery, shiv-
ers, and creeps squeezed out of them. They were gor-
geous ghost stories, for they were told by a man fully
informed as to all the legendary and gruesome details. At first I used to think he might have communicated it more effectively. Then I saw that the cool,
drawling manner, the level voice, were in reality the
highest art.

He told his stories in a half-amused, detached manner which imposed confidence more readily than any

amount of earnest asseveration. The mere fact of his own belief in what he said came to matter little. He was the vehicle by which was brought accurate knowledge. He had read all these things, and now reported them as he had read: each man could decide for himself as to their credibility.

At last the donkey engine was cleared and reinstalled, atop the cliff. The Nigger built under her a fire of black walnut; Captain Selover handed out grog all around; and we started her up with a cheer, just to see the wheels revolve.

Next we half buried some long hatches, end up, to serve as bitts for the lines, hitched our cables to them, and joyfully commenced the task of pulling the *Golden Horn* piece by piece up the side of the cliff.

The stores were badly damaged by the wet, and there was no liquor, for which I was sincerely grateful. We broke into the boxes, and arrayed ourselves in various garments—which speedily fell to pieces— and appropriated gim-cracks of all sorts. There were some arms, but the ammunition had gone bad. Perdosa, out of forty or fifty mis-fires, got one feeble sputter, and a tremendous *bang* which blew up his piece, leaving only the stock in his hand. A few tinned goods were edible; but all the rest was destroyed. A lot of hard woods, a thousand feet of chain cable, and a fairly good anchor might be considered as prizes. As for the rest, it was foolishness, but we hauled it up just the same until nothing at all remained. Then we shut off the donkey engine, and put on dry clothes. We had been quite happy for the eight months.

It was now well along toward spring. The winter had been like summer, and with the exception of a few rains of a week or so, we had enjoyed beautiful skies. The seals had thinned out considerably, but were now returning in vast numbers ready for their annual domestic arrangements.

Our Sundays we had mostly spent in resting, or in fishing. There were many deep sea fish to be had, of great palatability, but small gameness; they came like so many leaden weights. A few of us had climbed some of the hills in a half-hearted curiosity, but from their summits saw nothing to tempt weariness. Practically we knew nothing beyond the mile or so of beach on which we lived.

Captain Selover had made a habit of coming ashore at least once during the day. He had contented himself with standing aloof, but I took pains to seem to confer with him, so that the men might suppose that I, as mate, was engaged in carrying out his directions. The dread of him was my most potent influence over them.

During the last few days of our wrecking, Captain Selover had omitted his daily visit. The fact made me uneasy, so that at my first opportunity I sculled myself out to the schooner. I found him, moist-eyed as usual, leaning against the mainmast doing nothing.

"We've finished, sir," said I.

He looked at me.

"Will you come ashore and have a look, sir?" I inquired.

"I ain't going ashore again," he muttered thickly.

" What! " I cried.

" I ain't going ashore again," he repeated obstinately, " and that's all there is to it. It's too much of a strain on any man. Suit yourself. You run them. I shipped as captain of a vessel. I'm no dock walloper. I won't *do* it—for no man! "

I gasped with dismay at the man's complete moral collapse. It seemed incredible. I caught myself wondering whether he would recover tone were he again to put to sea.

" My God, man, but you *must!* " I cried at last.

" I won't, and that's flat," said he, and turned deliberately on his heel and disappeared in the cabin.

I went ashore thoughtful and a little scared. But on reflection I regained a great part of my ease of mind. You see, I had been with these men now eight months, during which they had been as orderly as so many primary schoolboys. They had worked hard, without grumbling, and had even approached a sort of friendliness about the camp fire. My first impression was overlaid. As I looked back on the voyage, with what I took to be a clearer vision, I could not but admit that the incidents were in themselves trivial enough— a natural excitement by a superstitious negro, a little tall talk that meant nothing. It must have been the glamour of the adventure that had deceived me; that, and the unusual stage setting and costuming. Certainly few men would work hard for eight months without a murmur, without a chance to look about them.

In that, of course, I was deceived by my inexperi-

ence. I realised later the wonderful effect Captain
Selover threw away with his empty brandy bottles.
The crew might grumble and plot during the watch
below; but when Captain Ezra Selover said *work,*
they worked. He had been saying work, for eight
months. They had, from force of experience, obeyed
him. It was all very simple.

THE EMPTY BRANDY BOTTLE

So there I was at once deprived of my chief support. Although no danger seemed imminent, nevertheless the necessity of acting on my own initiative and responsibility oppressed me somewhat.

Truth to tell, after the first, I was more relieved than dismayed at the captain's resolution to stay aboard. His drinking habit was growing on him, and afloat or ashore he was now little more than a figurehead, so that my chief asset as far as he was concerned, was rather his reputation than his direct influence. In contact with the men, I dreaded lest sooner or later he do something to lessen or destroy the awe in which they held him.

Of course Dr. Schermerhorn had been mistaken in his man: A real captain of men would have risen to circumstances wherever he found them. But who could have foretold? Captain Selover had been a rascal always, but a successful and courageous rascal. He had run desperate chances, dominated desperate crews. Who could know that a crumble of island beach and six months ashore would turn him into what he had become? Yet I believe such cases are not uncommon in other walks of life. A man and his work combine to mean something; yet both may be absolutely useless when separated. It was the weak link——

I put in some time praying earnestly that the eyes

of the crew might be blinded, and that the doctor would finish his experiments before the cauldron could boil up again.

My first act as real commander was to announce holiday. My idea was that the island would keep the men busy for a while. Then I would assign them more work to do. They proposed at once a tour into the interior.

We started up the west coast. After three or four miles along a mesa formation where often we had to circle long detours to avoid the gullies, we came upon another short beach, and beyond it a series of ledges on which basked several hundred seals. They did not seem alarmed. In fact one old bull, scarred by many battles, made toward us.

We left him, scaled the cliff, and turned up a broad, pleasant valley toward the interior.

There the later lava flow had been deflected. All that showed of the original eruption were occasional red outcropping rocks. Soil and grass had overlaid the mineral. Scattered trees were planted throughout the flat. Cacti and semi-tropical bushes mingled with brush on the rounded side hills. A number of brilliant birds fluttered at our approach.

Suddenly Handy Solomon, who was in advance, stopped and pointed to the crest of the hill. A file of animals moved along the sky line.

" Mutton! " said he, " or the devil's a preacher! "

" Sheep! " cried Thrackles. " Where did they come from? "

" *Golden Horn,* " I suggested. " Remember that wide, empty deck forward? They carried sheep there."

The men separated, intending fresh meat. The af

fair was ridiculous. These sheep had become as wild as deer. Our surrounding party with its silly bared knives could only look after them open-mouthed, as they skipped nimbly between its members.

"Get a gun of the Old Man, Mr. Eagen," suggested Pulz, "and we'll have something besides salt horse and fish."

I nodded.

We continued. The island was like this as far as we went. When we climbed a ridge, we found ourselves looking down on a spider-web of other valleys and cañons of the same nature, all diverging to broad downs and a jump into the sea, all converging to the outworks that guarded the volcano with its canopy of vapour.

On our way home we cut across the higher country and the heads of the cañons until we found ourselves looking down on the valley and Dr. Schermerhorn's camp. The steam from the volcanic blowholes swayed below us. Through its rifts we saw the tops of the buildings. Presently we made out Percy Darrow, dressed in overalls, his sleeves rolled back, and carrying a retort. He walked, very preoccupied, to one of the miniature craters, where he knelt and went through some operation indistinguishable at the distance. I looked around to see my companions staring at him fascinated, their necks craned out, their bodies drawn back into hiding. In a moment he had finished, and carried the retort carefully into the laboratory. The men sighed and stood erect, once more themselves. As we turned away Perdosa voiced what must have been in the minds of all.

"A man could climb down there," said he.

"Why should he want to?" I demanded sharply.

"*Quien sabe?*" shrugged he.

We turned in silence toward the beach. Each brooded his thoughts. The sight of that man dressed in overalls, carrying on some mysterious business, brought home to each of us the fact that our expedition had an object, as yet unknown to us. The thought had of late dropped into the background. For my part I had been so immersed in the adventure and the labour and the insistent need of the hour that I had forgotten why I had come. Dr. Schermerhorn's purpose was as inscrutable to me as at first. What had I accomplished?

The men, too, seemed struck with some such idea. There were no yarns about the camp fire that night. Percy Darrow did not appear, for which I was sincerely sorry. His presence might have created a diversion. For some unknown reason all my old apprehensions, my sense of impending disaster, had returned to me strengthened. In the firelight the Nigger's sullen face looked sinister, Pulz's nervous white countenance looked vicious. Thrackles' heavy, bulldog expression was threatening, Perdosa's Mexican cast fit for knife work in the back. And Handy Solomon, stretched out, leaning on his elbow, with his red headgear, his snaky hair, his hook nose, his restless eye and his glittering steel claw—the glow wrote across his aura the names of Kid, Morgan, Blackbeard.

They sat smoking, staring into the fire with mesmerised eyes. The silence got on my nerves. I arose impatiently and walked down the pale beach, where

" These sheep had become as wild as deer "

the stars glimmered in splashes along the wettest sands. The black silhouette of the hills against the dark blue of the night sky; the white of breakers athwart the indistinct heave of the ocean, a faint light marking the position of the *Laughing Lass*—that was everything in the world. I made out some object rolled about in the edge of the wash. At the cost of wet feet I rescued it. It was an empty brandy bottle.

X

CHANGE OF MASTERS

THE next day we continued our explorations by land, and so for a week after that. I thought it best not to relinquish all authority, so I organised regular expeditions, and ordered their direction. The men did not object. It was all good enough fun to them.

The net results were that we found a nesting place of sea birds—too late in the season for eggs; a hot spring near enough camp to be useful; and that was about all. The sheep were the only animals on the island, although there were several sorts of birds. In general, the country was as I have described it—either volcanic or overlaid with fertile earth. In any case it was cañon and hill. We soon grew tired of climbing and turned our attention to the sea.

With the surf boat we skirted the coast. It was impregnable except in three places: our own beach, that near the seal rookery, and on the south side of the island. We landed at each one of these places. But returning close to the coast we happened upon a cave mouth more or less guarded by an outlying rock.

The day was calm, so we ventured in. At first I thought it merely a gorge in the rock, but even while peering for the end wall we slipped under the archway and found ourselves in a vast room.

Our eyes were dazzled so we could make out little

at first. But through the still, clear water the light filtered freely from below, showing the bottom as through a sea glass. We saw the fish near the entrance, and coral and sea growths of marvellous vividness. They waved slowly as in a draught of air. The medium in which they floated was absolutely invisible, for, of course, there were no reflections from its surface. We seemed to be suspended in mid-air, and only when the dipping oars made rings could we realise that anything sustained us.

Suddenly the place let loose in pandemonium. The most fiendish cries, groans, shrieks, broke out, confusing themselves so thoroughly with their own echoes that the volume of sound was continuous. Heavy splashes shook the water. The boat rocked. The invisible surface was broken into facets.

We shrank, terrified. From all about us glowed hundreds of eyes like coals of fire—on a level with us, above us, almost over our heads. Two by two the coals were extinguished.

Below us the bottom was clouded with black figures, darting rapidly like a school of minnows beneath a boat. They darkened the coral and the sands and the glistening sea growths just as a cloud temporarily darkens the landscape—only the occultations and brightenings succeeded each other much more swiftly.

We stared stupefied, our thinking power blurred by the incessant whirl of motion and noise.

Suddenly Thrackles laughed aloud.

" Seals!" he shouted through his trumpeted hands.

Our eyes were expanding to the twilight. We could make out the arch of the room, its shelves, and hollows, and niches. Lying on them we could discern the seals, hundreds and hundreds of them, all staring at us, all barking and bellowing. As we approached, they scrambled from their elevations, and, diving to the bottom, scurried to the entrance of the cave.

We lay on our oars for ten minutes. Then silence fell. There persisted a tiny *drip, drip, drip* from some point in the darkness. It merely accentuated the hush. Suddenly from far in the interior of the hill there came a long, hollow *boo-o-o-m!* It reverberated, roaring. The surge that had lifted our boat some minutes before thus reached its journey's end.

The chamber was very lofty. As we rowed cautiously in, it lost nothing of its height, but something in width. It was marvellously coloured, like all the volcanic rocks of this island. In addition some chemical drip had thrown across its vividness long gauzy streamers of white. We rowed in as far as the faintest daylight lasted us. The occasional reverberating *boom* of the surges seemed as distant as ever.

This was beyond the seal rookery on the beach. Below it we entered an open cleft of some size to another squarer cave. It was now high tide; the water extended a scant ten fathoms to end on an interior shale beach. The cave was a perfectly straight passage following the line of the cleft. How far in it reached we could not determine, for it, too, was full of seals, and after we had driven them back a hundred feet or so their fiery eyes scared us out. We did not care to put them at bay.

The next day I rowed out to the *Laughing Lass* and got a rifle. I found the captain asleep in his bunk, and did not disturb him. Perdosa and I, with infinite pains, tracked and stalked the sheep, of which I killed one. We found the mutton excellent. The hunting was difficult, and the quarry, as time went on, more and more suspicious, but henceforward we did not lack for fresh meat. Furthermore we soon discovered that fine trolling was to be had outside the reef. We rigged a sail for the extra dory, and spent much of our time at the sport. I do not know the names of the fish. They were very gamy indeed, and ran from five to an indeterminate number of pounds in weight. Above fifty pounds our light tackle parted, so we had no means of knowing how large they may have been.

Thus we spent very pleasantly the greater part of two weeks. At the end of that time I made up my mind that it would be just as well to get back to business. Accordingly I called Perdosa and directed him to sort and clear of rust the salvaged chain cable. He refused flatly. I took a step toward him. He drew his knife and backed away.

"Perdosa," said I firmly, "put up that knife."

"No," said he.

I pulled the saw-barrelled Colt's 45 and raised it slowly to a level with his breast.

"Perdosa," I repeated, "drop that knife."

The crisis had come, but my resolution was fully prepared for it. I should not have cared greatly if I had had to shoot the man—as I certainly should have done had he disobeyed. There would then have been one less to deal with in the final accounting, which strangely enough I now for a moment never doubted would come. I had not before aimed at a man's life, so you can see to what tensity the baffling mystery had strung me.

Perdosa hesitated a fraction of an instant. I really think he might have chanced it, but Handy Solomon, who had been watching me closely, growled at him.

"Drop it, you fool!" he said.

Perdosa let fall the knife.

"Now, get at that cable," I commanded, still at white heat. I stood over him until he was well at work, then turned back to set tasks for the other men. Handy Solomon met me halfway.

"Begging your pardon, Mr. Eagen," said he, "I want a word with you."

"I have nothing to say to you," I snapped, still excited.

"It ain't reasonable not to hear a man's say," he advised in his most conciliatory manner, "I'm talking for all of us."

He paused a moment, took my silence for consent, and went ahead.

"Begging your pardon, Mr. Eagen," said he, "we ain't going to do any more useless work. There ain't no laziness about us, but we ain't going to be busy at nothing. All the camp work and the haulin' and cuttin' and cleanin' and the rest of it, we'll do gladly. But we ain't goin' to pound any more cable, and you can kiss the Book on that."

"You mean to mutiny?" I asked.

He made a deprecatory gesture.

"Put us aboard ship, sir, and let us hear the Old Man give his orders, and you'll find no mutiny in us.

But here ashore it's different. Did the Old Man give orders to pound the cable?"

"I represent the captain," I stammered.

He caught the evasion. "I thought so. Well, if you got any kick on us, please, sir, go get the Old Man. If he says to our face, pound cable, why pound cable it is. Ain't that right, boys?"

They murmured something. Perdosa deliberately dropped his hammer and joined the group. My hand strayed again toward the sawed-off Colt's 45.

"I wouldn't do that," said Handy Solomon, almost kindly. "You couldn't kill us all. And w'at good would it do? I asks you that. I can cut down a chicken with my knife at twenty feet. You must surely see, sir, that I could have killed you too easy while you were covering Pancho there. This ain't got to be a war, Mr. Eagen, just because we don't want to work without any sense to it."

There was more of the same sort. I had plenty of time to see my dilemma. Either I would have to abandon my attempt to keep the men busy, or I would have to invoke the authority of Captain Selover. To do the latter would be to destroy it. The master had become a stuffed figure, a bogie with which to frighten, an empty bladder that a prick would collapse. With what grace I could muster, I had to give in.

"You'll have to have it your own way, I suppose," I snapped.

Thrackles, grinned, and Pulz started to say something, but Handy Solomon, with a peremptory gesture, and a black scowl, stopped him short.

"Now that's what I calls right proper and handsome!" he cried admiringly. "We reely had no right to expect that, boys, as seamen, from our first officer! You can kiss the Book on it, that very few crews have such kind masters. Mr. Eagen has the right, and we signed to it all straight, to work us as he pleases; and w'at does he do? Why, he up and gives us a week shore leave, and then he gives us light watches, and all the time our pay goes on just the same. Now that's w'at I calls right proper and handsome conduct, or the devil's a preacher, and I ventures with all respect to propose three cheers for Mr. Eagen."

They gave them, grinning broadly. The villain stood looking at me, a sardonic gleam in the back of his eye. Then he gave a little hitch to his red head covering, and sauntered away humming between his teeth. I stood watching him, choked with rage and indecision. The humming broke into words.

> "'Oh, quarter, oh, quarter!' the jolly pirates cried.
> *Blow high, blow low! What care we?*
> But the quarter that we gave them was to sink them in the sea,
> *Down on the coast of the high Barbare-e-e.*"

"Here, you swab," he cried to Thrackles, "and you, Pancho! get some wood, lively! And Pulz, bring us a pail of water. Doctor, let's have duff to celebrate on."

The men fell to work with alacrity.

IX

THE CORROSIVE

THAT evening I smoked in a splendid isolation while the men whispered apart. I had nothing to do but smoke, and to chew my cud, which was bitter. There could be no doubt, however I may have saved my face, that command had been taken from me by that rascal, Handy Solomon. I was in two minds as to whether or not I should attempt to warn Darrow or the doctor. Yet what could I say? and against whom should I warn them? The men had grumbled, as men always do grumble in idleness, and had perhaps talked a little wildly; but that was nothing.

The only indisputable fact I could adduce was that I had allowed my authority to slip through my fingers. And adequately to excuse that, I should have to confess that I was a writer and no handler of men.

I abandoned the unpleasant train of thought with a snort of disgust, but it had led me to another. In the joy and uncertainty of living I had practically lost sight of the reason for my coming. With me it had always been more the adventure than the story; my writing was a by-product, a utilisation of what life offered me. I had set sail possessed by the sole idea of ferreting out Dr. Schermerhorn's investigations, but the gradual development of affairs had ended by absorbing my every faculty. Now, cast into an eddy by my change of fortunes, the original idea regained its force. I was out of the active government of affairs, with leisure on my hands, and my thoughts naturally turned with curiosity again to the laboratory in the valley.

Darrow's " devil fires " were again painting the sky. I had noticed them from time to time, always with increasing wonder. The men accepted them easily as only one of the unexplained phenomena of a sailor's experience, but I had not as yet hit on a hypothesis that suited me. They were not allied to the aurora; they differed radically from the ordinary volcanic emanations; and scarcely resembled any electrical displays I had ever seen. The night was cool; the stars bright: I resolved to investigate.

Without further delay I arose to my feet and set off into the darkness. Immediately one of the group detached himself from the fire and joined me.

" Going for a little walk, sir? " asked Handy Solomon sweetly. " That's quite right and proper. Nothin' like a little walk to get you fit and right for your bunk."

He held close to my elbow. We got just as far as the stockade in the bed of the arroyo. The lights we could make out now across the zenith; but owing to the precipitance of the cliffs, and the rise of the arroyo bed, it was impossible to see more. Handy Solomon felt the defences carefully.

" A man would think, sir, it was a cannibal island," he observed. " All so tight and tidy-like here. It would take a ship's guns to batter her down. A man might dig under these here two gate logs, if no one was against him. Like to try it, sir? "

"No," I answered gruffly.

From that time on I was virtually a prisoner; yet so carefully was my surveillance accomplished that I could place my finger on nothing definite. Someone always accompanied me on my walks; and in the evening I was herded as closely as any cattle.

Handy Solomon took the direction of affairs off my hands. You may be sure he set no very heavy tasks. The men cut a little wood, carried up a few pails of water—that was all.

Lacking incentive to stir about, they came to spend most of their time lying on their backs watching the sky. This in turn bred a languor which is the sickest, most soul- and temper-destroying affair invented by the devil. They could not muster up energy enough to walk down the beach and back, and yet they were wearied to death of the inaction. After a little they became irritable toward one another. Each suspected the other of doing less than he should. You who know men will realise what this meant.

The atmosphere of our camp became surly. I recognised the precursor of its becoming dangerous. One day on a walk in the hills I came on Thrackles and Pulz lying on their stomachs gazing down fixedly at Dr. Schermerhorn's camp. This was nothing extraordinary, but they started guiltily to their feet when they saw me, and made off, growling under their breaths.

All this that I have told you so briefly, took time. It was the eating through of men's spirits by that worst of corrosives, idleness. I conceive it unnecessary to weary you with the details——

The situation was as yet uneasy but not alarming. One evening I overheard the beginning of an absurd plot to gain entrance to the Valley—that was as far as detail went. I became convinced at last that I should in some way warn Percy Darrow.

That seems a simple enough proposition, does it not? But if you will stop to think one moment of the difficulties of my position, you will see that it was not as easy as at first it appears. Darrow still visited us in the evening. The men never allowed me even the chance of private communication while he was with us. One or two took pains to stretch out between us. Twice I arose when the assistant did, resolved to accompany him part way back. Both times men resolutely escorted us, and as resolutely separated us from the opportunity of a single word apart. The crew never threatened me by word or look. But we understood each other.

I was not permitted to row out to the *Laughing Lass* without escort. Therefore I never attempted to visit her again. The men were not anxious to do so; their awe of the captain made them only too glad to escape his notice. That empty shell of a past reputation was my only hope. It shielded the arms and ammunition.

As I look back on it now, the period seems to me to be one of merely potential trouble. The men had not taken the pains to crystallise their ideas. I really think their compelling emotion was that of curiosity. They wanted to *see*. It needed a definite impulse to change that desire to one of greed.

The impulse came from Percy Darrow and his idle

talk of voodoos. As usual he was directing his remarks to the sullen Nigger.

"Voodoos?" he said. "Of course there are. Don't fool yourself for a minute on that. There are good ones and bad ones. You can tame them if you know how, and they will do anything you want them to." Pulz chuckled in his throat. "You don't believe it?" drawled the assistant turning to him. "Well, it's so. You know that heavy box we are so careful of? Well, that's got a tame voodoo in it."

The others laughed.

"What he like?" asked the Nigger gravely.

"He's a fine voodoo, with wavery arms and green eyes, and red glows." Watching narrowly its effect he swung off into one of the genuine old crooning voodoo songs, once so common down South, now so rarely heard. No one knows what the words mean— they are generally held to be charm-words only—a magic gibberish. But the Nigger sprang across the fire like lightning, his face altered by terror, to seize Darrow by the shoulders.

"Doan you! Doan you!" he gasped, shaking the assistant violently back and forth. "Dat he King Voodoo song! Dat call him all de voodoo— all!"

He stared wildly about in the darkness as though expecting to see the night thronged. There was a moment of confusion. Eager for any chance I hissed under my breath; "Danger! Look out!"

I could not tell whether or not Darrow heard me. He left soon after. The mention of the chest had focussed the men's interest.

"Well," Pulz began, "we've been here on this spot o' hell for a long time."

"A year and five months," reckoned Thrackles.

"A man can do a lot in that time."

"If he's busy."

"They've been busy."

"Yes."

"Wonder what they've done?"

There was no answer to this, and the sea lawyer took a new tack.

"I suppose we're all getting double wages."

"That's so."

"And that's say four hunder' for us and Mr. Eagen here. I suppose the Old Man don't let the schooner go for nothing."

"Two hundred and fifty a month," said I, and then would have had the words back.

They cried out in prolonged astonishment.

"Seventeen months," pursued the logician after a few moments. He scratched with a stub of lead. "That makes over eleven thousand dollars since we've been out. How much do you suppose his outfit stands him?" he appealed to me.

"I'm sure I can't tell you," I replied shortly.

"Well, it's a pile of money, anyway."

Nobody said anything for some time.

"Wonder what they've done?" Pulz asked again.

"Something that pays big." Thrackles supplied the desired answer.

"Dat chis'——" suggested Perdosa.

"Voodoo——" muttered the Nigger.

"That's to scare us out," said Handy Solomon,

with vast contempt. " That's what makes me sure it
is the chest."

Pulz muttered some of the jargon of alchemy.

" That's it," approved Handy Solomon. " If we
could get——"

" We wouldn't know how to use it," interrupted
Pulz.

" The book——" said Thrackles.

" Well, the book——" asserted Pulz pugnaciously.
" How do you know what it will be? It may be the
Philosopher's Stone and it may be one of these other
damn things. And then where'd we be? "

It was astounding to hear this nonsense bandied
about so seriously. And yet they more than half believed, for they were deep-sea men of the old school,
and this was in print. Thrackles voiced approximately
the general attitude.

" Philosopher's stone or not, something's up. The
old boy took too good care of that box, and he's spend-
ing too much money, and he's got hold of too much
hell afloat to be doing it for his health."

" You know w'at I t'ink? " smiled Perdosa. " He
mak' di'mon's. He *say* dat."

The Nigger had entered one of his black, brooding
moods from which these men expected oracles.

" Get him ches'," he muttered. " I see him full—
full of di'mon's! "

They listened to him with vast respect, and were
visibly impressed. So deep was the sense of awe that
Handy Solomon unbent enough to whisper to me:

" I don't take any stock in the Nigger's talk *ordinarily*. He's a hell of a fool nigger. But when his eye

looks like that, then you want to listen close. He sees things then. Lots of times he's seen things. Even last year—the *Oyama*—he told about her three days ahead. That's why we were so ready for her," he chuckled.

Nothing more developed for a long time except a savage fight between Pulz and Perdosa. I hunted sheep, fished, wandered about—always with an escort tired to death before he started. The thought came to me to kill this man and so to escape and make cause with the scientists. My common sense forbade me. I begin to think that common sense is a very foolish faculty indeed.

It taught me the obvious—that all this idle, vapouring talk was common enough among men of this class, so common that it would hardly justify a murder, would hardly explain an unwarranted intrusion on those who employed me. How would it look for me to go to them with these words in my mouth:

" The captain has taken to drinking to dull the monotony. The crew think you are an alchemist and are making diamonds. Their interest in this fact seemed to me excessive, so I killed one of them, and here I am."

" And who are you? " they could ask.

" I am a reporter," would be my only truthful reply.

You can see the false difficulties of my position. I do not defend my attitude. Undoubtedly a born leader of men, like Captain Selover at his best, would have known how to act with the proper decision both now and in the inception of the first mutiny. At heart I never doubted the reality of the crisis.

Even Percy Darrow saw the surliness of the men's attitudes, and with his usual good sense divined the cause.

"You chaps are getting lazy," said he, "why don't you do something? Where's the captain?"

They growled something about there being nothing to do, and explained that the captain preferred to live aboard.

"Don't blame him," said Darrow, "but he might give us a little of his squeaky company occasionally. Boys, I'll tell you something about seals. The old bull seals have long, stiff whiskers—a foot long. Do you know there's a market for those whiskers? Well, there is. The Chinese mount them in gold and use them for cleaners for their long pipes. Each whisker is worth from six bits to a dollar and a quarter. Why don't you kill a few bull seal for the 'trimmings'?"

"Nothin' to do with a voodoo?" grunted Handy Solomon.

Darrow laughed amusedly. "No, this is the truth," he assured. "I'll tell you what: I'll give you boys six bits apiece for the whisker hairs, and four bits for the galls. I expect to sell them at a profit."

Next morning they shook off their lethargy and went seal-hunting.

I was practically commanded to attend. This attitude had been growing of late: now it began to take a definite form.

"Mr. Eagan, don't you want to go hunting?" or "Mr. Eagen, I guess I'll just go along with you to stretch my legs," had given way to, "We're going fishing: you'd better come along."

I had known for a long time that I had lost any real control of them; and that perhaps humiliated me a little. However, my inexperience at handling such men, and the anomalous character of my position to some extent consoled me. In the filaments brushed across the face of my understanding I could discover none so strong as to support an overt act on my part. I cannot doubt, that had the affair come to a focus, I should have warned the scientists even at the risk of my life. In fact, as I shall have occasion to show you, I did my best. But at the moment, in all policy I could see my way to little besides acquiescence.

We killed seals by sequestrating the bulls, surrounding them, and clubbing them at a certain point of the forehead. It was surprising to see how hard they fought, and how quickly they succumbed to a blow properly directed. Then we stripped the mask with its bristle of long whiskers, took the gall, and dragged the carcass into the surf where it was devoured by fish. At first the men, pleased by the novelty, stripped the skins. The blubber, often two or three inches in thickness, had then to be cut away from the pelt, cube by cube. It was a long, an oily, and odoriferous job. We stunk mightily of seal oil; our garments were shiny with it, the very pores of our skins seemed to ooze it. And even after the pelt was fairly well cleared, it had still to be tanned. Percy Darrow suggested the method, but the process was long, and generally unsatisfactory. With the acquisition of the fifth greasy, heavy, and ill-smelling piece of fur the men's interest in peltries waned. They confined themselves in all strictness to the " trimmings."

Percy Darrow showed us how to clean the whiskers. The process was evil. The masks were, quite simply, to be advanced so far in the way of putrefaction that the bristles would part readily from their sockets. The first batch the men hung out on a line. A few moments later we heard a mighty squawking, and rushed out to find the island ravens making off with the entire catch. Protection of netting had to be rigged. We caught seals for a month or so. There was novelty in it, and it satisfied the lust for killing. As time went on, the bulls grew warier. Then we made expeditions to outlying rocks.

Later Handy Solomon approached me on another diplomatic errand.

" The seals is getting shy, sir," said he.

" They are," said I.

" The only way to do is to shoot them," said he.

" Quite like," I agreed.

A pause ensued.

" We've got no cartridges," he insinuated.

" And you've taken charge of my rifle," I pointed out.

" Oh, not a bit, sir," he cried. " Thrackles, he just took it to clean it—you can have it whenever you want it, sir."

" I have no cartridges—as you have observed," said I.

" There's plenty aboard," he suggested.

" And they're in very good hands there," said I.

He ruminated a moment, polishing the steel of his hook against the other arm of his shirt. Suddenly he looked up at me with a humorous twinkle.

"You're afraid of us!" he accused.

I was silent, not knowing just how to meet so direct an attack.

"No need to be," he continued.

I said nothing.

He looked at me shrewdly; then stood off on another tack.

"Well, sir, I didn't mean just that. I didn't mean you was really scared of us. But we're gettin' to know each other, livin' here on this old island, brothers-like. There ain't no officers and men ashore—is there, now, sir? When we gets back to the old *Laughing Lass,* then we drops back into our dooty again all right and proper. You can kiss the Book on that. Old Scrubs, he knows that. He don't want no shore in his. *He* knows enough to stay aboard, where we'd all rather be."

He stopped abruptly, spat, and looked at me. I wondered whither this devious diplomacy led us.

"Still, in one way, an officer's an officer, and a seaman's a seaman, thinks you, and discipline must be held up among mates ashore or afloat, thinks you. Quite proper, sir. And I can see you think that the arms is for the afterguard except in case of trouble. Quite proper. You can do the shooting, and you can keep the cartridges always by you. Just for discipline, sir."

The man's boldness in so fully arming me was astonishing, and his carelessness in allowing me aboard with Captain Selover astonished me still more. Nevertheless I promised to go for the desired cartridges, fully resolved to make an appeal.

A further consideration of the elements of the game convinced me, however, of the fellow's shrewdness. It was no more dangerous to allow me a rifle —under direct surveillance—for the purposes of hunting, than to leave me my sawed-off revolver, which I still retained. The arguments he had used against my shooting Perdosa were quite as cogent now. As to the second point, I, finding the sun unexpectedly strong, returned from the cove for my hat, and so overheard the following between Thrackles and his leader:

"What's to keep him from staying aboard?" cried Thrackles, protesting.

"Well, he might," acknowledged Handy Solomon, "and then are we the worse off? You ain't going to make a boat attack against Old Scrubs, are you?"

Thrackles hesitated.

"You can kiss the Book on it, you ain't," went on Handy Solomon easily, "nor me, nor Pulz, nor the Greaser, nor the Nigger, nor none of us all together. We've had our dose of that. Well, if he goes aboard and *stays*, where are we the worse off? I asks you that. But he won't. This is w'ats goin' to happen. Says he to Old Scrubs, ' Sir, the men needs you to bash in their heads.' ' Bash 'em in yourself,' says he, ' that's w'at you're for.' And if he should come ashore, w'at could he do? I asks you that. We ain't disobeyed no orders dooly delivered. We're ready to pull halliards at the word. No, let him go aboard, and if he peaches to the Old Man, why all the better, for it just gets the Old Man down on him."

"How about Old Scrubs——"

"Don't you believe none in luck?" asked Handy Solomon.

"Aye."

"Well, so do I, with w'at that law-crimp used to call joodicious assistance."

I rowed out to the *Laughing Lass* very thoughtful, and a little shaken by the plausible argument. Captain Selover was lying dead drunk across the cabin table. I did my best to waken him, but failed, took a score of cartridges—no more—and departed sadly. Nothing could be gained by staying aboard; every chance might be lost. Besides, an opening to escape in the direction of the laboratory might offer—I, as well as they, believed in luck judiciously assisted.

In the ensuing days I learned much of the habits of seals. We sneaked along the cliff tops until over the rookeries; then lay flat on our stomachs and peered cautiously down on our quarry. The seals had become very wary. A slight jar, the fall of a pebble, sometimes even sounds unnoticed by ourselves, were enough to send them into the water. There they lined up just outside the surf, their sleek heads glossy with the wet, their calm, soft eyes fixed unblinkingly on us.

It was useless to shoot them in the water: they sank at once.

When, however, we succeeded in gaining an advantageous position, it was necessary to shoot with extreme accuracy. A bullet directly through the back of the head would kill cleanly. A hit anywhere else was practically useless, for even in death the animals seemed to retain enough blind instinctive vitality to flop them into the water. There they were lost.

Each rookery consisted of one tremendous bull who officiated apparently as the standing army; a number of smaller bulls, his direct descendants; the cows, and the pups. The big bull held his position by force of arms. Occasionally other, unattached, bulls would come swimming by. On arriving opposite the rookery the stranger would utter a peculiar challenge. It was never refused by the resident champion, who promptly slid into the sea, and engaged battle. If he conquered, the stranger went on his way. If, however, the stranger won, the big bull immediately struck out to sea, abandoning his rookery, while the new-comer swam in and attempted to make his title good with all the younger bulls. I have seen some fierce combats out there in the blue water. They gashed each other deep——

You can see by this how our hunting was never at an end. On Tuesday we would kill the boss bull of a certain establishment. By Thursday, at latest, another would be installed.

I learned curious facts about seals in those days. The hunting did not appeal to me particularly, because it seemed to me useless to kill so large an animal for so small a spoil. Still, it was a means to my all-absorbing end, and I confess that the stalking, the lying belly down on the sun-warmed grass over the surge and under the clear sky, was extremely pleasant. While awaiting the return of the big bull often we had opportunity to watch the others at their daily affairs, and even the unresponsive Thrackles was struck with their almost human intelligence. Did you know that seals kiss each other, and weep tears when grieved?

The men often discussed among themselves the narrow, dry cave. There the animals were practically penned in. They agreed that a great killing could be made there, but the impossibility of distinguishing between the bulls and the cows deterred them. The cave was quite dark.

Immerced in our own affairs thus, the days, weeks, and months went by. Events had slipped beyond my control. I had embarked on a journalistic enterprise, and now that purpose was entirely out of my reach.

Up the valley Dr. Schermerhorn and his assistant were engaged in some experiment of whose very nature I was still ignorant. Also I was likely to remain so. The precautions taken against interference by the men were equally effective against me. As if that were not enough, any move of investigation on my part would be radically misinterpreted, and to my own danger, by the men. I might as well have been in London.

However, as to my first purpose in this adventure I had evolved another plan, and therefore was content. I made up my mind that on the voyage home, if nothing prevented, I would tell my story to Percy Darrow, and throw myself on his mercy. The results of the experiment would probably by then be ready for the public, and there was no reason, as far as I could see, why I should not get the " scoop " at first hand.

Certainly my sincerity would be without question; and I hoped that two years or more of service such as I had rendered would tickle Dr. Schermerhorn's sense of his own importance. So adequate did this plan seem, that I gave up thought on the subject.

My whole life now lay on the shores. I was not again permitted to board the *Laughing Lass*. Captain Selover I saw twice at a distance. Both times he seemed to be rather uncertain. The men did not remark it. The days went by. I relapsed into that state so well known to you all, when one seems caught in the meshes of a dream existence which has had no beginning and which is destined never to have an end.

We were to hunt seals, and fish, and pry bivalves from the rocks at low tide, and build fires, and talk, and alternate between suspicion and security, between the danger of sedition and the insanity of men without defined purpose, world without end forever.

XII

"OLD SCRUBS" COMES ASHORE

THE inevitable happened. One noon Pulz looked up from his labour of pulling the whiskers from the evil-smelling masks.

"How many of these damn things we got?" he inquired.

"About three hunder' and fifty," Thrackles replied.

"Well, we've got enough for me. I'm sick of this job. It stinks."

They looked at each other. I could see the disgust rising in their eyes, the reek of rotten blubber expanding their nostrils. With one accord they cast aside the masks.

"It ain't such a hell of a fortune," growled Pulz, his evil little white face thrust forward. "There's other things worth all the seal trimmin's of the islands."

"Diamon's," gloomed the Nigger.

"You've hit it, Doctor," cut in Solomon.

There we were again, back to the old difficulty, only worse. Idleness descended on us again. We grew touchy on little things, as a misplaced plate, a shortage of firewood, too deep a draught at the nearly empty bucket. The noise of bickering became as constant as the noise of the surf. If we valued peace, we kept our mouths shut. The way a man spat, or ate, or slept, or even breathed became a cause of irritation to every other member of the company. We stood the outrage as long as we could; then we objected in a wild and ridiculous explosion which communicated its heat to the object of our wrath. Then there was a fight. It needed only liquor to complete the deplorable state of affairs.

Gradually the smaller things came to worry us more and more. A certain harmless singer of the cricket or perhaps of the tree-toad variety used to chirp his innocent note a short distance from our cabin. For all I know he had done so from the moment of our installation, but I had never noticed him before. Now I caught myself listening for his irregular recurrence with every nerve on the quiver. If he delayed by ever so little, it was an agony; yet when he did pipe up, his feeble strain struck to my heart cold and paralysing like a dagger. And with every advancing minute of the night I became broader awake, more tense, fairly sweating with nervousness. One night—good God, was it only last week? . . . it seems ages ago, another existence . . . a state cut off from this by the wonder of a transmigration, at least. . . . Last week!

I did not sleep at all. The moon had risen, had mounted the heavens, and now was sailing overhead. By the fretwork of its radiance through the chinks of our rudely-built cabin I had marked off the hours. A thunderstorm rumbled and flashed, hull down over the horizon. It was many miles distant, and yet I do not doubt that its electrical influence had dried the moisture of our equanimity, leaving us rattling husks for the winds of destiny to play upon. Certainly I can remember no other time, in a rather wide experience, when I have felt myself more on edge, more choked with the restless, purposeless nervous energy that leaves a man's tongue parched and his eyes staring. And still that infernal cricket, or whatever it was, chirped.

I had thought myself alone in my vigil, but when finally I could stand it no longer, and kicked aside my covering with an oath of protest, I was surprised to hear it echoed from all about me.

"Damn that cricket!" I cried.

And the dead shadows stirred from the bunks, and the hollow-eyed victims of insomnia crept out to curse their tormentor. We organised an expedition to hunt him down. It was ridiculous enough, six strong men prowling for the life of one poor little insect. We did not find him, however, though we succeeded in silencing him. But no sooner were we back in our bunks than he began it again, and such was the turmoil of our nerves that day found us sitting wan about a fire, hugging our knees.

We were so genuinely emptied, not so much by the cricket as by the two years of fermentation, that not one of us stirred toward breakfast, in fact not one of us moved from the listless attitude in which day found him, until after nine o'clock. Then we pulled ourselves together and cooked coffee and salt horse. As a significant fact, the Nigger left the dishes unwashed, and no one cared.

Handy Solomon finally shook himself and arose.

"I'm sick of this," said he, "I'm goin' seal-hunting."

They arose without a word. They were sick of it, too, sick to death. We were a silent, gloomy crew indeed as we thrust the surf boat afloat, clambered in, and shipped the oars. No one spoke a word; no one had a comment to make, even when we saw the rookery slide into the water while we were still fifty yards from the beach. We pulled back slowly along the coast. Beyond the rock we made out the entrance to the dry cave.

" There's seal in there," cried Handy Solomon, " lots of 'em! "

He thrust the rudder over, and we headed for the cave. No one expressed an opinion.

As it was again high tide, we rowed in to the steep shore inside the cave's mouth and beached the boat. The place was full of seals; we could hear them bellowing.

" Two of you stand here," shouted Handy Solomon, " and take them as they go out. We'll go in and scare 'em down to you."

" They'll run over us," screamed Pulz.

" No, they won't. You can dodge up the sides when they go by."

This was indeed well possible, so we gripped our clubs and ventured into the darkness.

We advanced four abreast, for the cave was wide enough for that. As we penetrated, the bellowing and barking became more deafening. It was impossible to see anything, although we *felt* an indistinguishable tumbling mass receding before our footsteps. Thrackles swore violently as he stumbled over a laggard. With uncanny abruptness the black wall of darkness in front of us was alive with fiery eyeballs. The seals had reached the end of the cave and had turned toward us. We, too, stopped, a little uncertain as to how to proceed.

The first plan had been to get behind the band and to drive it slowly toward the entrance to the cave. This was now seen to be impossible. The cavern was too narrow; its sides at this point too steep, and the animals too thickly congested. Our eyes, becoming accustomed to the twilight, now began to make out dimly the individual bodies of the seals and the general configuration of the rocks. One big boulder lay directly in our path, like an island in the shale of the cave's floor. Perdosa stepped to the top of it for a better look. The men attempted to communicate their ideas of what was to be done, but could not make themselves heard above the uproar. I could see their faces contorting with the fury of being baffled. A big bull made a dash to get by; all the herd flippered after him. If he had won past they would have followed as obstinately as sheep, and nothing could have stopped them, but the big bull went down beneath the clubs. Thrackles hit the animal two vindictive blows after it had succumbed.

This settled the revolt, and we stood as before. Pulz and Handy Solomon tried to converse by signs, but evidently failed, for their faces showed angry in the twilight. Perdosa, on his rock, rolled and lit a cigarette. Thrackles paced to and fro, and the Nigger leaned on his club, farther down the cave. They had been left at the entrance, but now in lack of results had joined their companions.

Now Thrackles approached and screamed himself black trying to impart some plan. He failed; but stooped and picked up a stone and threw it into the mass of seals. The others understood. A shower of stones followed. The animals milled like cattle, bellowed the louder, but would not face their tormentors. Finally an old cow flopped by in a panic. I thought they would have let her go, but she died a little beyond the bull. No more followed, although the men threw stones as fast and hard as they were able. Their faces were livid with anger, like that of an evil-tempered man with an obstinate horse.

Suddenly Handy Solomon put his head down, and with a roar distinctly audible even above the din that filled the cave, charged directly into the herd. I saw the beasts cringe before him; I saw his club rising and falling indiscriminately; and then the whole back of the cave seemed to rise and come at us.

This was no chance of sport now, but a struggle for very life. We realised that once down there would be no hope, for while the seals were more anxious to escape than to fight, we knew that their jaws were powerful. There was no time to pick and choose. We hit out with all the strength and quickness we possessed. It was like a bad dream, like struggling with an elusive hydra-headed monster, knee high, invulnerable. We hit, but without apparent effect. New heads rose, the press behind increased. We gave ground. We staggered, struggling desperately to keep our feet.

How long this lasted I cannot tell. It seemed hours. I know my arms became leaden from swinging my

club; my eyes were full of sweat; my breath gasped.
A sharp pain in my knee nearly doubled me to the
ground and yet I remember clamping to the thought
that I must keep my feet, keep my feet at any cost.
Then all at once I recalled the fact that I was armed. I
jerked out the short-barrelled Colt's 45 and turned it
loose in their faces.

Whether the flash and detonation frightened them;
whether Perdosa, still clinging to his rock, managed
to turn their attention by his flanking efforts, or
whether, quite simply, the wall of dead finally turned
them back, I do not know, but with one accord they
gave over the attempt.

I looked at once for Handy Solomon, and was surprised to see him still alive, standing upright on a
ledge the other side of the herd. His clothing was
literally torn to shreds, and he was covered with blood.
But in this plight he was not alone, for when I turned
toward my companions they, too, were tattered, torn,
and gory. We were a dreadful crew, standing there
in the half-light, our chests heaving, our rags dripping red.

For perhaps ten seconds no one moved. Then with
a yell of demoniac rage my companions clambered
over the rampart of dead seals and attacked the herd.

The seals were now cowed and defenceless. It was
a slaughter, and the most debauching and brutal I have
ever known. I had hit out with the rest when it had
been a question of defence, but from this I turned
aside in a sick loathing. The men seemed possessed of
devils, and of their unnatural energy. Perdosa cast
aside the club and took to his natural weapon, the knife.

I can see him yet rolling over and over embracing a big
cow, his head jammed in an ecstasy of ferocity between the animal's front flippers, his legs clasped to
hold her body, only his right arm rising and falling
as he plunged his knife again and again. She struggled,
turning him over and under, wept great tears, and
fairly whined with terror and pain. Finally she was
still, and Perdosa staggered to his feet, only to stare
about him drunkenly for a moment before throwing
himself with a screech on another victim.

The Nigger alone did not jump into the turmoil.
He stood just down the cave, his club ready. Occasionally a disorganised rush to escape would be made.
The Nigger's lips snarled, and with a truly mad en-
joyment he beat the poor animals back.

I pressed against the wall horrified, fascinated, unable either to interfere or to leave. A close, sticky
smell took possession of the air. After a little a tiny
stream, growing each moment, began to flow past my
feet. It sought its channel daintily, as streamlets do,
feeling among the stones in eddies, quiet pools, miniature falls, and rapids. For the moment I did not realise
what it could be. Then the light caught it down where
the Nigger waited, and I saw it was red.

At first the racket of the seals was overpowering.
Now, gradually, it was losing volume. I began to hear
the blasphemies, ferocious cries, screams of anger
hurled against the cave walls by the men. The thick,
sticky smell grew stronger; the light seemed to grow
dimmer, as though it could not burn in that fetid air.
A seal came and looked up at me, big tears rolling from
her eyes; then she flippered aimlessly away, out of her

poor wits with terror. The sight finished me. I staggered down the length of the black tunnel to the boat.

After a long interval a little three months' pup waddled down to the water's edge, caught sight of me, and with a squeal of fright dived far. Poor little devil! I would not have hurt him for worlds. As far as I know this was the only survivor of all that herd.

The men soon appeared, one by one, tired, sleepy-eyed, glutted, walking in a cat-like trance of satiety. They were blood and tatters from head to foot, and from drying red masks peered their bloodshot eyes. Not a word said they, but tumbled into the boat, pushed off, and in a moment we were floating in the full sunshine again.

We rowed home in an abstraction. For the moment Berserker rage had burned itself out. Handy Solomon continually wetted his lips, like an animal licking its chops. Thrackles stared into space through eyes drugged with killing. No one spoke.

We landed in the cove, and were surprised to find it in shadow. The afternoon was far advanced. Over the hill we dragged ourselves, and down to the spring. There the men threw themselves flat and drank in great gulps until they could drink no more. We built a fire, but the Nigger refused to cook.

"Someone else turn," he growled, "I cook aboard ship."

Perdosa, who had hewed the fuel, at once became angry.

"I cut heem de wood!" he said, "I do my share; eef I cut heem de wood you mus' cook heem de grub!"

But the Nigger shook his head, and Perdosa went

into an ecstasy of rage. He kicked the fire to pieces;
he scattered the unburned wood up and down the
beach; he even threw some of it into the sea.

"Eef you no cook heem de grub, you no hab my
wood!" he shrieked, with enough oaths to sink his
soul.

Finally Pulz interfered.

"Here you damn foreigners," said he, "quit it!
Let up, I say! We got to eat. You let that wood
alone, or you'll pick it up again!"

Perdosa sprang at him with a screech. Pulz was
small but nimble, and understood rough and tumble
fighting. He met Perdosa's rush with two swift blows
—a short arm jab and an upper-cut. Then they
clinched, and in a moment were rolling over and over
just beyond the wash of the surf.

The row waked the Nigger from his sullen abstraction. He seemed to come to himself with a start;
his eye fell surprisedly on the combatants, then lit up
with an unholy joy. He drew his knife and crept down
on the fighters. It was too good an opportunity to pay
off the Mexican.

But Thrackles interfered sharply.

"Come off!" he commanded. "None o' that!"

"Go to hell!" growled the Nigger.

A great rage fell on them all, blind and terrible, like
that leading to the slaughter of the seals. They fought
indiscriminately, hitting at each other with fists and
knives. It was difficult to tell who was against whom.
The sound of heavy breathing, dull blows, the tear of
cloth, and grunts of punishment received; the swirl of
the sand, the heave of struggling bodies, all riveted my

attention, so that I did not see Captain Ezra Selover until he stood almost at my elbow.

"Stop!" he shrieked in his high, falsetto voice.

And would you believe it, even through the blood haze of their combat the men heard him, and heeded. They drew reluctantly apart, got to their feet, stood looking at him through reeking brows half submissive and half defiant. The bull-headed Thrackles even took a half step forward, but froze in his tracks when Old Scrubs looked at him.

"I hire you men to fight when I tell you to, and only then," said the captain sternly. "What does this mean?"

He menaced them one after another with his eyes, and one after another they quailed. All their plottings, their threats, their dangerousness dissipated like mist before the command of this one resolute man. . These pirates who had seemed so dreadful to me, now were nothing more than cringing schoolboys before their master.

And then suddenly to my horror I, watching closely, saw the captain's eye turn blank. I am sure the men must have felt the change, though certainly they were too far away to see it, for they shifted by ever so little from their first frozen attitude. The captain's hand sought his pocket, and they froze again, but instead of the expected revolver, he produced a half-full brandy bottle.

The change in his eyes had crept into his features. They had turned foolishly amiable, vacant, confiding.

"'llo boys," said he appealingly, "you good fel-lowsh, ain't you? Have a drink. 'S good stuff. Good ol' bottl'," he lurched, caught himself, and advanced toward them, still with the empty smile.

They stared at him for ten seconds, quite at a loss. Then:

"By God, he's drunk!" Handy Solomon breathed, scarcely louder than a whisper.

There was no other signal given. They sprang as with a single impulse. One instant I saw clear against the waning daylight the bulky, foolish-swaying form of Captain Selover: the next it had disappeared, carried down and obliterated by the rush of attacking bodies. Knives gleamed ruddy in the sunset. There was no struggle. I heard a deep groan. Then the murderers rose slowly to their feet.

XIII

I MAKE MY ESCAPE

I HAD plenty of time to run away. I do not know why I did not do so; but the fact stands that I remained where I was until they had finished Captain Selover. Then I took to my heels, but was soon cornered. I drew my revolver, remembered that I had emptied it in the seal cave—and had time for no more coherent mental processes. A smothering weight flung itself on me, against which I struggled as hard as I could, shrinking in anticipation from the thirsty plunge of the knives. However, though the weight increased until further struggle was impossible, I was not harmed, and in a few moments found myself, wrists and ankles tied, beside a roaring fire. While I collected myself I heard the grate of a boat being shoved off from the cove, and a few moments later made out lights aboard the *Laughing Lass*.

The looting party returned very shortly. Their plundering had gone only as far as liquor and arms. Thrackles let down from the cliff top a keg at the end of a line. Perdosa and the Nigger each carried an armful of the 30-40 rifles. The keg was rolled to the fire and broached.

The men got drunk, wildly drunk, but not helplessly so. A flame communicated itself to them through the liquor. The ordinary characteristics of their compo-

174

sition sprung into sharper relief. The Nigger became more sullen; Perdosa more snake-like; Pulz more viciously evil; Thrackles more brutal; while Handy Solomon staggering from his seat to the open keg and back again, roaring fragments of a chanty, his red headgear contrasting with his smoky black hair and his swarthy hook-nosed 'countenance—he needed no further touch.

Their evil passions were all awake, and the plan, so long indefinite, developed like a photographer's plate.

"That's one," said Thrackles. "One gone to hell."

"And now the diamonds," muttered Pulz.

> "There's a ship upon the windward, a wreck upon the
> lee,
> *Down on the coast of the high Barbare-e-e*,"

roared Handy Solomon. "Damn it all, boys, it's the best night's work we ever did. The stuff's ours. Then it's me for a big stone house in Frisco O!"

"Frisco, hell," sneered Pulz, "that's all you know. You ought to travel. Paris for me and a little gal to learn the language from."

"I get heem a fine *caballo,* an' fine saddle, an' fine clo's," breathed Perdosa sentimentally. "I ride, and the silver jingle, and the *señorita* look——"

Thrackles was for a ship and the China trade.

"What you want, Doctor?" they demanded of the silent Nigger.

But the Nigger only rolled his eyes and shook his head. By and by he arose and disappeared in the dusk and was no more seen.

"Dam' fool," muttered Handy Solomon. "Well, here's to crime!"

He drank a deep cup of the raw rum, and staggered back to his seat on the sands.

"'I am not a man-o'-war, nor a privateer,' said he.
Blow high, blow low! What care we!
'But I am a jolly pirate and I'm sailing for my fee,'
Down on the coast of the high Barbare-e-e."

he sang. "We'll land in Valparaiso and we'll go every man his way; and we'll sink the old *Laughing Lass* so deep the mermaids can't find her."

Thrackles piled on more wood and the fire leaped high.

"Let's get after 'em," said he.

"To-morrow's jes' 's good," muttered Pulz. "Les' hav' 'nother drink."

"We'll stay here 'n see if our ol' frien' Percy don' show up," said Handy Solomon. He threw back his head and roared forth a volume of sound toward the dim stars.

"Broadside to broadside the gallant ships did lay,
Blow high, blow low! What care we?
'Til the jolly man-o'-war shot the pirate's mast away,
Down on the coast of the high Barbare-e-e."

I saw near me a live coal dislodged from the fire when Thrackles had thrown on the armful of wood. An idea came to me. I hitched myself to the spark, and laid across it the rope with which my wrists were tied. This, behind my back, was not easy to accomplish, and twice I burned my wrists before I succeeded.

Fortunately I was at the edge of illumination, and behind the group. I turned over on my side so that my
back was toward the fire. Then rapidly I cast loose
my ankle lashings. Thus I was free, and selecting a
moment when universal attention was turned toward
the rum barrel, I rolled over a sand dune, got to my
hands and knees, and crept away.

Through the coarse grass I crept thus, to the very
entrance of the arroyo, then rose to my feet. In the
middle distance the fire leaped red. Its glow fell intermittently on the surges rolling in. The men staggered or lay prone, either as gigantic silhouettes or as
tatterdemalions painted by the light. The keg stood
solid and substantial, the hub about which reeled the
orgy. At the edge of the wash I could make out something prone, dim, limp, thrown constantly in new
positions of weariness as the water ebbed and flowed
beneath it, now an arm thrown out, now cast back,
as though Old Scrubs slept feverishly. The drunkards
were getting noisy. Handy Solomon still reeled off
the verses of his song. The others joined in, fright-
fully off the key; or punctuated the performance by
wild staccato yells.

" Their coffin was their ship and their grave it was the
    sea,
    Blow high, blow low! What care we?
And the quarter that we gave them was to sink them
    in the sea,
    Down on the coast of the high Barbare-e-e,"

bellowed Handy Solomon.

I turned and plunged into the cool darkness of the
cañon.

XIV

AN ADVENTURE IN THE NIGHT

TEN seconds after entering the arroyo I was stumbling along in an absolute blackness. It almost seemed to me that I could reach out my hands and touch it, as one would touch a wall. Or perhaps not exactly that, for a wall is hard, and this darkness was soft and yielding, in the manner of enveloping hangings. Directly above me was a narrow, jagged, and irregular strip of sky with stars. I splashed in the brook, finding its waters strangely warm, rustled through the grasses, my head back, chin out, hands extended as one makes his way through a house at night. There were no sounds except the tinkle of the sulphurous stream: successive bends in the cañon wall had shut off even the faintest echoes of the bacchanalia on the beach.

The way seemed much longer than by daylight. Already in my calculation I had traversed many times the distance, when, with a jump at the heart, I made out a glow ahead, and in front of it the upright logs of the stockade.

To my surprise the gate was open. I ascended the gentle slope to the valley's level—and stumbled over a man lying prostrate, shivering violently, and moaning.

I bent over to discover whom it might be. As I did so a brilliant light seemed to fill the valley, throwing an illumination on the man at my feet. I saw it was the Nigger, and perceived at the same instant that he was almost beside himself with terror. His eyes rolled, his teeth chattered, his frame contracted in a strong convulsion, and the black of his complexion had faded to a washed-out dirty grey, revolting to contemplate. He felt my touch and sprang to his feet, clutching me by the shoulder as a man clutching rescue.

"My Gawd!" he shivered. "Look! Dar it is again!"

He fell to pattering in a tongue unknown to me— charms, spells, undoubtedly, to exorcise the devils that had hold of him. I followed the direction of his gaze, and myself cried out.

The doctor's laboratory stood in plain sight between the two columns of steam blown straight upward through the stillness of the evening. It seemed bursting with light. Every little crack leaked it in generous streams, while the main illumination appeared fairly to bulge the walls outward. This was in itself nothing extraordinary, and indicated only the activity of those within, but while I looked an irregular patch of incandescence suddenly splashed the cliff opposite. For a single instant the very substance of the rock glowed white hot; then from the spot a shower of spiteful flakes shot as from a pryotechnic, and the light was blotted out as suddenly as it came. At the same moment it appeared at another point, exhibited the same phenomena, died, flashed out at still a third place, and so was repeated here and there with bewildering rapidity until the walls of the valley crackled and spat sparks. Abruptly the darkness fell:

As abruptly it was broken again by a similar exhibition; only this time the fire was blue. Blue was followed by purple, purple by red. Then ensued the briefest possible pause, in which a figure moved across the bars of light escaping through the chinks of the laboratory, and then the whole valley blazed with patches of vari-coloured fire. It was not a reflection: it was actual physical conflagration of the solid rock, in irregular areas. Some of the fire shapes were most fantastic. And with the unexpectedness of a bursting shell the surface of the ground before our feet crackled into a ghastly blue flame.

The Nigger uttered a cry in his throat and disappeared. I felt a sharp breath on my neck, an ejaculation of surprise at my very ear. It was startling enough to scare the soul out of a man, but I held fast and was just about to step forward, when my collar was twisted tight from behind. I raised both hands, felt steel, and knew that I was in the grasp of Handy Solomon's claw.

The sailor had me foul. I did my best to twist around, to unbutton the collar, but in vain. I felt my wind leaving me, the ghastly blue light was shot with red. Distinctly I heard the man's sharp intaken breath as some new phenomenon met his eye, and his great oath as he swore.

" By the mother of God! " he cried, " it's the devil."

Then I was jerked off my feet, and the next I knew I was lying on my back, very wet, on the beach; the day was breaking, and the men, quite sober, were talking vehemently.

It was impossible to make out what they said, but

as Handy Solomon and the Nigger were the centre of discussion, I could imagine the subject. I felt very stiff and sore and hazy in my mind. My neck was lame from the dragging and my tongue dry from the choking. For some time I lay in a half-torpor watching the lilac of dawn change to the rose of sunrise, utterly indifferent to everything. They had thrown me down across the first rise of the little sand dunes back of the tide sands, and from it I could at once look out over the sea full of the restless shadows of dawn, and the land narrowing to the mouth of the arroyo. I remember wondering whether Captain Selover were up yet. Then with a sharp stab at the heart I remembered.

The thought was like a dash of cold water in clearing my faculties. I raised my head. Seaward a white gull had caught the first rays of the sun beyond the cliffs. Landward—I saw with a choke in my throat— a figure emerging from the arroyo.

At the sight I made a desperate attempt to move, but with the effort discovered that I was again bound. My stirring thus called Pulz's attention. Before I could look away he had followed the direction of my gaze. The discussion instantly ceased. They waited in grim silence.

I did not know what to do. Percy Darrow, carrying some sort of large book, was walking rapidly toward us. Perdosa had disappeared. Thrackles after an instant came and sat beside me and clapped his big hand over my mouth. It was horrible.

When within a hundred paces or so, I could see that Darrow laboured under some great excitement. His usual indifferent saunter had, as I have indicated,

given way to a firm and decided step; his ironical eye
glistened; his sallow cheek glowed.

"Boys," he shouted cheerfully. "The time's up.
We've succeeded. We'll sail just as soon as the Lord'll
let us get ready. Rustle the stuff aboard. The doctor'll
be down in a short time, and we ought to be loaded by
night."

Handy Solomon and Pulz laid hand on two of the
rifles near by and began surreptitiously to fill their
magazines. The Nigger shook his knife free of the
scabbard and sat with it in his left hand, concealed by
his body. I could feel Thrackles's muscles stiffen. Another fifty paces and it would be no longer necessary
to stop my mouth.

The thought made me desperate. I had failed as a
leader of these men, and I had been forced to stand by
at debauching, cruel, and murderous affairs, but now
it is over I thank Heaven the reproach cannot be made
against me that at any time I counted the consequences
to myself. Thrackles's hand lay heavy across my
mouth. I bit it to the bone, and as he involuntarily
snatched it away, I rolled over toward the sea.

Thus for an instant I had my mouth free.

"Run! Run!" I shouted. "For God's sake——"

Thrackles leaped upon me and struck me heavily
upon the mouth, then sprang for a rifle. I managed to
struggle back to the dune, whence I could see.

XV

FIVE HUNDRED YARDS' RANGE

PERCY DARROW, with the keenness that always characterised his mental apprehension, had understood enough of my strangled cry. He had not hesitated nor delayed for an explanation, but had turned track and was now running as fast as his long legs would carry him back toward the opening of the ravine. My companions stood watching him, but making no attempt either to shoot or to follow. For a moment I could not understand this, then remembered the disappearance of Perdosa. My heart jumped wildly, for the Mexican had been gone quite long enough to have cut off the assistant's escape. I could not doubt that he would pick off his man at close range as soon as the fugitive should have reached the entrance to the arroyo.

There can be no question that he would have done so had not his Mexican impatience betrayed him. He shot too soon. Percy Darrow stopped in his tracks. Although we heard the bullet sing by us, for an instant we thought he was hit. Then Perdosa fired a second time, again without result. Darrow turned sharp to the left and began desperately to scale the steep cliffs.

I once took part in a wild boar hunt on the coast of California. Our dogs had penned a small band at the head of a narrow *barranca,* from which a single steep trail led over the hill. We, perched on another hill some three or four hundred yards away, shot at the animals as they toiled up the trail. The range was long, but we had time, for the severity of the climb forced the boars to a foot pace.

It was exactly like that. Percy Darrow had two hundred feet of ascent to make. He could go just so fast; must consume just so much time in his snail-like progress up the face of the hill. During that time he furnished an excellent target, and the loose sandstone showed where each shot struck.

A significant indication was that the men did not take the trouble to get nearer, for which manœuvre they would have had time in plenty, but distributed themselves leisurely for a shooting match.

" First shot," claimed Handy Solomon, and without delay fired off-hand. A puff of dust showed to the right. " Nerve no good," he commented, " jerked her just as I pulled."

Pulz fired from the knee. The dust this time puffed below.

" Thought she'd carry up at that distance," he muttered.

The Nigger, too, missed, and Thrackles grinned triumphantly.

" I get a show," said he.

He spread his massive legs apart, drew a deep breath, and raised his weapon. It lay in his grasp steady as a log, and I saw that Percy Darrow's fate was in the hands of that dangerous class of natural marksman that possesses no nerves. But for the second time my teeth saved his life. The trigger guard slipped against Thrackles's lacerated hand almost at the instant of discharge. He missed; and the bullet went wide.

Darrow had climbed a matter of twenty feet.

Now the seamen distributed themselves for more leisurely and accurate marksmanship. Handy Solomon lay flat on his stomach, resting the rifle muzzle across the top of a sand dune. Pulz sat down, an elbow on either knee for the greater steadiness. The Nigger knelt; but Thrackles remained on his feet. No rest could be steadier than the stone-like rigidity of his thick arms.

The firing now became miscellaneous. No one paid any attention to anyone else. Each discovered what I could have told them, that even the human figure at five hundred yards is a small mark for a strange rifle. The constant correction of elevation, however, brought the puffs of dust always closer, and I could not but realise that the doctrine of chances must bring home some of the bullets. I soon discovered by way of comfort that only Thrackles and Handy Solomon really understood firearms; and of those two Thrackles alone had had much experience at long range. He told me afterward he had hunted otter.

About halfway up the cliff Thrackles fired his fifth shot. No dust followed the discharge; and I saw Percy Darrow stagger and almost lose his hold. The men yelled savagely, but the assistant pulled himself together and continued his crawling.

The sun had been shining in our faces. I could imagine its blurring effect on the sights. Now abruptly it was blotted out, and a semi-twilight fell. We all looked up, in spite of ourselves. An opaque veil had been drawn quite across the heavens, through which we could not make out even the shape of the sun. It was like a thunder cloud except that its under surface instead of being the usual grey-black was a deep earth-brown. As we looked up, a deep bellow stirred the air, which had fallen quite still, long forks of lightning shot horizontally from the direction of the island's interior, and flashes of dull red were reflected from the canopy of cloud.

The men stared with their mouths open. Undoubtedly the change had been some time in preparation, but all had been so absorbed in the affair of the doctor's assistant that no one had noticed. It came to our consciousness with the suddenness of a theatrical change. A dull roaring commenced, grew in volume, and then a great explosion shook the very ground under our feet.

We stared at each other, our faces whitening.

"What kind of hell has broke loose?" muttered Pulz.

The Nigger fell flat on his face, uttering deep lamentations.

"Voodoo! Voodoo!" he groaned.

A gentle shower of white flakes began, powdering the surface of everything. Far out to sea we could make out the sun on the water. Gradually the roaring died down; the lightning ceased. Comparative peace ensued. We looked again toward the cliff. Percy Darrow had not for one instant ceased to climb. He was just topping the edge of the bluff. Handy Solomon,

The firing now became miscellaneous.   No one paid any
attention to any one else

with a cry of rage, seized another rifle and emptied the magazine at him as fast as the lever could be worked. The dust flew wild in a half dozen places. Darrow drew himself up to the sky line, raised his hat ironically, and disappeared.

"Damn his soul!" cried Handy Solomon, his face livid. He threw his rifle to the beach and danced on it in an ecstasy of rage.

"What do we care," growled Thrackles, "he's no good to us. W'at I want to know is, wat's up here, anyhow!"

"Didn't you never see a volcano go off, you swab?" snapped Handy Solomon.

"Easy with your names, mate. No, I never did. We better get out."

"Without the chest?"

"S'pose we go up the gulch and get it, then," suggested Thrackles.

But at this Handy Solomon drew back in evident terror.

"Up that hole of hell?" he objected. "Not I. You an' Pulz go."

They wrangled over it, Pulz joining. Perdosa, shaken to the soul, crept in, and made a bee-line for the rum barrel. He and the Nigger were frankly scared. They had the nervous jumps at every little noise or unexpected movement; and even the natural explanation of these phenomena gave them very little reassurance. I knew that Darrow would hurry as fast as he could back to the valley by way of the upper hills; I knew that he had there several sporting rifles; and I hoped greatly that he and Dr. Schermerhorn might accomplish something before the men had recovered their wits to the point of foreseeing his probable attack. The uncanny cloud in the heavens, the weird half-light, and the explosions, which now grew more frequent, had their strong effect in spite of explanation. The men were not really afraid to venture in quest of the supposed treasure; but they were in a frame of mind that dreaded the first plunge. And time was going by.

But the fates were against us, as always in this ill-starred voyage. I, watching from my sand dune, saw a second figure emerge from the arroyo's mouth. It appeared to stagger as though hurt; and every eight or ten paces it stopped and rested in a bent-over position. The murky light was too dim for me to make out details; but after a moment a rift in the veil enabled me to identify Dr. Schermerhorn carrying, with great difficulty, the chest.

XVI

THE MURDER

I took no chances, but began at once to shout, as soon
as I saw the men had noticed his coming. It was impossible for me to tell whether or not Dr. Schermerhorn heard me. If he did, he misunderstood my intention, for he continued painfully to advance. The only
result I gained was to get myself well gagged with my
own pocket handkerchief, and thrown in a hollow between the dunes. Thence I could hear Handy Solomon speaking fiercely and rapidly.

"Now you let me run this," he commanded; "we
got to find out somethin'. It ain't no good to us without we knows—and we want to find out how he's
got the rest hid."

They assented.

"I'm goin' out to help him carry her in," announced
the seaman.

A long pause ensued, in which I watched the deep
canopy of red-black thicken overhead. A strange and
unearthly light had fallen on the world, and the air
was quite still. After a while I heard Handy Solomon
and Dr. Schermerhorn join the group.

"There you are, Perfessor," cried Handy Solomon,
in tones of the greatest heartiness. "I'll put her right
there, and she'll be as safe as a babby at home. She's
heavy, though."

Dr. Schermerhorn laughed a pleased and excited laugh. I could tell by the tone of his voice that he was strung high, and guessed that his triumph needed an audience.

"You may say so well!" he said. "It iss heafy; and it iss heafy with the world-desire, the great substance than can do efferything. Where iss Percy?"

"He's gone aboard."

"We must embark. The time is joost right. A day sooner and the egsperiment would haf been spoilt; but now"—he laughed—"let the island sink, we do not care. We must embark hastily."

"It'll take a man long time to carry down all your things, Perfessor."

"Oh, led them go! The eruption has alretty swallowed them oop. The lava iss by now a foot deep in the valley. Before long it flows here, so we must embark."

"But you've lost all them vallyable things, Perfessor," said Handy Solomon. "Now, I call that hard luck."

Dr. Schermerhorn snapped his fingers.

"They do not amoundt to that!" he cried. "Here, here, in this leetle box iss all the treasure! Here iss the labour of ten years! Here iss the *Laughing Lass,* and the crew, and all the equipmendt comprised. Here iss the world!"

"I'm a plain seaman, Perfessor, and I suppose I got to believe you; but she's a main small box for all that."

"With that small box you can haf all your wishes," asserted the Professor, still in the German lyric strain

over his triumph. " It iss the box of enchantments.
You haf but to will the change you would haf taig
place—it iss done. The substance of the rocks, the
molecule—all!"

" Could a man make diamonds?" asked Pulz abruptly. I could hear the sharp intake of the men's
breathing as they hung on the reply.

" Much more wonderful changes than that it can
accomplish," replied the doctor, with an indulgent
laugh. " That change iss simple. Carbon iss coal; carbon iss diamond. You see? One has but to change the
form, not the substance."

" Then it'll change coal to diamonds?" asked
Handy Solomon.

" Yes, you gather my meanings——"

I heard a sharp squeak like a terrified mouse. Then
a long, dreadful silence; then two dull, heavy blows,
spaced with deliberation. A moment later I caught a
glimpse of Handy Solomon bent forward to the labour
of dragging a body toward the sea, his steel claw
hooked under the angle of the jaw as a man handles
a fish. Pulz came and threw off my bonds and gag.

" Come along!" said he.

All kept looking fearfully toward the arroyo. A
dense white steam marked its course. The air was
now heavy with portent. Successive explosions, some
light, some severe, shook the foundations of the island. Great rocks and boulders bounded down the
hills. The flashes of lightning had become more frequent. We moved, exaggerated to each other's vision
by the strange light, uncouth and gigantic.

" Let's get out of this!" cried Thrackles.

We turned at the word and ran, Thrackles staggering under the weight of the chest. All our belongings we abandoned, and set out for the *Laughing Lass* with only the tatters in which we stood. Luckily for us a great part of the ship's stores had been returned to her hold after the last thorough scrubbing, so we were in subsistence, but all our clothes, all our personal belongings, were left behind us on the beach. For after once we had topped the cliff that led over to the cove, I doubt if any consideration on earth would have induced us to return to that accursed place.

The row out to the ship was wet and dangerous. Seismic disturbances were undoubtedly responsible for high pyramidic waves that lifted and fell without onward movement. We fairly tumbled up out of the dory, which we did not hoist on deck, but left at the end of the painter to beat her sides against the ship.

XVII

THE OPEN SEA

OUR haste, however, availed us little, for there was no wind at all. We lay for over two hours under the weird light, over-canopied by the red-brown cloud, while the explosions shook the foundations of the world. Nobody ventured below. The sails flapped idly from the masts: the blocks and spars creaked: the three-cornered waves rose straight up and fell again as though reaching from the deep.

When the men first began to sweat the sails up, evidently in preparation for an immediate departure, I objected vehemently.

"You aren't going to leave him on the island," I cried. "He'll die of starvation."

They did not answer me; but after a little more, when my expostulations had become more positive, Handy Solomon dropped the halliard, and drew me to one side.

"Look here, you," he snarled, "you'd better just stow your gab. You're lucky to be here yourself, let alone botherin' your thick head about anybody else, and you can kiss the Book on that! Do you know why you ain't with them carrion?" He jerked his thumb toward the beach. "It's because Solomon Anderson's your friend. Thrackles would have killed you in a minute 'count of his bit hand. I got you your chance.

Now don't you be a fool, for I ain't goin' to stand between you and them another time. Besides, he won't last long if that volcano keeps at it."

He left me. Whatever truth lay in his assumption of friendship, and I doubted there existed much of either truth or friendship in him, I saw the common sense of his advice. I was in no position to dictate a course of action.

After the sails were on her we gathered at the starboard rail to watch the shore. There the hills ran into inky blackness, as the horizon sometimes merges into a thunder squall. A dense white steam came from the creek bed within the arroyo. The surges beat on the shore louder than the ordinary, and the foam, even in these day hours, seemed to throw up a faint phosphorescence. Frequent earthquakes oscillated the landscape. We watched, I do not know for what, our eyes straining into the murk of the island. Nobody thought of the chest, which lay on the cabin table aft. I contributed maliciously my bit to their fear.

" These volcanic islands sometimes sink entirely," I suggested, " and in that case we'd be carried down by the suction."

It was intended merely to increase their uneasiness, but, strangely enough, after a few moments it ended by imposing itself on my own fears. I began to be afraid the island would sink, began to watch for it, began to share the fascinated terror of these men.

The suspense after a time became unbearable, for while the portent—whether physical or moral we were too far under its influence to distinguish—grew momentarily, our own souls did not expand in due correspondence. We talked of towing, of kedging out, of going to any extreme, even to small boats. Then just as we were about to move toward some accomplishment, a new phenomenon chained our attention to the shore.

In the mouth of the arroyo appeared a red glow. A moment later a wave of lava, white-hot, red, iridescent, cooling to a black crust cracked in incandescence, rolled majestically out over the grassy plain. Each instant it grew in volume, until the ravine must have been flowing half full.

Before its scorching the grasses even at the edge of the sea were smoking, and our camp had already burst into flames. We had to shield our faces against the heat, and the wooden railing under our hands was growing warm.

Pulz turned an ashy countenance toward us.

"My God," he screamed. "What's going to happen when she hits the sea?"

She hit the sea, and immediately a great cloud of steam arose, and the hissing as of a thousand serpents. We felt the strong suction under our keel, and staggered under the jerk of the ship's cable as she swung toward the beach. The paint was beginning to crackle along the rail. We could see nothing for the scalding white veil that enveloped us; we could hear nothing for the roar of steam, the bombardment of explosions, and the crash of thunder; but our nostrils were assaulted by a most unearthly medley of smells.

"Hell's loose," growled Thrackles.

We were clinging hard as the ship reeled. Huge

surges were racing in from seaward, growing larger
with each successive billow.

Handy Solomon raised his head, listened intently,
and struck his forehead.

"Wind," he screamed at the top of his voice, and
jumped for the halliards.

Thrackles followed him, but no one else moved. In
an instant the two were back, striking and kicking savagely, rousing their companions to the danger. We all
laid into the canvas like mad, and in no time had
snugged down to a staysail and the peak of our mainsail. Thrackles drew his knife and jumped for the
cable, while Handy Solomon, his eyes snapping, seized
the wheel.

We finished just in time. I was turning away after
tying the last gasket on the foresail, when the deck
up-ended and tipped me headforemost into the starboard scupper. At the same time a smother of salt
water blew over the port rail, now far above me, to
drench me as thoroughly as though I had fallen overboard. I brushed out my eyes to find the ship smack
on her beam ends, and the wind howling by from the
sea.

I had company enough in the scuppers. Only
Handy Solomon clung desperately to the wheel, jam-
ming his weight to port in the hope she might pay
up: Thrackles, too, his eye squinted along some bearing of his own, was waiting for her to drag. Presently it became evident that she was doing so,
whereupon he drew his knife across our hawser.

"My God," chattered Pulz at my ear. "If we go
ashore——"

He did not need to finish. Unless the *Laughing Lass* could recover before the squall had driven her to leeward a scant half mile, we should be cooked alive in the boiling cauldron at the shore's edge.

For an interminable time, as it seemed to me, we lay absolutely motionless. The scene is stamped indelibly on my memory—the bulwarks high above me, the steep, sleek deck, the piratical figure tense at the wheel, the snarling water racing from beneath us, the lurid glow to landward crawling up on us inch by inch like a hungry wild beast. Then almost imperceptibly the brave schooner righted. The strained lines on Handy Solomon's carven features relaxed little by little. Thrackles, staring over the side, let out a mighty roar.

"Steerage way," he shouted, and executed an awkward clog dance on the reeling deck.

She moved forward, there was no doubt of that, for gradually we were eating toward the wind—but we made considerable leeway as well. Handy Solomon, taut as the weather rigging, took his little advantages one by one like precious gifts. Light there was none; the land was blotted out by the steam and murk which had crept to sea and now was hurled back by the wind. All we could do was to hang there, tasting the copper of excitement, waiting for these different forces to adjust themselves. Inch by inch we crept forward: foot by foot we made leeway. The intensest of the lava glow worked its way from directly abeam to the quarter. By this we knew we must be nearly opposite the cove. At once a new doubt sprang up in our minds.

A moment ago all the energy of our desires had

gone up in the ambition to avoid being cast on the beach. Now we saw that that was not enough. It was necessary to squeeze around the point where lay the *Golden Horn,* in order to avoid the fate that had overtaken her. Handy Solomon yelled something at us. We could not hear, but our own knowledge told us what it must be, and with one accord we turned to on the foresail. With the peak of it hoisted we moved a trifle faster, though the schooner lay over at a perilous angle. A moment later the fogs parted to show us the cliffs looming startlingly near. There were the donkey engine and the works we had constructed for wrecking—and there beside them, watching· us reflectively, stood Percy Darrow.

For ten minutes we stared at him fascinated, during which time the ship laboured against the staggering winds, gained and lost in its buffeting with the great surges. The breakers hurling themselves in wild abandon against the rocks sent their back-wash of tumbling peaks to our very bilges. The few remains of the *Golden Horn,* alternately drenched and draining, seemed to picture to us our inevitable end.

I think we had all selected the same two points for our " bearings," a rock and a drop of the cliff bolder than the ordinary. If the rock opened from the cliff to eastward, we were lost; if it remained stationary, we were at least holding our own; if it opened out to westward, we were saved. We watched with a strained eagerness impossible to describe. At each momentary gain or rebuff we uttered ejaculations. The Nigger mumbled charms. Every once in a while one of us would snatch a glance to leeward at the cruel, white waters, the whirl of eddies where the sea was beaten, only to hurry back to the rock and the point of the cliff whence our message of safety or destruction was to be flung. Once I looked up. Percy Darrow was leaning gracefully against a stanchion, watching. His soft hat was pulled over his eyes; he stroked softly his little moustache; I caught the white puff of his cigarette. During the moment of my inattention something happened. A wild shout burst from the men. I whirled, and saw to my great joy a strip of sky westward between the cliff and the rock. And at that very instant a billow larger than the ordinary rolled beneath us, and in the back suction of its passage I could dimly make out cruel, dangerous rocks lying almost under our keel.

Slowly we crept away. Our progress seemed infinitesimal, and yet it was real. In a while we had gained sea room; in a while more we were fairly under sailing way, and the cliffs had begun to drop from our quarter. With one accord we looked back. Percy Darrow waved his hand in an indescribably graceful and ironic gesture; then turned square on his heel and sauntered away to the north valley, out of the course of the lava. That was the last I ever saw of him.

As we made our way from beneath the island, the weight of the wind seemed to lessen. We got the foresail on her, then a standing jib; finally little by little all her ordinary working canvas. Before we knew it, we were bowling along under a stiff breeze, and the island was dropping astern.

From a distance it presented a truly imposing sight.

The centre shot intermittent blasts of ruddy light; explosions, deadened by distance, still reverberated strongly; the broad canopy of brown-red, split with lightnings, spread out like a huge umbrella. The lurid gloom that had enveloped us in the atmosphere apparently of a nether world had given place to a twilight. Abruptly we passed from it to a sun-kissed, sparkling sea. The breeze blew sweet and strong; the waves ran untortured in their natural long courses.

At once the men seemed to throw off the superstitious terror that had cowed them. Pulz and Thrackles went to bail the extra dory, alongside, which by a miracle had escaped swamping. The Nigger disappeared in the galley. Perdosa relieved Handy Solomon at the wheel; and Handy Solomon came directly over to me.

XVIII

THE CATASTROPHE

HE approached me with a confidence that proclaimed the new leader. A brace of Colt's revolvers swung from his belt, the tatters of his blood-stained garments hung about him.

" Well, here we are," he remarked.

I nodded, waiting for what he had to disclose.

" And lucky for you that you're here at all, say I," he continued. " And now that you're here, w'at are you going to do? That's the question—w'at are you going to do?" He cocked his head sidewise and looked at me speculatively as a cat might look at a rather large mouse. " We been a little rough," he went on after a moment, " and some folks is strait-laced. There might be trouble. And you know a heap too much."

" What do you want of me?" I demanded.

" It's just this," he returned briskly. " If you'll lay us our course to San Salvador, we'll let you go as one of us and no questions asked."

" If not?" I inquired.

He shrugged his shoulders. " I leave it to you."

" There's always the sea," I suggested.

" And it's deep," he agreed.

We looked out to the horizon in a diplomatic silence. I did not know whether to be angry, amused, or alarmed that the man estimated my cleverness so slightly. Why, the hook was barely concealed, and the bait of the coarsest. That I would go safe to a sight of San Salvador I did not doubt: that I would never enter the harbour I was absolutely certain. The choice offered me was practically whether I preferred being thrown overboard now or several hundred miles to southeastward.

I thought rapidly. It might be possible to announce a daily false reckoning to the crew, to sail the ship within rowing distance of some coast; and then to escape while the men believed themselves many hundred miles at sea. It would take nice calculation to prevent suspicion, but as it was the only chance I resolved upon it immediately.

"That's all very well," I said firmly, "but you can't get anywhere without me, and I'm not going to put in two years and then keep my mouth shut for nothing. I want a share in the swag—an even share with the rest of you."

"Oh, that'll be all right," he cried; "you can have it."

If anything was needed to convince me of the man's sinister intentions, this too ready acquiescence would have been enough. I knew him too well. If he had had the slightest intention of permitting me to go free, he would have bargained.

The Nigger called us to mess. We ate in the after cabin. The chest was locked and the men had as yet been unable to break into it. Pulz professed some skill in locksmithing and promised to experiment later. After mess we went on deck again. The island had

dropped down to the horizon and showed as a brilliant glow under a dark canopy. I leaned over the rail
looking at it. Below me the extra dory bumped along.
The idea came to me that if I could escape that night,
I could row back to Percy Darrow. The two of us
could make shift to live on fish and shellfish and mutton. The plan rapidly defined itself in my brain. From
the remains of the *Golden Horn* we could construct
some kind of a craft in which to run free to the summer trades. Thus we might in time reach some one
or another of the Sandwich Islands, whence a passing
trader could take us back to civilisation. There were
many elements of uncertainty in the scheme, but it
seemed to me less desperate than trusting to the ca-
prices of these men, especially since they now had free
access to the liquor stores.

While I leaned over the rail engrossed in these
thoughts, one of the black thunder clouds that had
been gathering and dissipating over the island during the entire afternoon suddenly glowed overhead
with a strange white incandescence startlingly akin
to Darrow's so-called " devil fires." Strangely enough,
this illumination, unlike the volcanic glows, appeared
to be cast on the clouds from without rather than shot
through them from within, as were the other volcanic
emanations. At the same instant I experienced a
sharp interior revulsion of some sort, most briefly
momentary, but of a character that shook me from
head to toe.

I had no time to analyse these various impressions,
however, for my attention was almost instantly dis-
tracted. From the cabin came the sound of a sharp

fall, then a man cried out, and on the heels of it Pulz
darted from the cabin, screaming horribly. We were
all on deck, and as the little man rushed toward the
stern Handy Solomon twisted him deftly from his
feet.

" My God, mate, what is it? " he cried, as he pinned
the sufferer to the deck.

But Pulz could not answer. He shivered, stiffened,
and lay rigid, his eyes rolled back.

" Fits," remarked Thrackles impatiently.

The excitement died. Rum was forced between the
victim's lips. After a little he recovered, but could
tell us nothing of his seizure.

After the dishes had been swept aside from supper,
Handy Solomon announced a second attempt to open
the chest.

" Pancho, here, says he's been a mechanic," said
he. " I right well know he's been a housebreaker. So
he's got the *sabe* for the job, and you can kiss the
Book on that."

Perdosa, with a grin, leaned over the cover from
behind and began to pick away at the lock with a long,
crooked wire. The others drew close about. I slipped
nearer the door, imagining that in their riveted interest I saw my opportunity. To my surprise I caught
a glimpse of legs disappearing up the companion. I
took stock. Pulz had gone on deck.

This surprised me, for I should have thought every
man interested enough in the supposed treasure to
wish to be present at its uncovering; and it annoyed
me still more—the success of my plan demanded a
clear deck. However, there was nothing for it now

but to trust that Pulz had wished to visit the forecastle, and that I might find the afterworks empty.

I paused at the foot of the companion and looked back. A breathlessness of excitement held the pirates in a vise. From above, the hanging lamp threw strong shadows across their faces, bringing out the deep lines, accentuating the dominant passions. With their rags and blood, their unshaven faces, their firearms, their filth, they showed in violent antithesis to the immaculate white of Old Scrubs's cabin, its glittering brass, and its shining leather. I darted up the steps.

The contrast of the starry night with the glare of the cabin lamp dazzled my eyes. I stood stock still for a moment, during which the only sounds audible were the singing of the winds through the rigging, the wash of the sea, and the small, sharp click of Perdosa's instrument as he worked at the chest.

Presently I could see better. I looked forward and aft for Pulz, but could see nothing of him, and had just about concluded that he had gone forward when I happened to glance aloft. There, to my astonishment, I made him out, huddled in silhouette against the stars, close to the main truck. What he was doing there I could not imagine. However, I did not have time to bother my head about him, further than to rejoice that he could not obstruct me.

I should very much have liked to get hold of a rifle and ammunition, or at least to lay in biscuit and water, but for this there was no time. It was not absolutely essential. The dull glow of the island was still visible. I had my pillar of fire and smoke to guide me.

Without further delay I jerked loose the painter and drew the extra dory alongside.

I had proceeded just so far in my movements, when the most extraordinary thing happened. I shall try to tell you of it as accurately as possible, and in the exact order of its occurrence. First a long, straight shaft of white light shot straight up *through* the cabin roof to a great height. It shone through the wooden planks as an ordinary light shines through glass. By contrast the surrounding blackness was thrown into a deeper shade, and yet the shaft itself was so brilliant as almost to scotch the sight. Curiously enough, it was defined accurately, being exactly in shape like one of the rectangular tin air-shafts you see so often in city hotels. At the instant of its appearance, the wind fell quite calm.

Almost immediately the rectangle on the roof through which the light made its passage began to splay out, like lighted oil, although the column retained still the integrity of its outline. The fire, if such it could be called, ran with incredible rapidity along the seams between the planks, forward and aft, until the entire deck was sketched like a pyrotechnic display in thin, vivid lines of incandescence. From each of these lines then the fire began again to spread, as though soaking through the planks.

All took place practically in an instant of time. I had no opportunity to move nor to cry out; indeed, my perceptions were inadequate to the task of mere observation. Up to now there had been no sound. The wind had fallen; the waters passed unnoticed. A stillness of death seemed to have descended on the ship. It was broken by a sharp double report, one as of the fall of a metallic substance, the other caused by the body of Pulz, which, shaken loose from the truck by a heavy roll, smashed against the rail of the ship and splashed overboard. Someone cried out sharply. An instant later the entire crew struggled out from the companionway, rushed in grim silence to the side of the vessel, and threw themselves into the sea.

My own ideas were somewhat confused. The fire had practically enveloped the ship. I thought to feel it; and yet my skin was cool to the touch. The ship's outlines became blurred. A dizziness overtook me; and then all at once a great desire seized and shook my very soul. I cannot tell you the vehemence of this desire. It was a madness; nothing could stand in the way of its gratification. Whatever happened, I must have water. It was not thirst, nor yet a purpose to allay the very real physical burning of which I was now dimly conscious; but a craving for the liquid itself as something apart from and unconnected with anything else. Without hesitation, and as though it were the most natural thing in the world, I vaulted the rail to cast myself into the ocean. I dimly remember a last flying impression of a furnace of light, then a great shock thudded through me, and I lost consciousness.

PART THREE

THE MAROON

I

IN THE WARDROOM

OVER the wardroom of the *Wolverine* had fallen a silence. It held after Slade had finished. Captain Parkinson, stiff and erect in his chair, staring fixedly at a spot two feet above the reporter's head, seemed to weigh, as a judge weighs, the facts so picturesquely set forth. Dr. Trendon, his sturdy frame half in shadow, had slouched far down into himself. Only the regard of his keen eyes fixed upon Slade's face, unwaveringly and a bit anxiously, showed that he was thinking of the narrator as well as of the narrative. The others had fallen completely under the spell of the tale. They sat, as children in a theatre, absorbed, forgetful of the world around them, wrapped in a more vivid element. At the close, they stirred and blinked, half dazed by the abrupt fall of the curtain.

Slade had told his story with fire, with something of passion, even. Now he felt the sharp reflex. He muttered uncertainly beneath his breath and glanced from one to another of the circled faces.

" That's all," he said unsteadily.

There passed through the group a stir and a murmur. Someone broke into sharp coughing. Chairs, shoved back, grated on the floor.

" Well, of all the extraordinary——" began a voice, ruminatingly, and broke short off, as if abashed at its own infraction of the silence.

"That's all," repeated Slade, a note of insistence in his voice. "Why don't you say something? Confound you, why don't you say something?" His speech rose husky and cracked. "Don't you believe it?"

"Hold on," said the surgeon quietly. "No need to get excited."

"Oh, well," muttered the reporter, with a sudden lapse. "Possibly you think I'm romancing. It doesn't matter. I don't suppose I'd believe it myself, in your place."

"But we're heading for the island," suggested Forsythe.

"That's so," cried Slade. "Well, that's all right. Believe or disbelieve as much as you like. Only get Percy Darrow off that island. Then we'll have his version. There are a few things I want to find out about, myself."

"There are several that promise to be fairly interesting," said Forsythe, under his breath.

Slade turned to the captain. "Have you any questions to put to me, sir?" he asked formally.

"Just one moment," interrupted Trendon. "Boy, a pony of brandy for Mr. Slade."

The reporter drank the liquor and again turned to Captain Parkinson.

"Only about our men," said the commanding officer, after a little thought.

Slade shook his head.

"I'm sorry I can't help you there, sir."

"Dr. Trendon said that you knew nothing about Edwards."

"Edwards?" repeated Slade inquiringly. His mind, still absorbed in the events which he had been relating, groped backward.

Trendon came to his aid. "Barnett asked you about him, you remember. It was when you recovered consciousness. Our ensign. Took over charge of the *Laughing Lass.*"

"Oh, of course. I was a little dazed, I fancy."

"We put Mr. Edwards aboard when we first picked up the deserted schooner," explained the captain.

"Pardon me," said the other. "My head doesn't seem to work quite right yet. Just a moment, please." He sat silent, with closed eyes. "You say you picked up the *Laughing Lass.* When?" he asked presently.

"Four—five—six days ago, the first time."

"Then you put out the fire."

The circle closed in on Slade, with an unconscious hitching forward of chairs. He had fixed his eyes on the captain. His mouth worked. Obviously he was under a tensity of endeavour in keeping his faculties set to the problem. The surgeon watched him, frowning.

"There was no fire," said the captain.

Slade leaped in his chair. "No fire! But I saw her, I tell you. When I went overboard she was one living flame!"

"You landed in the small boat. Knocked you senseless," said Trendon. "Concussion of the brain. Idea of flame might have been a retroactive hallucination."

"Retroactive rot," cried the other. "I beg your pardon, Dr. Trendon. But if you'd seen her as I saw her—— Barnett!"

He turned in appeal to his old acquaintance.

"There was no fire, Slade," replied the executive officer gently. "No sign of fire that we could find, except that the starboard rail was blistered."

"Oh, that was from the volcano," said Slade. "That was nothing."

"It was all there was," returned Barnett.

"Just let me run this thing over," said the free lance slowly. "You found the schooner. She wasn't afire. She didn't even seem to have been afire. You put a crew aboard under your ensign, Edwards. Storm separated you from her. You picked her up again deserted. Is that right?"

"Day before yesterday morning."

"Then," cried the other excitedly, "the fire was smouldering all the time. It broke out and your men took to the water."

"Impossible," said Barnett.

"Fiddlesticks!" said the more downright surgeon.

"I hardly think Mr. Edwards would be driven overboard by a fire which did not even scorch his ship," suggested the captain mildly.

"It drove *our* lot overboard," insisted Slade. "Do you think we were a pack of cowards? I tell you, when that hellish thing broke loose, you *had* to go. It wasn't fear. It wasn't pain. It was—— What's the use. You can't explain a thing like that."

"We certainly saw the glow the night Billy Edwards was—disappeared," mused Forsythe.

"And again, night before last," said the captain.

"What's that!" cried Slade. "Where *is* the *Laughing Lass?*"

"I'd give something pretty to know," said Barnett.

"Isn't she in tow?"

"In tow?" said Forsythe. "No, indeed. We hadn't adequate facilities for towing her. Didn't you tell him, Mr. Barnett?"

"Where is she, then?" Slade fired the question at them like a cross-examiner.

"Why, we shipped another crew under Ives and McGuire that noon. We were parted again, and haven't seen them since."

"God forgive you!" said the reporter. "After the warnings you'd had, too. It was—it was——"

"My orders, Mr. Slade," said Captain Parkinson, with quiet dignity.

"Of course, sir. I beg your pardon," returned the other. "But—you say you saw the light again?"

"The first night they were out," said Barnett, in a low voice.

"Then your second crew is with your first crew," said Slade, shakily. "And they're with Thrackles, and Pulz and Solomon, and many another black-hearted scoundrel and brave seaman. Down there!"

He pointed under foot. Captain Parkinson rose and went to his cabin. Slade rose, too, but his knees were unsteady. He tottered, and but for the swift aid of Barnett's arm, would have fallen.

"Overdone," said Dr. Trendon, with some irritation. "Cost you something in strength. Foolish performance. Turn in now."

Slade tried to protest, but the surgeon would not hear of it, and marched him incontinently to his berth. Returning, Trendon reported, with growls of discontent, that his patient was in a fever.

" Couldn't expect anything else," he fumed. " Pack of human interrogation points hounding him all over the place."

" What do you think of his story? " asked Forsythe.

The grizzled surgeon drew out a cigar, lighted it, took three deliberate puffs, turned it about, examined the ash end with concentration, and replied:

" Man's telling a straight story."

" You think it's all true? " cried Forsythe.

" Humph! " grunted the other. " *He* thinks it's all true."

An orderly appeared and knocked at the captain's cabin.

" Beg pardon, sir," they heard him say. " Mr. Carter would like to know how close in to run. Volcano's acting up pretty bad, sir."

Captain Parkinson went on deck, followed by the rest.

II

THE JOLLY ROGER

FEELING the way forward, the cruiser was soon caught
in a maze of cross currents. Hither and thither she
was borne, a creature bereft of volition. Order followed order like the rattle of quick-fire, and was
obeyed with something more than the *Wolverine's*
customary smartness. From the bridge Captain Parkinson himself directed his ship. His face was placid:
his bearing steady and confident. This in itself was
sufficient earnest that the cruiser was in ticklish case.
For it was an axiom of the men who sailed under
Parkinson that the calmer that nervous man grew, the
more cause was there for nervousness on the part of
others.

The approach was from the south, but suspicious
aspects of the water had fended the cruiser out and
around, until now she stood prow-on to a bold headland at the northwest corner of the island. Above
this headland lay a dark pall of vapour. In the shifting breeze it swayed sluggishly, heavily, as if riding
at anchor like a logy ship of the air. Only once did
it show any marked movement.

"It's spreading out toward us," said Barnett to
his fellow officers, gathered aft.

"Time to move, then," grunted Trendon.

The others looked at him inquiringly.

"About as healthful as prussic acid, those volcanic gases," explained the surgeon.

The ship edged on and inward. Presently the sing-song of the leadsman sounded in measured distinctness through the silence. Then a sudden activity and bustle forward, the rattle of chains, and the *Wolverine* was at anchor. The captain came down from the bridge.

"What do you think, Dr. Trendon?" he asked.

More explicit inquiry was not necessary.

The surgeon understood what was in his superior's mind.

"Never can tell about volcanoes, sir," he said.

"Of course," agreed the captain. "But—well, do you recognise any of the symptoms?"

"Want me to diagnose a case of earthquake, sir?" grinned Trendon. "She might go off to-day, or she might behave herself for a century."

"Well, it's all chance," said the other, cheerfully. "The man *might* be alive. At any rate we must do our best on that theory. What do you make of that cloud on the peak?"

"Poisonous vapours, I suppose. Thought we'd have a chance to make sure just now. Seemed to be coming right for us. Wind's shifted it since."

"There couldn't be anything alive up there?"

"Not so much as a bug," replied the doctor positively.

"Yet I thought when the vapour lifted a bit that I saw something moving."

"When was that, sir?"

"Ten or fifteen minutes back."

"We'll see soon enough, sir," put in Forsythe. "The wind is driving it down to the south'ard."

Sullenly, reluctantly, the forbidding mass moved across the headland. All glasses were bent upon it. Without taking his binocular from his eyes, Trendon began to ruminate aloud.

"If he could have got to the beach. . . . No vapour there. . . . Signal, though. . . . Perhaps he hadn't time. . . . And I'd hate to risk good men on that hell's cauldron. . . . Just as much risk here, perhaps. Only it seems——"

"There it is," cried Forsythe. "Look. The highest point."

Dull, gray wisps of murk, the afterguard of the gaseous cloud, were twisting and spiraling in a witch-dance across the landscape, and, seen by snatches and glimpses through it, something flapped darkly in the breeze. Suddenly the veil parted and fled. A flag stood forth in the sharp gust, rigid, and appalling. It was black.

"The *Jolly Roger,* by God! They've come back!" exclaimed Forsythe.

"And set up the sign of their shop," added Barnett.

"If they stuck to their flag—good-bye," observed Trendon grimly.

"Dr. Trendon," said Captain Parkinson, "you will arm yourself and go with me in the gig to make a landing."

"Yes, sir," responded the surgeon.

"Mr. Barnett."

" Yes, sir."

" Should we be overtaken by the vapour while on the highland and be unable to get back to the beach, you are to send no rescuing party up there until the air has cleared."

' But, sir, may we not——"

" Do you understand? "

" Yes, sir."

" In case of an attack you will at once send in another boat with a howitzer."

" Yes, sir."

" Dr. Trendon, will you see Mr. Slade and inquire of him the best point for landing? "

Trendon hesitated.

" I suppose it would hardly do to take him with us? " pursued the commanding officer.

" If he is roused now, even for a moment, I won't answer for the consequences, sir," said the surgeon bluntly.

" Surely you can have him point out a landing place," said the captain.

" On your responsibility," returned the other, obstinately. " He's under opiate now."

" Be it so," said Captain Parkinson, after a time.

Going in, they saw no sign of life along the shore. Even the birds had deserted it. For the time the volcano seemed to have pretermitted its activity. Now and again there was a spurtle of smoke from the cone, followed by subterranean growlings, but, on the whole, the conditions were reassuring.

" Penny-pop-pinwheel of a volcano, anyhow," remarked Trendon, disparagingly. " Real man-size eruption would have wiped the whole thing off the map, first whack."

As they drew in, it became apparent that they must scale the cliff from the boat. Farther to the south opened out a wide cove that suggested easy beaching, but over it hung a cloud of steam.

"Lava pouring down," said Trendon.

Fortunately at the point where the cliff looked easiest the seas ran low. Ropes had been brought. After some dainty manœuvring two of the sailors gained foothold and slung the ropes so that the remainder of the disembarcation was simple. Nor was the ascent of the cliff a harsh task. Half an hour after the landing the exploring party stood on the summit of the hill, where the black flag waved over a scene of utter desolation. The vegetation was withered to pallid rags: even the tiniest weedling in the rock crevices had been poisoned by the devastating blast.

In the midst of that deathly scene, the flag seemed instinct with a sinister liveliness. Whoever had set it there had accurately chosen the highest available point on that side of the island, the spot of all others where it would make good its signal to the eye of any chance farer upon those shipless seas. For the staff a ten-foot sapling, finely polished, served. A mound of rock-slabs supported it firmly. Upon the cloth itself was no design. It was of a dull black, the hue of soot. Captain Parkinson, standing a few yards off, viewed it with disfavour.

"Furl that flag," he ordered.

Congdon, the coxswain of the gig, stepped forward and began to work at the fastenings. Presently he turned a grinning face to the captain, who was scanning the landscape through his glass.

" Beggin' your pardon, sir," he said.

" Well, what is it?" demanded Captain Parkinson.

" Beggin' your pardon, sir, that ain't rightly no flag. That's what you might rightly call a garment, sir. It's an undershirt, beggin' your pardon."

" Black undershirt's a new one to me," muttered Trendon.

" No, sir. It ain't rightly black, look."

Wrenching the object from its fastenings, he flapped it violently. A cloud of sooty dust, beaten out, spread about his face. With a strangled cry the sailor cast the shirt from him and rolled in agony upon the ground.

" You fool!" cried Trendon. " Stand back, all of you."

Opening his medicine case, he bent over the racked sufferer. Presently the man sat up, pale and abashed.

" That's how poisonous volcanic gas is," said the surgeon to his commanding officer. " Only inhaled remnants of the dust, too."

" An ill outlook for the man we're seeking," the captain mused.

" Dead if he's anywhere on this highland," declared Trendon. " Let's look at his flag-pole."

He examined the staff. " Came from the beach," he pronounced. " Waterworn. H'm! Maybe he ain't so dead, either."

" I don't quite follow you, Dr. Trendon."

" Why, I guess our man has figured this thing all out. Brought this pole up from the beach to plant it

With a strangled cry the sailor cast the shirt from him

here. Why? Because this was the best observation
point. No good as a permanent residence, though.
Planted his flag and went back."

" Why didn't we see him on the beach, then? "

" Did you notice a cave around to the north? Good
refuge in case of fumes."

" It's worth trying," said the captain, putting up
his glass.

" Hold on, sir. What's this? Here's something.
Look here."

Trendon pointed to a small bit of wood rather
neatly carved to the shape of an indicatory finger,
and lashed to the staff, at the height of a man's face.
The others clustered around.

" Oh, the devil!" cried Trendon. " It must have
got twisted. It's pointing straight down."

" Strange performance," said the captain. " However, since it points that way—heave aside those rocks,
men."

The first slab lifted brought to light a corner of
cardboard. This, on closer examination, proved to be
the cover of a book. The rocks rolled right and left,
and as the flag-staff, deprived of its support, tottered
and fell, the trove was dragged forth and handed to
the captain. While the ground jarred with occasional
tremors and the mountain puffed forth its vaporous
threats, he and the surgeon, seated on a rock, gave
themselves with complete absorption to the reading.

III

THE CACHE

OUTWARDLY the book accorded ill with its surroundings. In that place of desolation and death, it typified
the petty neatness of office processes. Properly placed,
it should have been found on a desk, with pens, rulers,
and other paraphernalia forming exact angles or par-
allels to it. It was a quarto, bound in marbled paper,
with black leather over the hinges. No external label
suggested its ownership or uses, but through one corner, blackened and formidable in its contrast to the
peaceful purposes of the volume, a hole had been bored.
The agency of perforation was obvious. A bullet had
made it.

"Seen someth ng of life, I reckon," said Trendon,
as the captain tu ned the volume about slowly in his
hands.

"And of death," returned Captain Parkinson solemnly. "Do you know, Trendon, I almost dread to
open this."

"Pshaw!" returned the other. "What is it to us?"

He threw the cover back. Neatly lettered on the inside, in the fine and slightly angular writing char-
acteristic of the Teutonic scholar, was the legend:

Karl Augustus Schermerhorn,
1409½ *Spruce Street,*
Philadelphia, Pa.

The opposite page was blank. Captain Parkinson turned half a dozen leaves.

"German!" he cried, in a note of disappointment, "Can you read German script?"

"After a fashion," replied the other. "Let's see. *Es wonnte sechs—und—dreissig unterjacke,*" he read. "Why, blast it, was the man running a haberdashery? What have three dozen undershirts to do with this?"

"A memorandum for outfitting, probably," suggested the captain. "Try here."

"Chemical formulæ," said Trendon. "Pages of 'em. The devil! Can't make a thing of it."

"Well, here's something in English."

"Good," said the other. "*By combining the hypersulphate of iridium with the fumes arising from oxide of copper heated to 1000 C. and combining with picric acid in the proportions described in formula x 18, a reaction, the nature of which I have not fully determined, follows. This must be performed with extreme care owing to the unstable nature of the benzene compounds.*"

"Picric acid? Benzene compounds? Those are high explosives," said Captain Parkinson. "We should have Barnett go over this."

"Here's a name under the formula. *Dr. A. Mardenter, Ann Arbor, Mich.* That explains its being in English. Probably copied from a letter."

"This must have been one of the experiments in the valley that Slade told us of," said the captain, thoughtfully. "Why, see here," he cried, with something like exultation. "That's what Dr. Schermerhorn was doing here. He has the clue to some explosive so terrific that he goes far out of the world to experiment with its manufacture. For companions he chooses a gang of cutthroats that the world would never miss in case anything went wrong. Possibly it was some trial of the finished product that started the eruption, even. Do you see?"

"Don't explain enough," grunted Trendon. "Deserted ship. Billy Edwards. Mysterious lights. Slade and his story. Any explosives in those? Good enough, far as it goes. Don't go far enough."

"It certainly leaves gaps," admitted the other.

He turned over a few more pages.

"Formulæ, formulæ, formulæ. What's this? Here are some marginal annotations."

"*Unbehasslich*," read Trendon. "Let's see. That means 'highly unsatisfactory,' or words to that effect. Hi! Here's where the old man loses his temper. Listen: '*May the devil take Carroll and Crum for careless*'—h'm—well, '*pig-dogs.*' Now, where do Carroll and Crum come in?"

"They're a firm of analytical chemists in Washington," said the captain. "When I was on the ordnance board I used to get their circulars."

"Fits in. What? More English? Worse than the German, this is."

The writing, beginning evenly enough at the top of a page, ran along for a line or two, then fell, sprawling in huge, ragged characters the full length. Trendon stumbled among them, indignantly.

"*June* 1, 1904," he read. "*It is done. Triumph.* (German word.) *Eureka. Es ist gefüllt. From the* (can't make out that word) *of the inspiration—god-*

like power—solution of the world-problems. Why, the old fool is crazy! And his writing is crazier. Can't make head or tail of it."

The captain turned several more pages. They were blank. " At any rate, it seems to be the end," he said.

" I should hope so," returned the other, disgustedly.

He took the book on his knees, fluttering the leaves between thumb and finger. Suddenly he checked, cast back, and threw the book wide open.

" Here beginneth a new chapter," said he, quietly.

No imaginable chirography could have struck the eye with more of contrast to the professor's small and nervous hand. Large, rounded, and rambling, it filled the page with few and careless words.

June 2, 1904. On this date I find myself sole occupant and absolute monarch of this valuable island. This morning I was a member of a community, interesting if not precisely peaceful. To-night I am the last leaf. ' All his lovely companions are faded and gone,' the sprightly Solomon, the psychic Nigger, the amiable Thrackles, the cheerful Perdosa, the genial Pulz, and the high-minded Eagen. Undoubtedly the social atmosphere has cleared; moreover, I am for the first time in my life a landed proprietor. Item: several square miles of grass land; item: several dozen head of sheep; item: a cove full of fish; item: a handsomely decorated cave; item: a sportive though somewhat unruly volcano. At times, it may be, I shall feel the lack of company. The seagulls alone are not distrustful of me. Undoubtedly the seagull is an estimable creature, but he leaves something to be desired in the way of companionship. Hence this diary, the inevitable refuge

*of the empty-minded. Materially, I shall do well enough,
though I face one tragic circumstance. My cigarette material, I find, is short. Upon counting up——"*

"Damn his cigarettes!" cried the surgeon. "This
must be Darrow. Finicky beast! Let's see if it's
signed."

He whirled the leaves over to the last sheet, glanced
at it, and sprang to his feet. There, sprawled in tremu-
lous characters, as by a hand shaken with agony or
terror, was written:

> *Look for me in the cave.*
> *Percy Darrow.*

The bullet hole in the corner furnished a sinister
period to the signature.

Trendon handed the ledger back to the captain, who
took one quick look, closed it, and handed it to Congdon.

"Wrap that up and carry it carefully," he said.

"Aye, aye, sir," said the coxswain, swathing it in
his jacket and tucking it under his arm.

"Now to find that cave," said Captain Parkinson
to the surgeon.

"The cave in the cliff, of course," said Trendon.
"Noticed it coming in, you know."

"Where?"

"On the north shore, about a mile to the east of
here."

"Then we'll cut directly across."

"Beg your pardon, sir," put in Congdon, "but I don't think we can make it from this side, sir."

"Why not?"

"No beach, sir, and the cliff's like the side of a ship. Looks to be deep water right into the cave's mouth."

"Back to the boat, then. Bring that flag along."

The descent was swift, at times reckless, but the party embarked without accident. Soon they were forging through the water at racing speed, the boat leaping to the impulsion of the sailorman's strongest motives, curiosity and the hope of saving a life.

IV

THE TWIN SLABS

WITHIN half an hour the gig had reached the mouth of the cave. As the coxswain had predicted, the seas ran into the lofty entrance. Elsewhere the surf fell whitely, but through the arch the waves rolled unbroken into a heavy stillness. Only as the boat hovered for a moment at the face of the cliff could the exploring party hear, far within, the hollow boom that told of breakers on a distant, subterranean beach.

"Run her in easy," came the captain's order. "Keep a sharp lookout for hidden rocks."

To the whispering plash of the oars they moved from sunlight into twilight, from twilight into darkness. Of a sudden the oars jerked convulsively. A great roar had broken upon the ears of the sailors; the invisible roof above them, the water heaving beneath them, the walls that hemmed them in, called, with a multiplication of resonance, upon the name of Darrow. The boat quivered with the start of its occupants. Then one or two laughed weakly as they realised that what they had heard was no supernatural voice. It was the captain hailing for the marooned man.

No vocal answer came. But an indeterminable space away they could hear a low splash followed by a second and a third. Something coughed weakly in front and to the right. Trendon's hand went to his revolver. The men sat, stiffened. One of them swore, in a whisper, and the oath came back upon them, echoing the name of the Saviour in hideous sibilance.

"Silence in the boat," said the captain, in such buoyant tones that the men braced themselves against the expected peril.

"Light the lantern and pass it to me," came the order. "Keep below the gunwale, men."

As the match spluttered: "Do you see something, a few rods to port?" asked the captain in Trendon's ear.

"Pair of green lights," said Trendon. "Eyes. Seals!"

"Seals! Seals! Seals!" shouted the walls, for the surgeon had suddenly released his voice. And as the mockery boomed, the green lights disappeared and there was more splashing from the distance. The crew sat up again.

The lantern spread its radiance. It was reflected from battlements of fairy beauty. Everywhere the walls were set, as with gems, in broad wales of varied and vivid hues. Dazzled at first, the explorers soon were able to discern the general nature of the subterranean world which they had entered. In most places the walls rose sheer and unscaleable from the water. In others, turretted rocks thrust their gleaming crags upward. Over to starboard a little beach shone with Quaker greyness in that spectacular display. The end of the cavern was still beyond the area of light.

"Must have been a swimmer to get in here," commented Trendon, glancing at the walls.

"Unless he had a boat," said the captain. "But why doesn't he answer?"

"Better try again. No telling how much more there is of this."

The surgeon raised his ponderous bellow, and the cave roared again with the summons. Silence, formidable and unbroken, succeeded.

"House to house search is now in order," he said. "Must be in here somewhere—unless the seals got him."

Cautiously the boat moved forward. Once she grazed on a half submerged rock. Again a tiny islet loomed before her. Scattered bones glistened on the rocky shore, but they were not human relics. Occasional beaches tempted a landing, but all of these led back to percipitous cliffs except one, from the side of which opened two small caves. Into the first the lantern cast its glare, revealing emptiness, for the arch was wide and the cave shallow. The entrance to the other was so narrow as to send a visitor to his knees. But inside it seemed to open out. Moreover, there were fish bones at the entrance. The captain, the surgeon, and Congdon, the coxswain, landed. Captain Parkinson reached the spot first. Stooping, he thrust his head in at the orifice. A sharp exclamation broke from him. He rose to his feet, turning a contorted face to the others.

"Poisonous," he cried.

"More volcano," said Trendon. He bent to the black hole and sniffed cautiously.

"I'll go in, sir," volunteered Congdon. "I've had fire-practice."

" My business," said Trendon, briefly. " Decomposition; unpleasant, but not dangerous."

Pushing the lantern before him, he wormed his way until the light was blotted out. Presently it shone forth from the funnel, showing that the explorer had reached the inner open space. Captain Parkinson dropped down and peered in, but the evil odour was too much for him. He retired, gagging and coughing. Trendon was gone for what seemed an interminable time. His superior officer fidgetted uneasily. At last he could stand it no longer.

" Dr. Trendon, are you all right? " he shouted.

" Yup," answered a choked voice. " Cubbing oud dow."

Again the funnel was darkened. A pair of feet appeared; then the surgeon's chunky trunk, his head, and the lantern. Once, twice, and thrice he inhaled deeply.

" Phew! " he gasped. " Thought I was tough, but —Phee-ee-ee-ew! "

" Did you find——"

" No, sir. Not Darrow. Only a poor devil of a seal that crawled in there to die."

The exploration continued. Half a mile, as they estimated, from the open, they reached a narrow beach, shut off by a perpendicular wall of rock. Skirting this, they returned on the other side, minutely examining every possible crevice. When they again reached the light of day, they had arrived at the certain conclusion that no living man was within those walls.

" Would a corpse rise to the surface soon in waters such as these, Dr. Trendon? " asked the captain.

" Might, sir. Might not. No telling that."

The captain ruminated. Then he beat his fist on his knee.

"The other cave!"

"What other cave?" asked the surgeon.

"The cave where they killed the seals."

"Surely!" exclaimed Trendon. "Wait, though. Didn't Slade say it was between here and the point?"

"Yes. Beyond the small beach."

"No cave there," declared the surgeon positively.

"There must be. Congdon, did you see an opening anywhere in the cliff as we came along?"

"No, sir. This is the only one, sir."

"We'll see about that," said the captain, grimly. "Head her about. Skirt the shore as near the breakers as you safely can."

The gig retraced its journey.

"There's the beach, as Slade described it," said Captain Parkinson, as they came abreast of the little reach of sand.

"And what are those two bird-roosts on it?" asked Trendon. "See 'em? Dead against that patch of shore-weed."

"Bits of wreckage fixed in the sand."

"Don't think so, sir. Too well matched."

"We have no time to settle the matter now," said the captain impatiently. "We must find that cave, if it is to be found."

Hovering just outside the final drag of the surf, under the skilful guidance of Congdon, the boat moved slowly along the line of beach to the line of cliff. All was open as the day. The blazing sun picked out each detail of jut and hollow. Evidently the poisonous vapours from the volcano had not spread their blight here, for the face of the precipice was bright with many flowers. So close in moved the boat that its occupants could even see butterflies fluttering above the bloom. But that which their eager eyes sought was still denied them. No opening offered in that smiling cliff-side. Not by so much as would admit a terrier did the mass of rock and rubble gape.

"And Slade described the cave as big enough to ram the *Wolverine* into," muttered Trendon.

Up to the point of the headland, and back, passed the boat. Blank disappointment was the result.

"What is your opinion now, Dr. Trendon?" asked the captain of the older man.

"Don't know, sir," answered the surgeon hopelessly. "Looks as if the cave might have been a hallucination."

"I shall have something to say to Mr. Slade on our return," said the captain crisply. "If the cave was an hallucination, as you suggest, the seal-murder was fiction."

"Looks so," agreed the other.

"And the murder of the captain. How about that?"

"And the mutiny of the men," added the surgeon.

"And the killing of the doctor. Your patient seems to be a romantic genius."

"And the escape of Darrow. Hold hard," quoth Trendon. "Darrow's no romance. Nothing fictional about the flag and ledger."

"True enough," said the captain, and fell to consideration.

"Anyway," said Trendon vigorously, "I'd like to have a look at those bird-roosts. Mighty like sign-posts, to my mind."

"Very well," said the captain. "It'll cost us only a wetting. Run her in, Congdon."

With all the coxswain's skill, and the oarsmen's technique, the passage of the surf was a lively one, and little driblets of water marked the trail of the officers as they shuffled up the beach.

The two slabs stood less than fifty yards beyond high water tide. Nearing them, the visitors saw that each marked a mound, but not until they were close up could they read the neat carving on the first. It ran as follows:

Here lies
SOLOMON ANDERSON
alias
HANDY SOLOMON
who murdered his employer, his captain, and his ship- mates, and was found, dead of his deserts, on these shores, June 5, 1904.
   This slab is erected as a memento of admiring esteem
by
the last of his victims.
   "And you can kiss the Book on that."

"Percy Darrow *fecit*," said the surgeon. "You can kiss the Book on *that*, too."

"Then Slade was telling the truth!"

"Apparently. Seems good corroboration."

The captain turned to the other mound. Its slab was carved by the same hand.

> *Sacred to the memory of an Ensign of the U. S. Navy, whose body, washed upon this coast, is here buried with all reverence, by strange hands; whose soul may God rest. "The seas shall sing his requiem." June the Sixth, MXMIV.*

"Billy Edwards," said the captain, very low.

He uncovered. The surgeon did likewise. So, for a space, they stood with bared heads between the twin graves.

V

THE PINWHEEL VOLCANO

THE surgeon spoke first.

"Another point," said he. "Darrow was alive within a few days."

Captain Parkinson turned slowly away from the grave. "You are right," he said, with an effort. "Our business is with the living now. The dead must wait."

"Hide and seek," growled Trendon. "If he's here why don't he show himself?"

The other shook his head.

"Place is all trampled up with his footprints," said Trendon. "He's plodded back and forth like a prisoner in a cell."

"The ledger," said the captain. "I'd forgotten it. That grave drove everything else out of my mind."

"Bring the book here," called Trendon.

Congdon unwrapped it from his jacket and handed it to him. The sailors cast curious glances at the two headstones.

"Mount guard over Mr. Edwards's grave," commanded the captain.

The coxswain saluted and gave an order. One of the sailors stepped forward to the first mound.

"Not that one," rasped the officer. "The other." The man saluted and moved on.

"With your permission, sir," said Trendon.

On a nod from his superior officer he opened the
ledger and took up Darrow's record.

"Here it is. Entry of June 3d."

*"Everything lovely. Schooner lost to sight. Query
—to memory dear? Not exactly. Though I shouldn't
mind having her under orders for a few days. Queer
glow in the sky last night: if they've been investigating
they may have got what's coming to them. Volcano
exhibiting fits of temper. Spouted out considerable fire
about nine o'clock. Quite spectacular, but no harm done.
Can foresee short rations of tobacco. Lava in valley still
too hot for comfort. No sign of Dr. Schermerhorn.
Still sleep on beach.*

"Not much there," sniffed Trendon.

"Go on," said the captain.

*"June 3. Evening. Thick and squally weather again.
Local atmospheric conditions seem upset. Volcano still
leading strenuous life. Climbed the headland this afternoon. Wind very shifty. Got an occasional whiff of
volcanic output. One in particular would have sent a
skunk to the camphor bottle. No living on the headland.
Will explore cave to-morrow with a view to domicile.
Have come down to an allowance of seven cigarettes per
diem.*

*"June 4. Explored cave to-day. Full of dead seals.
Not only dead, but all bitten and cut to pieces. Must
have been lively doings in Seal-Town. Not much choice
between air in the cave and vapours from the volcano.
Barring seals, everything suitable for light housekeeping,
such as mine. Undertook to clean house. Dragged late
lamented out into the water. Some sank and were swept*

away by the sea-puss. Others, I regret to say, floated. Found trickle of fresh water in depth of cave, and little sand-ledge to sleep on. So far, so good: we may be 'appy yet. If only I had my cigarette supply. Once heard a botanist say that leaves of the white shore-willow made fair substitute for tobacco. Fair substitute for nux vomica! Would like to interview said botanist.

"The fellow is a tobacco maniac," growled Trendon, feeling in his breast pocket. "The devil," he cried, bringing forth an empty hand.

Silently the captain handed him a cigar. "Thank you, sir," he said, lighted it, and continued reading.

"*June 5. Had a caller to-day. Climbed the headland this morning. Found volcano taking a day off. Looking for sign of* Laughing Lass, *noticed something heliographing to me from the waves beyond the reef. Seemed to be metal. I guessed a tin can. Caught in the swirl, it rounded the cape, and I came down to the shore to meet it. Halfway down the cliff I had a better view. I saw it was not a tin can. There was a dark body under it, which the waves were tossing about, and as the metal moved with the body, it glinted in the sun. Suddenly it was borne in upon me that an arm was doing the signalling, waving to me with a sprightly, even a jocular friendliness. Then I saw what it really was. It was Handy Solomon and his steel hook. He was riding quite high. Every now and again he would bow and wave. He grounded gently on the sand beach. I planted him promptly. First, however, I removed a bag of tobacco from his pocket. Poor stuff, and water soaked, but still tobacco. Spent a quiet afternoon carving a headstone for the dear departed. Pity it were that virtues so shin-*

ing should be uncommemorated. Idle as the speculation is, I wonder who my next visitor will be. Thrackles, I hope. Evidently some of them have been playing the part of Pandora. Spent last night in the cave. Air quite fresh.

"*June 6. Saw the glow again last night.*

The surgeon paused in his reading. "That would be the night of the 5th: the night before we picked her up empty."

"Yes," agreed Captain Parkinson. "That was the night Billy Edwards—— Go on."

"*Saw the glow again last night. Don't understand it. Once should have been enough for them. This matter of hoarding tobacco may be a sad error. If Old Spitfire keeps on the way she has to-day I shan't need much more. It would be a raw jest to be burned or swallowed up with a month's supply of unsmoked cigarettes on one. Cave getting shaky. Still, I think I'll stick there. As between being burned alive and buried alive, I'm for the respectable and time honoured fashion of interment. Bombardment was mostly to the east to-day, but no telling when it may shift.*

"*June 7. This morning I found a body rolling in the surf. It was the body of a young man, large and strongly built, dressed in the uniform of an ensign of our navy. Surely a strange visitor to these shores! There was no mark of identification upon him except a cigarette case graven with an undecipherable monogram in Tiffany's most illegible style of arrow-headed inscription. This I buried with him, and staked the grave with a headboard. An officer and a gentleman, a youth of friendly ways and*

*kindly living, if one may judge by the face of the dead;
and he comes by the same end to the same goal as Handy
Solomon. Why not? And why should one philosophise
in a book that will never be read? Hold on! Perhaps—
just perhaps—it may be read. The officer was not long
dead. Ensigns of the U. S. navy do not wander about
untraversed waters alone. There must be a warship
somewhere in the vicinity. But why, then, an unburied
officer floating on the ocean? I will smoke upon this,
luxuriously and plentifully. (Later.) No use. I can't
solve it. But one thing I do. I put up a signal pole on
the headland and caché this record under it this afternoon.
From day to day, with the kindly permission of the volcano, I will add to it. . . . Bad doings by Old Spitfire.
The cloud is coming down on me. Also seems to be
moving along the cliff. I will retire hastily to my private
estate in the cave.*

" That's all, except the scrawl on the last page,"
said Trendon. " Some action of the volcano scared
him off. He just had time to scrawl that last message
and drop the book into the cache. The question is, did
he get back alive? "

" I doubt it," said the captain. " We will search the
headland for his body."

" But the cave," insisted the surgeon. " We ought
to have found some sign of him there."

" Slade is the solution," said the captain. " We must
ask him."

They put back to the ship. Barnett was anxiously
awaiting them.

" Your patient has been in a bad way, Dr. Trendon," he said.

"What's wrong?" asked Trendon, frowning.

"He came up on deck, wild-eyed and staggering. There was a sheet of paper in his hand which seemed to have some bearing on his trouble. When he found you had gone to the island without him he began to rage like a maniac. I had to have him carried down by force. In the rumpus the paper disappeared. I assumed the responsibility of giving him an opiate."

"Quite right," approved Trendon. "I'll go down. Will you come with me, sir?" he said to the captain.

They found Slade in profound slumber.

"Won't do to wake him now," growled Trendon. "Hello, what's here?"

Lying in the hollow of the sick man's right hand, where it had been crushed to a ball, was a crumpled mass of tracing paper. Trendon smoothed it out, peered at it and passed it to the captain.

"It's a sketch of an Indian arrow-head," he exclaimed in surprise, at the first glance. "What are all these marks?"

"Map of the island," barked Trendon. "Look here."

The drawing was a fairly careful one, showing such geographical points as had been of concern to the two-year inhabitants. There was the large cavern, indicated as they had found it, and at a point between it and the headland the legend, "Seal Cave."

"But it's wrong," cried Captain Parkinson, setting finger to the spot. "We passed there twice. There's no opening."

"No guarantee that there may not have been," returned the other. "This island has been considerably shaken up lately. Entrance may have been closed by a landslide down the cliff. Noticed signs myself, but didn't think of it in connection with the cave."

"That's work for Barnett, then," said the captain, brightening. "We'll blow up the whole face of the cliff, if necessary, but we'll get at that cave."

He hurried out. Order followed order, and soon the gig, with the captain, Trendon, and the torpedo expert, was driving for the point marked "Seal Cave" on the map over which they were bent.

VI

MR. DARROW RECEIVES

"You say the last entry is June 7th?" asked Barnett, as the boat entered the light surf.

Trendon nodded.

"That was the night we saw the last glow, and the big burst from the volcano, wasn't it?"

"Right."

"The island would have been badly shaken up."

"Not so violently but that the flag-pole stood," said the captain.

"That's true, sir. But there's been a good deal of volcanic gas going. The man's been penned up for four days."

"Give the fellow a chance," growled Trendon. "Air may be all right in the cave. Good water there, too. Says so himself. By Slade's account he's a pretty capable citizen when it comes to looking after himself. Wouldn't wonder if we'd find him fit as a fiddle."

"There was no clue to Ives and McGuire?" asked Barnett presently.

"None." It was the captain who answered.

The gig grated, and the tide being high, they waded to the base of the cliff, Barnett carrying his precious explosives aloft in his arms.

"Here's the spot," said the captain. "See where the water goes in through those crevices."

"Opening at the top, too," said Trendon.

245

He let out his bellow, roaring Darrow's name.

" I doubt if you could project your voice far into a cave thus blocked," said Captain Parkinson. " We'll try this."

He drew his revolver and fired. The men listened at the crevices of the rock. No sound came from within.

" Your enterprise, Mr. Barnett," said the commander, with a gesture which turned over the conduct of the affair to the torpedo expert.

Barnett examined the rocks with enthusiasm.

" Looks like moderately easy stuff," he observed. " See how the veins run. You could almost blow a design to order in that."

" Yes; but how about bringing down the whole cave?"

" Oh, of course there's always an element of uncertainty when you're dealing with high explosives," admitted the expert. " But unless I'm mistaken, we can chop this out as neat as with an axe."

Dropping his load of cartridges carelessly upon a flat rock which projected from the water, he busied himself in a search along the face of the cliff. Presently, with an " Ah," of satisfaction, he climbed toward a hand's breadth of platform where grew a patch of purple flowers.

" Throw me up a knife, somebody," he called.

" Take notice," said Trendon, good-naturedly, " that I'm the botanist of this expedition."

" Oh, you can have the flowers. All I want is what they grow in."

Loosening a handful of the dry soil, he brought it

down and laid it with the explosives. Next he called one of the sailors to "boost" him, and was soon perched on the flat slant of a huge rock which formed, as it were, the keystone to the blockade.

"Let's see," he ruminated. "We want a slow charge for this. One that will exert a widespread pressure without much shattering force. The No. 3, I think."

"How is that, Mr. Barnett?" asked the captain, with lively interest.

"You see, sir," returned the demonstrator, perched high, like a sculptor at work on some heroic masterpiece, "what we want is to split off this rock." He patted the flank of the huge slab. "There's a lovely vein running at an angle inward from where I sit. Split that through, and the rock should roll, of its own weight, away from the entrance. It's held only by the upper projection that runs under the arch here."

"Neat programme," commented Trendon, with a tinge of sardonic scepticism.

"Wait and see," retorted Barnett blithely, for he was in his element now. "I'll appoint you my assistant. Just toss me up that cartridge: the third one on the left."

The surgeon recoiled.

"Supposing you don't catch it?"

"Well, supposing I don't."

"It's dynamite, isn't it?"

"Something of the same nature. Joveite, it's called."

Still the surgeon stared at him. Barnett laughed.

"Oh, you've got the high explosives superstition,"

he said lightly. " Dynamite don't go off as easy as
people think. You could drop that stuff from the cliff-
head without danger. Have I got to come down for
it ? "

With a wry face Trendon tossed .up the package.
It was deftly caught.

" Now wet that dirt well. Put it in the canvas bag
yonder, and send one of the men up with it. I'm going
to make a mud pie."

Breaking the package open, he spread the yellow
powder in a slightly curving line along the rock. With
the mud he capped this over, forming a little arched
roof.

" To keep it from blowing away," surmised
Trendon.

" No; to make it blow down instead of blowing up."

" Oh, rot! " returned the downright surgeon.
" That pound of dirt won't make the shadow of a
feather's difference."

" Won't it! " retorted the other. " Curious thing
about high explosives. A mud-cap will hold down the
force as well as a ton of rock. Wait and see what happens to the rock beneath."

He slid off his perch into the ankle-deep water and
waded out to the boat. Here he burrowed for a moment, presently emerging with a box. This he carried
gingerly to a convenient rock and opened. First he
lifted out some soft padding. A small tin box honey-
combed inside came to light. With infinite precaution
Barnett picked out an object that looked like a 22-
calibre short cartridge, wadded some cotton batten in
his hand, set the thing in the wadding, laid it on the

rock, carefully returned the small box to the large box and the large box to the boat, took up the cartridge again and waded back to the cliff. They watched him in silence.

"This is the little devil," he said, indicating his delicate burden. "Fulminate of mercury. This is the stuff that'll remove your hand with neatness and despatch. It's the quickest tempered little article in the business. Just give it one hard look and it's off."

"Here," said Trendon, "I resign. From now on I'm a spectator."

Barnett swung the fulminate in his handkerchief and gave it to a sailor to hold. The man dandled it like a new-born infant. Back to his rock went Barnett. Producing some cord, he let down an end.

"Tie the handkerchief on, and get out of the way," he directed.

With painful slowness the man carried out the first part of the order; the latter half he obeyed with sprightly alacrity. Very slowly, very delicately, the expert drew in his dangerous burden. Once a current of air puffed it against the face of the rock, and the operator's head was hastily withdrawn. Nothing happened. Another minute and he had the tiny shell in hand. A fuse was fixed in it and it was shoved under the mud-cap. Barnett stood up.

"Will you kindly order the boat ready, Captain Parkinson?" he called.

The order was given.

"As soon as I light the fuse I will come down and we'll pull out fifty yards. Leave the rest of the Joveite where it is. All ready? Here goes."

He touched a match to the fuse. It caught. For a moment he watched it.

"Going all right," he reported, as he struck the water. "Plenty of time."

Some seventy yards out they rested on their oars. They waited. And waited. And waited.

"It's out," grunted Trendon.

From the face of the cliff puffed a cloud of dust. A thudding report boomed over the water. Just a wisp of whitish-grey smoke arose, and beneath it the great rock, with a gapping seam across its top, rolled majestically outward, sending a shower of spray on all sides, and opening to their eager view a black chasm into the heart of the headland. The experiment had worked out with the accuracy of a geometric problem.

"That's all, sir," Barnett reported officially.

"Magic! Modern magic!" said the captain. He stared at the open door. For the moment the object of the undertaking was forgotten in the wonder of its exact accomplishment.

"Darrow'll think an earthquake's come after him," remarked Trendon.

"Give way," ordered the captain.

The boat grated on the sand. Captain Parkinson would have entered, but Barnett restrained him.

"It's best to wait a minute or two," he advised. "Occasionally slides follow an explosion tardily, and the gases don't always dissipate quickly."

Where they stood they could see but a short way into the cave. Trendon squatted and funnelled his hands to one eye.

"Sorry not to have met you at the door," he said courteously

"There's fire inside," he said.

In a moment they all saw it, a single, pin-point glow, far back in the blackness, a Cyclopean eye, that swayed as it approached. Alternately it waned and brightened. Suddenly it illuminated the dim lineaments of a face. The face neared them. It joined itself to reality by a very solid pair of shoulders, and a man sauntered into the twilit mouth of the cavern, removed a cigarette from his lips, and gave them greeting.

"Sorry not to have met you at the door," he said, courteously. "It was you that knocked, was it not? Yes? It roused me from my siesta."

They stared at him in silence. He blinked in the light, with unaccustomed eyes.

"You will pardon me for not asking you in at once. Past circumstances have rendered me—well—perhaps suspicious is not too strong a word."

They noticed that he held a revolver in his hand.

Captain Parkinson came forward a step. The host half raised his weapon. Then he dropped it abruptly.

"Navy men!" he said, in an altered voice. "I beg your pardon. I could not see at first. My name is Percy Darrow."

"I am Captain Parkinson of the United States cruiser *Wolverine*," said the commander. "This is Mr. Barnett, Mr. Darrow. Dr. Trendon, Mr. Darrow."

They shook hands all around.

"Like some damned silly afternoon tea," Trendon said later, in retailing it to the mess. A pause followed.

"Won't you step in, gentlemen?" said Darrow, "May I offer you the makings of a cigarette?"

"Wouldn't you be robbing yourself?" inquired the captain, with a twinkle.

"Oh, you found the diary, then," said Darrow easily. "Rather silly of me to complain so. But really, in conditions like these, tobacco becomes a serious problem."

"So one might imagine," said Trendon drily. He looked closely at Darrow. The man's eyes were light and dancing. From the nostrils two livid lines ran diagonally. Such lines one might make with a hard blue pencil pressed strongly into the flesh. The surgeon moved a little nearer.

"Can you give me any news of my friend Thrackles?" asked Darrow lightly. "Or the esteemed Pulz? Or the scholarly and urbane Robinson of Ethiopian extraction?"

"Dead," said the captain.

"Ah, a pity," said the other. He put his hand to his forehead. "I had thought it probable." His face twitched. "Dead? Very good. In fact—really—er—amusing."

He began to laugh, quite to himself. It was not a pleasant laugh to hear. Trendon caught and shook him by the shoulder.

"Drop it," he said.

Darrow seemed not to hear him. "Dead, all dead!" he repeated. "And I've outlasted 'em! God damn 'em, I've outlasted 'em!" And his mirth broke forth in a strangely shocking spasm.

Trendon lifted a hand and struck him so powerfully

between the shoulder blades that he all but plunged forward on his face.

"Quit it!" he ordered again. "Get hold of yourself!"

Darrow turned and gripped him. The surgeon winced with the pain of his grasp. "I can't," gasped the maroon, between paroxysms. "I've been living in hell. A black, shaking, shivering hell, for God knows how long. . . . What do *you* know? Have *you* ever been buried alive?" And again the agony of laughter shook him.

"This, then," muttered the doctor, and the hypodermic needle shot home.

During the return Darrow lay like a log in the bottom of the gig. The opiate had done its work. Consciousness was mercifully dead within him.

VII

THE SURVIVORS

REST and good food quickly brought Percy Darrow back to his normal poise. One inspection satisfied Dr. Trendon that all was well with him. He asked to see the captain, and that gentleman came to Ives's room, which had been assigned to the rescued man.

"I hope you've been able to make yourself comfortable," said the commander, courteously.

"It would be strange indeed if I could not," returned Darrow, smiling. "You forget that you have set a savage down in the midst of luxury."

"Make yourself free of Ives's things," invited Captain Parkinson. "Poor fellow; he will not use them again, I fear."

"One of your men lost?" asked Darrow. "Ah, the young officer whose body I found on the beach, perhaps?"

"No; but we have to thank you for that burial," said the captain.

Darrow made a swift gesture. "Oh, if thanks are going," he cried, and paused in hopelessness of adequate expression.

"This has been a bitter cruise for us," continued the captain. He sighed and was silent for a moment. "There is much to tell and to be told," he resumed.

"Much," agreed the other, gravely.

"You will want to see Slade first, I presume," said the captain.

"One of your officers whom I have not yet had the pleasure of meeting?"

The captain stared. "Slade," he said. "Ralph Slade."

"Apparently there's a missing link. Or—I fear I was not wholly myself yesterday for a time. Possibly something occurred that I did not quite take in."

"Perhaps we'd better wait," said Captain Parkinson, with obvious misgiving. "You're not quite rested. You will feel more like——"

"If you don't mind," said Darrow composedly, "I'd like to get at this thing now. I'm in excellent understanding, I assure you."

"Very well. I am speaking of the man who acted as mate in the *Laughing Lass*. The journalist who— good heavens! What arrant stupidity! I have to beg your pardon, Mr. Darrow. It has just occurred to me. He called himself Eagen with you."

"Eagen! What is this? Is Eagen alive?"

"And on this ship. We picked him up in an open boat."

"And you say he calls himself Slade?"

"He is Ralph Slade, adventurer and journalist. Mr. Barnett knows him and vouches for him."

"And he was on our island under an assumed name," said Darrow in tones that had the smoothness and the rasp of silk. "Rather annoying. Not good form, quite, even for a pirate."

"Yet, I believe he saved your life," suggested the captain.

Darrow looked up sharply. "Why, yes," he admitted. "So he did. I had hoped——" He checked himself. "I had thought that all of the crew went the same way. You didn't find any of the others?"

"None."

Darrow got to his feet. "I think I'd like to see Eagen—Slade—whatever he calls himself."

"I don't know," began the captain. "It might not be——" He hesitated and stopped.

Darrow drew back a little, misinterpreting the other's attitude. "Do I understand that I am under restraint?" he asked stiffly.

"Certainly not. Why should you be?"

"Well," returned the other contemplatively, "it really might be regarded as a subject for investigation. Of course I know only a small part of it. But there have certainly been suspicious circumstances. Piracy there has been: no doubt of that. Murder, too, if my intuitions are not at fault. Or at least, a disappearance to be accounted for. Robbery can't be denied. And there's a dead body or two to be properly accredited." He looked the captain in the eye.

"Well?"

"You'll find my story highly unsatisfactory in detail, I fancy. I merely want to know whether I'm to present it as a defence, or only an explanation."

"We shall be glad to hear your story when you are ready to tell it—after you have seen Mr. Slade."

"Thank you," said Darrow simply. "You have heard his?"

"Yes. It needs filling in."

"When may I see him?"

"That's for Dr. Trendon to say. He came to us almost dead. I'll find out."

The surgeon reported Slade much better, but all a-quiver with excitement.

"Hate to put the strain on him," said he. "But he'll be in a fever till he gets this thing off his mind. Send Mr. Darrow to him."

After a moment's consideration Darrow said: "I should like to have you and Dr. Trendon present, Captain Parkinson, while I ask Eagen one or two questions."

"Understand one thing, Mr. Darrow," said Trendon briefly. "This is not to be an inquisition."

"Ah," said Darrow, unmoved. "I'm to be neither defendant nor prosecutor."

"You are to respect the condition of Dr. Trendon's patient, sir," said Captain Parkinson, with emphasis. "Outside of that, your attitude toward a man who has twice thought of your life before his own is for you to determine."

No little cynicism lurked in Darrow's tones as he said:

"You have confidence in Mr. Slade, alias Eagen."

"Yes," replied Captain Parkinson, in a tone that closed that topic.

"Still, I should be glad to have you gentlemen present, if only for a moment," insisted Darrow, presently.

"Perhaps it would be as well—on account of the patient," said the surgeon significantly.

"Very well," assented the captain.

The three went to Slade's cabin. He was lying

propped up in his bunk. Trendon entered first, followed by the captain, then Darrow.

"Here's your prize, Slade," said the surgeon.

Darrow halted, just inside the door. With an eager light in his face Slade leaned forward and stretched out his hand.

"I couldn't believe it until I saw you, old man," he cried.

Darrow's eyebrows went up. Before Slade had time to note that there was no response to his outstretched hand, the surgeon had jumped in and pushed him roughly back upon his pillow.

"What did you promise?" he growled. "You were to lie still, weren't you? And you'll do it, or out we go."

"How are you, Eagen?" drawled Darrow.

"Not Eagen. I'm done with that. They've told you, haven't they?"

Darrow nodded. "Are you the only survivor?" he inquired.

"Except yourself."

"The Nigger? Pulz? Thrackles? The captain? All drowned?"

"Not the captain. They murdered him."

"Ah," said Darrow softly. "And you—I beg your pardon—your—er—friends disposed of the doctor in the same way?"

"Handy Solomon," replied Slade with shaking lips. "Hell's got that fiend, if there's a hell for human fiends. They threw the doctor's body in the surf."

"You didn't notice whether there were any papers?"

"If there were they must have been destroyed with the body when the lava poured down the valley into the sea."

"The lava: of course," assented Darrow, with elaborate nonchalance. "Well, he was a kind old boy. A cheerful, simple, wise old child."

"I would have given my right hand to save him," cried Slade. "It was so sudden—so damnable——"

"Better to have saved him than me," said Darrow. He spoke with the first touch of feeling that he exhibited. "I have to thank you for my life, Eagen—I beg your pardon: Slade. It's hard to remember."

Dr. Trendon arose, and Captain Parkinson with him.

"Give you two hours, Mr. Darrow," said the surgeon. "No more. If he seems exhausted, give him one of these powders. I'll look in in an hour."

At the end of an hour he returned. Slade was lying back on his pillow. Darrow was talking, eagerly, confidentially. In another hour he came out.

"The whole thing is clear," he said to Captain Parkinson. "I am ready to report to you."

"This evening," said the captain. "The mess will want to hear."

"Yes, they will want to hear," assented Darrow. "You've had Slade's story. I'll take it up where he left off, and he'll check me. Mine's as incredible as —as Slade's was. And it's as true."

VIII

THE MAKER OF MARVELS

As they had gathered to hear Ralph Slade's tale, so now the depleted mess of the *Wolverine* grouped themselves for Percy Darrow's sequel. Slade himself sat directly across from the doctor's assistant. Before him lay a paper covered with jotted notes. Trendon slouched low in the chair on Slade's right. Captain Parkinson had the other side. Convenient to Darrow's hand lay the material for cigarettes. As he talked he rolled cylinder after cylinder, and between sentences consumed them in long, satisfying puffs.

"First you will want to learn of the fate of your friends and shipmates," he began. "They are dead. One of them, Mr. Edwards, fell to my hands to bury, as you know. He lies beside Handy Solomon. The others we shall probably not see: any one of a score of ocean currents may have swept them far away. The last great glow that you saw was the signal of their destruction. So the work of a great scientist, a potent benefactor of the race, a gentle and kindly old heart, has brought about the death of your friends and of my enemies. The innocent and the guilty . . . the murderer with his plunder, the officer following his duty . . . one and the same end . . . a paltry thing our vaunted science is in the face of such tangled fates." He spoke low and bitterly. Then he squared his shoulders and his manner became businesslike.

"Interrupt me when any point needs clearing up," he said. "It's a blind trail at best. You've the right to see it as plain as I can make it—with Slade's help. Cut right in with your questions: There'll be plenty to answer and some never will be answered . . .

"Now let me get this thing laid out clearly in my own mind. You first saw the glow—let me see——"

"Night of June 2d," said Barnett.

"June 2d," agreed Darrow. "That was the end of Solomon, Thrackles & Co. A very surprising end to them, if they had time to think," he added grimly.

"Surprising enough, from the survivor's viewpoint," said Slade.

"Doubtless. They've had that story from you; I needn't go over it. This ship picked up the *Laughing Lass*, deserted, and put your first crew aboard. That night, was it not, you saw the second pillar of fire?"

Barnett nodded.

"So your men met their death. Then came the second finding of the empty schooner. . . . Captain Parkinson, they must have been brave men who faced the unknown terrors of that prodigy."

"They volunteered, sir," said the Captain, with simple pride.

Darrow bowed with a suggestion of reverence in the slow movement of his head. "And that night— or was it two nights later?—you saw the last appearance of the portent. Well, I shall come to that. . . .

Slade has told you how they lived on the beach.
With us in the valley it was different. Almost from
the first I was alone. The doctor ceased to be a
companion. He ceased to be human, almost. A machine, that's what he was. His one human instinct
was—well, distrust. His whole force of being was cen-
tred on his discovery. It was to make him the foremost scientist of the world; the foremost individual
entity of his time—of all time, possibly. Even to outline it to you would take too much time. Light, heat,
motive power in incredible degrees and under such
control as has never been known: these were to be the
agencies at his call. The push of a button, the turn of
a screw—oh, he was to be master of such power as
no monarch ever wielded! Riches—pshaw! Riches
were the least of it. He could create them, practically.
But they would be superfluous. Power: unlimited, absolute power was his goal. With his end achieved he
could establish an autocracy, a dynasty of science:
whatever he chose. Oh, it was a rich-hued, golden,
glowing dream; a dream such as men's souls don't
formulate in these stale days—not our kind of men.
The Teutonic mysticism—you understand. And it
was all true. Oh, quite."

"Do you mean us to understand that he had this
power you describe?" asked Captain Parkinson.

"In his grasp. Then comes a practical gentleman
with a steel hook. A follower of dreams, too, in his
way. Conflicting interests—you know how it is. One
well-aimed blow from the more practical dreamer, and
the greater vision passes. . . . I'm getting ahead
of myself. Just a moment."

His cigarette glowed fiercely in the dimness before he took up his tale again.

"You all know who Dr. Schermerhorn was. None of you know—I don't know myself, though I've been his factotum for ten years—along how many varied lines of activity that mind played. One of them was the secret of energy: concentrated, resistless energy. Man's contrivances were too puny for him. The most powerful engines he regarded as toys. For a time high explosives claimed his attention. He wanted to harness them. Once he got to the point of practical experiment. You can see the ruins yet: a hole in southern New Jersey. Nobody ever understood how he escaped. But there he was on his feet across a ten-foot fence in a ploughed field—yes, he flew the fence—and running, running furiously in the opposite direction, when the dust cleared away. Someone stopped him finally. Told him the danger was over. 'Yet, I will not return,' he said firmly, and fainted away. That disgusted him with high explosives. What secrets he discovered he gave to the government. They were not without value, I believe."

"They were not, indeed," corroborated Barnett.

"Next his interest turned to the natural phenomena of high energy. He studied lightning in an open steel network laboratory, with few results save a succession of rheumatic attacks, and an improved electric interrupter, since adopted by one of the great telegraph companies. The former obliged him to stop these experiments, and the invention he considered trivial. Probably the great problem of getting at the secret of energy led him into his attempts to study the mys-

terious electrical waves radiated by lightning flashes;
at any rate he was soon as deep into the subject of
electrical science as his countryman, Hertz, had ever
been. He used to tell me that he often wondered why
he hadn't taken up this line before—the world of
energy he now set out to explore, waves in that tremendous range between those we hear and those we
see. It was natural that he should then come to the
most prominent radio-active elements, uranium, tho-
rium, and radium. But though his knowledge sur-
passed that of the much-exploited authorities, he was
never satisfied with any of his results.

"'Pitchblende; no!' he would exclaim. 'It has not
the great power. The mines are not deep enough,
yet!'

"Then suddenly the great idea that was to bring
him success, and cost him his life, came to him. The
bowels of the earth must hold the secret! He took up
volcanoes. . . . Does all this sound foolish? It
was not if you knew the man. He was a mighty enthusiast, a born martyr. Not cold-blooded, like the
rest of us. The fire was in his veins. . . . A
light, please. Thank you.

"We chased volcanoes. There was a theory under it
all. He believed that volcanic emanations are caused
by a mighty and uncomprehended energy, something
that achieves results ascribable neither to explosions
nor heat, some eternal, inner source. . . . Radium, if you choose, only he didn't call it that. Radium
itself, as known to our modern scientists, he regarded
as the harmless plaything of people with time hanging heavy on their hands. He wasn't after force in

pin-point quantities: he wanted bulk results. Yet I
believe that, after all, what he sought was a sort of
higher power of radium. The phenomena were re-
lated. And he had some of that concentrated essence
of pitchblende in the chest when we started. Oh, not
much: say about twenty thousand dollars' worth.
Maybe thirty. For use? No; rather for comparison,
I judge.

"Yes, we chased volcanoes. I became used to camp-
ing between sample hells of all known varieties. I got
so that the fumes of a sulphur match seemed like a
draught of pure, fresh air. Wherever any of the
earth's pimples showed signs of coming to a head,
there were we, taking part in the trouble. By and by
the doctor got so thoroughly poisoned that he had
to lay off. Back to Philadelphia we came. There an
aged seafaring person, temporarily stranded, mulcted
the Professor of a dollar—an undertaking that required no art—and in the course of his recital touched
upon yonder little cesspool of infernal iniquities. An
uncharted volcanic island: one that he could have all
for his own; you may guess whether Dr. Schermerhorn was interested.

"'That iss for which we haf so-long-in-vain
sought, Percy,' he said to me in his quaint, link-chain
style of speech. 'A leedle prifate volcano-laboratory
to ourselves to have. Totally unknown: undescribed,
not-on-the-chart-to-be-found. To-morrow we start. I
make a list of the things-to-get.'

"He began his list, as I remember, with three dozen
undershirts, a gallon of pennyroyal for insect bites, a
box of assorted fish hooks, thirty pounds of tea, and a

case of carpet tacks. When I hadn't anything else to worry over, I used to lie awake at night and speculate on the purpose of those carpet tacks. He had something in mind: if there was anything on which he prided himself, it was his practical bent. But the list never got any further: it ceased short of one page in the ledger, as you may have noticed. I outfitted by telegraph on the way across the continent.

"The doctor didn't ask me whether I'd go. He took it for granted. That's probably why I didn't back out. Nor did I tell him that the three life insurance companies which had foolishly and trustingly accepted me as a risk merely on the strength of a good constitution were making frantic efforts to compromise on the policies. They felt hurt, those companies: my healthy condition had ceased to appeal to them. What's a good constitution between earthquakes? No, there was no use telling the doctor. It would only have worried him. Besides, I didn't believe that the island was there. I thought it was a myth of that stranded ancient mariner's imagination. When it rose to sight at the proper spot, none were more astounded than the bad risk who now addresses you.

"Yet, I must say for the island that it came handsomely up to specifications. Down where you were, Slade, you didn't get a real insight into its disposition. But in back of us there was any kind of action for your money. Geysers, hell-spouts, fuming fissures, cunning little craterlets with half-portions of molten lava ready to serve hot; more gases than you could create in all the world's chemical laboratories: in fact, everything to make the place a paradise for Old Nick

—and Dr. Schermerhorn. He brought along in his precious chest, besides the radium, some sort of raw material: also, as near as I could make out, a sort of cage or guardianship scheme for his concentrated essence of cussedness, when he should get it out of the volcano.

"In the first seven months he puttered around the little fumers, with an occasional excursion up to the main crater. It was my duty to follow on and drag him away when he fell unconscious. Sometimes I would try to get him before he was quite gone. Then he would become indignant, and fight me. Perhaps that helped to lose me his confidence. More and more he withdrew into himself. There were days when he spoke no word to me. It was lonely. Do you know why I used to visit you at the beach, Slade? I suppose you thought I was keeping watch on you. It wasn't that, it was loneliness. In a way, it hurt me, too: for one couldn't help but be fond of the old boy; and at times it seemed as if he weren't quite himself. Pardon me, if I may trouble you for the matches? Thanks. . . .

"Matters went very wrong at times: the doctor fumed like his little craters; growled out long-winded, exhaustive German imprecations: wouldn't even eat. Then again the demon of work would drive him with thong and spur: he would rush to his craters, to his laboratories, to his ledger for the purpose of entering unintelligible commentaries. He had some peculiar contrivance, like a misshapen retort, with which he collected gases from the craterlets. Whenever I'd hear one of those smash, I knew it was a bad day.

Meantime, the volcano also became—well, what you might call temperamental.

"It got to be a year and a quarter—a year and a half. I wondered whether we should ever get away. My tobacco was running short. And the bearing of the men was becoming fidgetty. My visits to the beach became quite interesting—to me. One day the doctor came running out of his laboratory with so bright a face that I ventured to ask him about departure.

"'Not so long, now, Percy,' he said, in his old, kind manner. 'Not so long. The first real success. It iss made. We have yet under-entire-control to bring it, but it iss made.'

"'And about time, sir,' said I. 'If we don't do something soon we may have trouble with the men.'

"'So?' said he in surprise. 'But they could do nothing. Nothing.' He wagged his great head confidently. 'We are armed.'

"'Oh, yes, armed. So are they.'

"'We are armed,' he repeated obstinately. 'Such as no man was ever armed, are we armed.'

"He checked himself abruptly and walked away. Well, I've since wondered what would have happened had the men attacked us. It would have been worth seeing, and—and surprising. Yes: I'm quite certain it would have been surprising. Perhaps, too, I might have learned more of the Great Secret . . . and yet, I don't know. It's all dark . . . a hint here . . . theory . . . mere glints of light. . . . Where did I put . . . Ah, thank you."

IX

THE ACHIEVEMENT

For some moments Darrow sat gazing fixedly at the table before him. His cigarette tip glowed and failed. Someone suggested drinks. The captain asked Darrow what he would have, but the question went unnoted.

" How I passed the next six months I could hardly tell you," he began again, quite abruptly. " At times I was bored—fearfully bored. Yet the element of mystery, of uncertainty, of underlying peril, gave a certain zest to the affair. In the periods of dulness I found some amusement in visiting the lower camp and baiting the Nigger. Slade will have told you about him; he possessed quite a fund of bastard Voodooism: he possessed more before I got through with him. Yes; if he had lived to return to his country, I fancy he would have added considerably to Afro-American witch-lore. You remember the vampire bats, Slade? And the devil-fires? Naturally I didn't mention to you that the devil-fire business wasn't altogether as clear to me as I pretended. It wasn't, though. But at the time it served very well as an amusement. All the while I realised that my self-entertainment was not without its element of danger, too: I remember glances not altogether friendly but always a little doubtful, a little awed. Even Handy Solomon, practical as he was, had a scruple or two of superstition in his make-up, on which one might work. Only Eagen—Slade, I mean—was beyond me there. You puzzled me not a little in those days, Slade. Well . . .

"Did I say that I was sometimes annoyed by the doctor's attitude? Yes: it seemed that he might have given me a little more of his confidence; but one can't judge such a man as he was. Among the ordinary affairs of life he had relied on me for every detail. Now he was independent of me. Independent! I doubt if he remembered my existence at times. Even in his blackest moods of depression he was sufficient unto himself. It was strange. . . . How he did rage the day the chemicals from Washington went wrong! I was washing my shirt in the hot water spring when he came bolting out of the laboratory and keeled me over. I came out pretty indignant. Apologise? Not at all. He just sputtered. His nearest approach to coherence seemed to indicate a desire that I should go back to Washington at once and destroy a perfectly reputable firm of chemists. Finally he calmed down and took it out in entering it in his daily record. He was quite proud of that daily record and remembered to write in it on an average of once a week.

"Then the chest went wrong. Whether it had rusted a bit, or whether the chemicals had got in their work on the hinges, I don't know; but one day the Professor, of his own initiative, recognised my existence by lugging his box out in the open and asking me to fix it. Previously he had emptied it. It was rather a complicated thing, with an inner compartment over which was a hollow cover, opening along one rim. That, I conjectured, was designed to hold some chemical compound or salt. There were many minor openings, too, each guarded by a similar hollow door. My business was with the heavy top cover.

" ' It should shut and open softly, gently,' explained the Professor. ' So. Not with-a-grating-sound-to-be-accompanied,' he added, with his curious effect of linked phraseology.

" Half a day's work fixed it. The lid would stand open of itself until tipped at a considerable angle, when it would fall and lock. Only on the outer shell was there a lock: that one was a good bit of craftsmanship.

" ' So, Percy, my boy,' said the doctor kindly. ' That will with-sufficient-safety guard our treasure. When we obtain it, Percy. When it entirely-finished-and-completed shall be.'

" ' And when will that be? ' I asked.

" ' God knows,' he said cheerfully. ' It progresses.'

" Whenever I went strolling at night, he would produce his curious lights. Sometimes they were fairly startling. One fact I made out by accident, looking down from a high place. They did not project from the laboratory. He always worked in the open when the light was to be produced. Once the experiment took a serious turn. The lights had flickered and gone. Dr. Schermerhorn had returned to his laboratory. I came up the arroyo as he flung the door open and rushed out. He was a grotesque figure, clad in an undershirt and a worn pair of trousers, fastened with an old bit of tarred rope in lieu of his suspenders, which I had been repairing. About his waist flickered a sort of aura of radiance which was extinguished as he flung himself headforemost into the cold spring. I hauled him out. He seemed dazed. To my questions he replied only by mumblings, the burden of which was:

" ' I do not understand. It is a not-to-be-comprehended accident.' It appears that he didn't quite know why he had taken to the water. Or if he did, he didn't want to tell.

" Next day he was as good as new. Just as silent as before, but it was a smiling, satisfied silence. So it went for weeks, for months, with the accesses of depression and anger always rarer. Then came an afternoon when, returning from a stalk after sheep, I heard strange and shocking noises from the laboratory. Strict as was the embargo which kept me outside the door, I burst in, only to be seized in a suffocating grip. Of a sudden I realised that I was being embraced. The doctor flourished a hand above my head and jigged with ponderous steps. The dismal noises continued to emanate from his mouth. He was singing. I wish I could give you a notion of the amazement, the paralysing wonder with which. . . . No, you did not know Dr. Schermerhorn: you would not understand. . . .

" We polkaed into the open. There he cast me loose. He stopped singing and burst into a rhapsody of disjointed words. Mostly German, it was—a wondrous jumble of the scientific and poetic. ' Eureka ' occurred at intervals. Then he would leap in the air. It was weird, it was distressing. Crazy? Oh, quite. For the time, you understand. If any of us should suddenly become the most potent individual in the world, wouldn't he be apt to lose balance temporarily? One must make allowances. There was excuse for the doctor. He had reached the goal.

"'Percy, you shall be rewarded,' he said. 'You haf like-a-trump-card stuck by me. You shall haf riches, gold, what you will. You are young; your blood runs red. With such riches nothing is beyond you. You could the ancient-tombs-of-Egypt explore. It is open to you such collections-as-have-never-been-gathered to make. What shall it be? Scarabs? Missals? Prehistoric implements? Amuse yourself, *mein kind*. We shall be able the-bills-with-usurious-interest to pay. What will you haf?'

"I said I'd like a vacation, if convenient.

"'Presently,' he replied. 'There yet remains the guardianship to be perfected. Then to-a-world-aston-ished-and-respectful we return. To-night we celebrate. I play you a rubber of pinochle.'

"We played. With the greatest secret of science resting at our elbows, we played. The doctor won; my mind was not strictly on the game. In the morning the doctor sang once more. . . . I shall never hear its like again. Was it a week, or a month, after that? . . . I cannot remember. I fancy I was excited. Then, too, there was something in the atmosphere about the laboratory . . . I don't know; imagination, possibly. Once we had a little manifesta-tion: the night that the Nigger and Slade were terrified by the rock fires. Days of excitement and pleasant work, with the little volcano grumbling more sulkily all the time . . . I have spent worse days.

"Such indifference as the doctor displayed toward the volcano I have never known. If I ventured to wa⁻n him he would assure me that there was no cause for alarm. I think he regarded that little hell's kitchen as merely a feed-spout for his vast enterprise. He felt a sort of affection toward it; he was tolerant of its petty fits of temper. That he completed his work before the destruction came was sheer luck. Nothing else. The day before the outburst he came to me with a tiny phial of complicated design.

"'Percy, I will at-a-reasonable-price sell this to you,' he said.

"'How much?' I inquired, responding to his playfulness.

"'A bargain,' he cried gaily. 'Five millions dollars. No! Shall I upon-a-needy-friend hard-press? Never. One million. One little million dollars.'

"'I haven't that amount with me,' I began.

"'Of no account,' he declared airily. 'Soon we shall haf many more times as that. Gif me your C. O. D.'

"'My I. O. U.?' I inquired.

"'It makes no matter. See. I will gif it to you gratis.'

"He handed me the metal contrivance. It was closed.

"'Inside iss a little, such a very little. Not yet iss it arranged the motive-power to give-forth. One more change-to-be-made that shall require. But the other phenomena are all in this little half-grain comprised. Later I shall tell you more. Take it. It iss without price.' He laid his hand on my shoulder. ' Like the love of friends,' he said gently."

Feeling in his upper waistcoat pocket, Darrow brought out a phial, so tiny that it rolled in the palm of his hand. He contemplated it, lost in thought.

" Radium? " queried Barnett, with the keen interest of the scientist.

" God knows *what* it is," said Darrow, rousing himself. " Not the perfected product; the doctor said that when he gave it to me. If I could remember one-tenth of what he told me that night! It is like a disordered dream, a phantasmagoria of monstrous powers, lit up with an intolerable, almost an infernal radiance. This much I did gather: that Dr. Schermerhorn had achieved what the greatest minds before him had barely outlined. Yes, and more. Becquerel, the Curies, Rutherford—they were playing with the letters of the Greek alphabet, Alphas, Gammas, and Rhos, while the simple, gentle old boy that I served had read the secret. From the molten eruptions of the racked earth he had taken gases and potencies that are nameless. By what methods of combination and refining I do not know, he produced something that was to be the final word of power. Control—control—that was all that lacked.

" Reduced to its simplest terms, it meant this: the doctor had something as much greater than radium as radium is greater than the pitchblende of which a thousand tons are melted down to the one ounce of extract. And the incredible energies of this he proposed to divide into departments of activity. One manifestation should be light, a light that would illuminate the world. Another was to make motive power so cheap that the work of the world could be done in an hour out of the day. Some idea he had of healing properties. Yes; he was to cure mankind. Or kill, kill as no man had ever killed, did he choose. The armies and navies of the powers would be at his mercy. Magnetism was to be his slave. Aërial navigation, transmutation of metals, the screening of gravity—does this sound like delirium? Sometimes I think it was.

" That night he turned over to me the key of the large chest and his ledger. The latter he bade me read. It was a complete jumble. You have seen it. . . . We were up a good part of the night with our pet volcano. It was suffering from internal disturbances. ' So,' the doctor would say indulgently, when a particularly active rock came bounding down our way. ' Little play-antics-to-exhibit now that the work iss finished.'

" In the morning he insisted on my leaving him alone and going down to give the orders. I took the ledger, intending to send it aboard. It saved my life possibly: Solomon's bullet deflected slightly, I think, in passing through the heavy paper. Slade has told you about my flight. I ought to have gone straight up the arroyo. . . . Yet I could hardly have made it. . . . I did not see him again, the doctor. My last glimpse . . . the old man—I remember now how the grey had spread through his beard—he was growing old—it had been ageing labour. He stood there at his laboratory door and the mountain spouted and thundered behind.

"'We will a name-to-suit-properly gif it,' he said, as I left him. 'It shall make us as the gods. We will call it celestium.'

"I left him there smiling. Smiling happily. The greatest force of his age—if he had lived. Very wise, very simple—a kind old child. May I trouble you for a light? Thanks."

X

THE DOOM

" Nothing remained but to search for his body. I was sure they had killed him and taken the chest. I had little expectation of finding him, dead or alive. None after I saw the stream of lava pouring into the sea. One saves his own life by instinct, I suppose. There I was. I had to live. It did not matter much, but I continued to do it by various shifts. That last day on the headland the fumes nearly got me. You may have noted the rather excited scrawl in the back of the ledger? Yes, I thought I was gone that time. But I got to the cave. It was low tide. Then the earthquake, and I was walled in. . . . Mr. Barnett's very accurate explosives—Slade's insistence—your risking your lives as you did, mites on the crust of a red-hot cheese—I hope you know how I feel about it all. One can't thank a man properly for the life . . .

" Oh, the pirates. Necessarily it must be a matter of theory, but I think we have it right. Slade and I built it up. For what it's worth, here it is. Let me see: you sighted the glow on the night of the 2d. Next day came the deserted ship. It must have puzzled you outrageously."

" It did," said Captain Parkinson, drily.

"Not an easy problem, even with all the data at hand. You, of course, had none. On Slade's showing, Handy Solomon and his worthy associates thought they had a chest full of riches when they got the doctor's treasure; believed they owned the machinery for making diamonds or gold or what-not of ready-to-hand wealth. It's fair to assume a certain eagerness on their part. Disturbed weather keeps them busy until they're well out from the island. Then to the chest. Opening it isn't so easy: I had the key, you know." He brought a curious and delicately wrought skeleton from his pocket. "Tipped with platinum," he observed. "Rather a gem of a key, I think. You see, there must have been some action, even through the keyhole, or he wouldn't have used a metal of this kind. But the crew was rich in certain qualities, it seems, which I failed, stupidly, to recognise in my acquaintance with them. Both Pulz and Perdosa appear to have been handy men where locks were concerned. First Pulz sneaks down and has his turn at the chest. He gets it open. Small profit for him in that: the next we know of him he is scandalising Handy Solomon by having a fit on the deck."

"That is what I couldn't figure out to save my life," said Slade eagerly.

"If you recollect, I told you of the Professor's plunge in the cold spring, in a sort of paroxysm, one day," said Darrow. "That was the physiological action of the celestium. At other times, I have seen him come out and deliberately roll in the creek, head under. Once he explained that the medium he worked in caused a kind of uncontrollable longing for water;

something having none of the qualities of burning or thirst, but an irresistible temporary mania. It worried him a good deal; he didn't understand it. That, then, was what ailed Pulz. When he opened the chest there was, as I surmise, a trifling quantity of this stuff lying in the inner lid. It wasn't the celestium itself, as I imagine, but a sort of by-product with the physiological and radiant effects of the real thing, and it had been set there on guard, a discouragement to the spirit of investigation, as it were. So, when the top was lifted, our little guardian gets in its work, producing the light phenomenon that so puzzled Slade, and inspiring Pulz with a passion for the rolling wave, which is only interrupted by Handy Solomon's tackling him. As he fled he must have pulled down the cover."

" He did," said Slade. " I heard the clang. But I saw the radiance on the clouds. And the whole thickness of a solid oak deck was in between the sky and the chest."

" Oh, a little thing like an oak deck wouldn't interrupt the kind of rays the doctor used. He had his own method of screening, you understand. However, this inconsiderable guardian affair must have used itself up, which true celestium wouldn't have done. So when Perdosa sets his genius for lock-picking to the task, the inner box, full of the genuine article, has no warning sign-post, so to speak. Everything's peaceful until they raise the compound-filled hollow layer of the inner cover, which serves to interrupt the action. Then comes the general exit and the superior fireworks."

"That's when the rays ran through the ship," said Slade. "It seemed to follow the deck-lines."

"The stuff had a strange affinity for tar," said Darrow. "I told you of the circle of fire about Professor Schermerhorn's waist the day he gave me such a scare. That was the celestium working on the tarred rope he wore for a belt. It made a livid circle on his skin. Did I tell you of his experiments with pitch? It doesn't matter. Where was I?"

"At the place where we all jumped," said Slade.

"Oh, yes. And you dove into the small boat, trying to reach the water."

"Wait a bit," said Barnett. "If that was the exhibition of radiance we saw, it died out in a few minutes. How was that? Did they close the chest before they ran?"

"Probably not," replied Darrow. "Slade spoke of Pulz taking to the maintop and being shaken out by the sudden shock of a wave. That may have been a volcanic billow. Whatever it was, it undoubtedly heeled the ship sufficiently to bring down both lids, which were rather delicately balanced."

"Yes, for Billy Edwards found the chest closed and locked," said Barnett.

"Of course; it was a spring lock. You sent Mr. Edwards and his men aboard. No such experts as Pulz or Perdosa were in your crew. Consequently it took longer to get the chest open. When at length the lid was raised, there was a repetition of the tragedy. Mr. Edwards and his men leaped. Probably they were paralysed almost before they struck the water. Your bos'n, whom Slade picked up, was the only one who had time even to grab a life preserver before the impulse toward water became irresistible. There was no element of fright, you understand: no desertion of their post. They were dragged as by the sweep of a tornado." Darrow spoke direct to Captain Parkinson. "If there is any feeling among you other than sorrow for their death, it is unjust and unworthy."

"Thank you, Mr. Darrow," returned the captain quietly.

"We found the chest closed again when the empty ship came back," observed Barnett.

"Being masterless, the schooner began to yaw," continued Darrow. "The first time she came about would have heeled her enough to shut the chest. Now came the turn of your other men."

"Ives and McGuire," said the Captain, as Darrow paused.

"The glow came again that night, and the next day we picked up Slade," said Barnett.

"You know what the glow meant for your companions," said Darrow.

"But the ship. The *Laughing Lass,* man. She's vanished. No one has seen her since."

"You are wrong there," said Darrow. "I have seen her."

In a common impulse the little circle leaned to him.

"Yes, I have seen her. I wish I had not. Let me bring my story back to the cave on the island. After the volcanic gases had driven me to the refuge, I sat near the mouth of the cave looking out into the darkness. That was the night of the 7th, the night you saw the last glow. It was very dark, except for occasional bursts of fire from the crater. Judge of my incredulous amazement when, in an access of this illumination, I saw plainly a schooner hardly a mile off shore, coming in under bare poles."

" Under bare poles? " cried Slade.

" The halliards must have disintegrated from some slow action of the celestium. It could be destructive: terrifically destructive. You shall judge. There was the schooner, naked as your hand. Possibly I might have thought it a hallucination but for what came after. Darkness fell again. I supposed then that Handy Solomon's crew were managing—or mismanaging—the *Laughing Lass* without the aid of their leader, whom I had satisfactorily buried. I hoped they would come ashore on the rocks. Yes I was vengeful . . . then.

" Of a sudden there sprang from the darkness a ship of light. You have all seen those great electric effects at expositions. Someone touches a button . . . you know. It was like that. Only that the piercingly brilliant jewelled wonder of a ship was set in the midst of a swirl of vari-coloured radiance such as I can't begin to describe. You saw it from a distance. Imagine what it was, coming close upon you that way—dead on, out of the night. A living glory, a living terror. . . ."

His voice sank. With a shaking hand he fumbled amid his cigarette papers.

" It came on. A human figure, glowing like a diamond ablaze, leaped out from it; another shot down from the foremast. I don't know how many I saw go. It was like a theatric effect, unreal, unconvincing, incredible. The end fitted it."

Darrow's eye roved. It fell upon a quaintly modelled ship, hung above the door.

"What's that?" he cried.

"Fool thing some Malay gave me," grunted Trendon. "Pretended to be grateful because I cut his foot off. No good. Go on with the story."

"No good? You don't care what happens to it?"

"Meant to heave it overboard before now," growled the other.

Someone handed it down to Darrow.

"If I had something to hold enough water," muttered he, "I'd like to float it. I'd like to see for myself how it worked out. I'd like to see that devil-work in action."

He spoke feverishly.

"Boy, fill the portable rubber tub in Mr. Forsythe's cabin and bring it here," ordered the captain.

"That will do." said Darrow, recovering himself.

He floated the model in the tub.

"Now, I don't know how this will come out," he said. "Nor do I know why the *Laughing Lass* met her fate under Ives and McGuire, and not before. Perhaps the chest lay open longer . . . long enough, anyway. We'll try it."

From his pocket he took a curious small phial.

"Is that what Dr. Schermerhorn gave you?" asked Slade.

"Yes," said Darrow. He set it carefully inside the

little model and slipped a lever. Slade quietly turned down the light.

A faint glow shot up. It grew bright and eddied in lovely, variant colours. As if set to a powder train, it ran through the ship. The pale faces of the spectators shone ghastly in its radiance. From someone burst a sudden gasp.

" There is not enough for danger," said Darrow, quietly.

" As a point of interest," grunted Trendon.

Everyone looked at his outstretched hand. A little pocket compass lay in the palm. The needle spun madly, projecting blue, vivid sparklings.

" My God! " cried Slade, and covered his eyes for a moment.

He snatched away his hands as a suppressed cry went up from the others.

" As I expected," said Darrow quietly.

The little craft opened out; it disintegrated. All that radiance dissolved and with its going the substance upon which it shaped itself vanished. The last glow showed a formless pulp, spreading upon the water.

" So passed the *Laughing Lass*," said Darrow solemnly.

" And the chest is at the bottom of the sea," said Barnett.

" Good place for it," muttered Trendon.

" In all probability it closed as the ship dissolved around it," said Darrow. " Otherwise we should see the effects in the water."

" It might be recovered," cried Slade, excitedly.

" Could you chart it, Darrow? Think of the possibilities——"

" Let it lie," said the captain. " Has it not cost enough? Let it lie."

The water in the tub fumed and sparkled faintly and was still. Darkness fell, except where Darrow's cigarette point glowed and faded.

THE END

SCIENCE FICTION

An Arno Press Collection

FICTION

About, Edmond. **The Man with the Broken Ear.** 1872

Allen, Grant. **The British Barbarians:** A Hill-Top Novel. 1895

Arnold, Edwin L. **Lieut. Gullivar Jones:** His Vacation. 1905

Ash, Fenton. **A Trip to Mars.** 1909

Aubrey, Frank. **A Queen of Atlantis.** 1899

Bargone, Charles (Claude Farrere, pseud.). **Useless Hands.** [1926]

Beale, Charles Willing. **The Secret of the Earth.** 1899

Bell, Eric Temple (John Taine, pseud.). **Before the Dawn.** 1934

Benson, Robert Hugh. **Lord of the World.** 1908

Beresford, J. D. **The Hampdenshire Wonder.** 1911

Bradshaw, William R. **The Goddess of Atvatabar.** 1892

Capek, Karel. **Krakatit.** 1925

Chambers, Robert W. **The Gay Rebellion.** 1913

Colomb, P. et al. **The Great War of 189—.** 1893

Cook, William Wallace. **Adrift in the Unknown.** n.d.

Cummings, Ray. **The Man Who Mastered Time.** 1929

[DeMille, James]. **A Strange Manuscript Found in a Copper Cylinder.** 1888

Dixon, Thomas. **The Fall of a Nation:** A Sequel to the Birth of a Nation. 1916

England, George Allan. **The Golden Blight.** 1916

Fawcett, E. Douglas. **Hartmann the Anarchist.** 1893

Flammarion, Camille. **Omega:** The Last Days of the World. 1894

Grant, Robert et al. **The King's Men:** A Tale of To-Morrow. 1884

Grautoff, Ferdinand Heinrich (Parabellum, pseud.). **Banzai!** 1909

Graves, C. L. and E. V. Lucas. **The War of the Wenuses.** 1898

Greer, Tom. **A Modern Daedalus.** [1887]

Griffith, George. **A Honeymoon in Space.** 1901

Grousset, Paschal (A. Laurie, pseud.). **The Conquest of the Moon.** 1894

Haggard, H. Rider. **When the World Shook.** 1919

Hernaman-Johnson, F. **The Polyphemes.** 1906

Hyne, C. J. Cutcliffe. **Empire of the World.** [1910]

In The Future. [1875]

Jane, Fred T. **The Violet Flame.** 1899

Jefferies, Richard. **After London; Or, Wild England.** 1885

Le Queux, William. **The Great White Queen.** [1896]

London, Jack. **The Scarlet Plague.** 1915

Mitchell, John Ames. **Drowsy.** 1917

Morris, Ralph. **The Life and Astonishing Adventures of John Daniel.** 1751

Newcomb, Simon. **His Wisdom The Defender:** A Story. 1900

Paine, Albert Bigelow. **The Great White Way.** 1901

Pendray, Edward (Gawain Edwards, pseud.). **The Earth-Tube.** 1929

Reginald, R. and Douglas Menville. **Ancestral Voices:** An Anthology of Early Science Fiction. 1974

Russell, W. Clark. **The Frozen Pirate.** 2 vols. in 1. 1887

Shiel, M. P. **The Lord of the Sea.** 1901

Symmes, John Cleaves (Captain Adam Seaborn, pseud.). **Symzonia.** 1820

Train, Arthur and Robert W. Wood. **The Man Who Rocked the Earth.** 1915

Waterloo, Stanley. **The Story of Ab:** A Tale of the Time of the Cave Man. 1903

White, Stewart E. and Samuel H. Adams. **The Mystery.** 1907

Wicks, Mark. **To Mars Via the Moon.** 1911

Wright, Sydney Fowler. **Deluge: A Romance** and **Dawn.** 2 vols. in 1. 1928/1929

SCIENCE FICTION

NON-FICTION
Including Bibliographies,
Checklists and Literary Criticism

Aldiss, Brian and Harry Harrison. **SF Horizons.** 2 vols. in 1. 1964/1965

Amis, Kingsley. **New Maps of Hell.** 1960

Barnes, Myra. **Linguistics and Languages in Science Fiction-Fantasy.** 1974

Cockcroft, T. G. L. **Index to the Weird Fiction Magazines.** 2 vols. in 1 1962/1964

Cole, W. R. **A Checklist of Science-Fiction Anthologies.** 1964

Crawford, Joseph H. et al. **"333": A Bibliography of the Science-Fantasy Novel.** 1953

Day, Bradford M. **The Checklist of Fantastic Literature in Paperbound Books.** 1965

Day, Bradford M. **The Supplemental Checklist of Fantastic Literature.** 1963

Gove, Philip Babcock. **The Imaginary Voyage in Prose Fiction.** 1941

Green, Roger Lancelyn. **Into Other Worlds:** Space-Flight in Fiction, From Lucian to Lewis. 1958

Menville, Douglas. **A Historical and Critical Survey of the Science Fiction Film.** 1974

Reginald, R. **Contemporary Science Fiction Authors,** First Edition. 1970

Samuelson, David. **Visions of Tomorow:** Six Journeys from Outer to Inner Space. 1974